THE MENAGERIE

Catherine Cookson

CORGI BOOKS

THE MENAGERIE
A CORGI BOOK : 0 552 14830 X

Originally published in Great Britain by
Macdonald & Co (Publishers) Ltd

PRINTING HISTORY
Macdonald edition published 1958
Corgi edition published 1971

23 25 27 29 30 28 26 24

This book is set in 11/13½ pt Sabon by
Kestrel Data, Exeter, Devon.

Corgi Books are published by Transworld Publishers,
61–63 Uxbridge Road, London W5 5SA,
a division of The Random House Group Ltd,
in Australia by Random House Australia (Pty) Ltd,
20 Alfred Street, Milsons Point, Sydney, NSW 2061, Australia,
in New Zealand by Random House New Zealand Ltd,
18 Poland Road, Glenfield, Auckland 10, New Zealand
and in South Africa by Random House (Pty) Ltd,
Endulini, 5a Jubilee Road, Parktown 2193, South Africa.

Reproduced, printed and bound in Great Britain by
Cox & Wyman Ltd, Reading, Berkshire.

To
MY VERY DEAR HUSBAND

CONTENTS

THE MENAGERIE

1

AUNT LOT

'Hello, Aunt Lot.'

'Oh! Hello, Stanley.'

'How's it going, Aunt Lot?'

'Oh, fine, Stanley.'

'That's the ticket.'

The man, laughing to himself, moved on through the press in the High Street while the woman, adjusting with the air of a fine lady the moth-eaten cape on her shoulders, turned again to the shop window and gazed with loving intensity at the cheap and bright dresses displayed. Oh, they were lovely. If she saved up hard enough she could get the red one by the end of the summer. But that was a long time away . . . If she could only depend upon the generosity of the others as she could upon Larry's five shillings every week, she could have it in a month or so; not that she expected anything from the others, for they were married and had families to look after.

'Hello, Aunt Lot. Goin' t'buy the shop?'

'Oh, hello, Mrs Preston. Hello, Mr Preston. No, I'm just lookin'.'

'Nothing could make you bonnier than you are, Lottie.'

11

'Oh, Mr Preston!'

With gratified pleasure she watched the couple for a moment before they were covered by the crowd; then again turned to the window . . . People were nice, weren't they; they said nice things. Perhaps she didn't need the frock, her own was good enough. Hadn't Mr Preston said she'd looked bonny? She knew he wasn't referring to her face but to her attire. She moved and stood in front of a navy-blue dress in order to see her reflection the better, and to her eyes it looked bonny. The large biscuit straw hat, its brim layered with faded silk roses that had been made before the century began; the green-spotted artificial silk dress, quite modern but obviously suited to some young girl and in whom she saw herself perfectly; and the grey sandals with the high heels and straps displaying the distorted toe joints were smart; but overshadowing all was the refined elegance of the fur cape.

Once again she adjusted the cape and moved on, walking slowly in and out of the crowd, enjoying seeing and being seen and answering the frequent hails with her usual smile and cheery replies.

It would be true to say that no-one in all Fellburn was greeted so often as Aunt Lot – even those who didn't greet her smiled in her direction. You could tell a stranger to the town if he were seen to stand and gape at the tall, skinny woman with the mop of fuzzy, fair hair, dressed in a conglomeration of clothes, the colours of which never ceased to yell at

12

each other, but which, strangely enough, were carried with a definite semblance of dignity.

Fellburn on a Saturday morning was always crowded. It was as if the two pits, the Phoenix at one end of the town and the Venus at the other, had spewed their slaves into its centre; there allowing them to get rid of the money they had earned in order to ensure their return. It was the present prosperity of the pits that had created the extended shopping centre of good-class shops. No longer did the miner's wife buy the cheap and tawdry, she was now as good as the next; the next, in Fellburn, meaning the ladies from Brampton Hill.

The ladies from the Hill shopped mostly by phone, but should they go into the town it would be no later than a Friday morning. For this social arrangement Aunt Lot was always sorry for she could never come out on a Friday – Jinny wouldn't let her – and she so liked looking at the pots.

She was now standing outside Fenwick's bookshop, always the last shop she looked into before returning home. She liked looking in the bookshop, not that she read books, she was incapable of reading, but because the sight of them always fascinated her. They created a feeling of excitement inside her and stirred some dormant desire to the point of awakening. She had never read a book in her life, but the feeling told her she knew all that was in them, for what are books made of but people. In a deep and normal part of her make-up she knew people, and it was in the mixed-up, fuddled layers near the surface that this knowledge formed itself into an unquestioning love for them. She was incapable of analysing any of her feelings. To her, the reason she looked at the books was because one day Larry was going to write one – well, not one, but dozens. Larry was clever; he had once been at the Grammar School.

The thought of her nephew brought her mind to razor blades. Eeh! now, she had nearly forgot to get his razor blades again. It was as Jinny said, she couldn't be trusted to remember a thing to the end of the back lane. She'd go to Johnson's right away this very minute. She turned from the window in a flurry and hurried as fast as the crowd allowed towards the chemist's.

The girl behind the counter smiled broadly at her.

'Hello, Aunt Lot,' she said. 'The same?'

'Yes, please. Gillettes, mind.'

'Oh yes, Aunt Lot, Gillettes. There you are.' She put the packet on the counter. 'And how's that big Gregory Peck of yours?' she said, laughing saucily into Aunt Lot's face.

'Eeh!' Lottie laughed back, 'you'll get it, calling him Gregory Peck, you will.'

'Ask him does he want a nice quiet platonic friend. There's your change. Now don't forget, mind.'

'I'll do no such thing.' Lottie left the shop laughing, with the girl's laugh following her, and again she thought, Aren't folks nice.

Happiness was now whirling through her entire body. A kindly word or a joke had the power to inject

14

joy into her veins, and to her mind she had so many things to make her happy. Was there not Jinny who cooked so nice and looked after them all? Jinny might go for her at times, but then it was because she had a lot to do. And who minded a sister going for you, anyway. And there was Frank. Where could there be a brother-in-law like Frank? Why, Frank was the best man alive, and he was good was Frank. Yes, deep down he was good. And there were her nieces, Florence and Gracey and their bairns, and her nephew Jack and his wife. On the thought of Lena, a tiny shadow flittered over the joy. Lena didn't like her – no, that was silly, everybody liked her, it was just that Lena was newly married and was bad-tempered because she couldn't have a house of her own. Lena liked her all right. And . . . then there was Larry. Her joy mounted and her step became tripping. Larry was all the children she had ever had. He was the prince who was ever searching for her, he was the friend she could go to and who had the power to release a part of her which she thought of as strange, she did not class it as sensible; Larry was her lord, her master, her judge. Others of the family had the power to dim her sky by their censure, but one word from Larry and the sun would be blotted out. And finally in her world there was Jessie. Jessie wasn't of the family but she should have been. She loved Jessie better than her sister Jinny or anybody except Larry – this thought was always accompanied by a feeling of guilt, which caused her to exclaim, Eeh, I shouldn't think this way. Eeh! it's bad. But there it was, she couldn't help it, and she rarely thought of Larry without thinking of Jessie.

As she passed Duke's Park she turned and smiled on the children playing there. A boy racing over the grass, touched the low wall dividing the park from the street and flinging up his arm and crossing his fingers, yelled, 'Jinks!' to his pursuers. Then added breathlessly, 'Hello, Aunt Lot.'

'Hello, Charlie. You're havin' a fine game.'

The other participants leaped on to the wall and added their greetings. 'Hello, Aunt Lot.' 'Hello, Aunt Lot.'

Lottie stopped and beamed on them. 'My, you're all out of puff.'

'Where you going, Aunt Lot?'

'Home.'

'Is your Jack gonna play for the town today?'

'Yes, likely, if he doesn't go and see Newcastle. Eeh! I must be gettin' along.'

'So long, Aunt Lot.'

'Goodbye, Aunt Lot.'

'Toodleloo, Aunt Lot.'

She answered this bright spark in his own vein, saying 'To-dil-loo,' whereupon the boys burst into roars of laughter, and she went from them with a step like a girl's and with pursed-up lips which lent further ludicracy to her long, lined face. Bairns were lovely; all bairns were lovely. There were no bad bairns only not so nice ones, like Florence's Monica.

She stopped on the kerb at the foot of Brampton Hill in order to allow a large car to pass. It moved slowly, waiting its chance to get into the main road. It was a long, low-built, powerful-looking car; it had something to draw all eyes, and its colours drew Lottie's. The thick cream enamel contrasted strikingly with the scarlet upholstery of its interior, and she was thinking 'Eeh! isn't it bonny' when her gaze fell upon one of its occupants. In an instant her surprise registered and dropped her mouth into a wide gape. The girl inside the car turned and looked at her. There was no smile on her face, but in the depth of her large eyes there was recognition.

The car, free now to move into the stream of traffic, shot away, leaving Lottie still gaping. Her eyes were stretched to their widest and when her mouth closed on a gasping Eeh! her eyes blinked. Then exclaiming aloud 'No, no!' she ran across the road, stopped for a moment, undecided which way to go, then to the amazement of the passers-by, who had never seen Lottie run, she zig-zagged among them exclaiming as she went, 'Eeh, no!' Then turning up a side street and taking all subsequent short cuts she reached home almost in a state of exhaustion.

Florence Quigley was paying her weekly visit to her mother. She came into the town once a week and dutifully called, as she always remarked, to see if they were still alive. This particular Saturday morning Florence had a grievance. It was an old one, yet it had been dormant for some time, but the sight of Aunt Lot arrayed in all her finery parading the High Street that morning had brought it to the fore again.

Of all the Broadhursts it was Florence alone who had always resented her aunt. Perhaps because in appearance she was the only member of the family who resembled her.

She stood now, pulling on her cotton gloves preparatory to her departure, and looking towards her mother who was setting the table for dinner she asked tensely, 'Look, Mum, aren't you going to do something?'

Jinny Broadhurst laid out with methodical precision six knives and forks and headed them with six spoons and forks before saying heavily, 'What do you want me to do?'

'You could burn those clothes of hers.'

'It's too late in the day; she's been like it too long. Anyway, they make her happy.'

'Happy!' Florence compressed her lips. 'It doesn't matter about other people's happiness, does it? I'm ashamed to go down the High Street, everybody saying "Hello, Aunt Lot" and laughing at her.'

'Well, by the sound of things,' said Jinny with a sigh, 'you won't be in the town much longer to be laughed at, and I don't think they're laughing at her anyway, they like her.'

'Like her!' Florence jerked back her head. 'Like her! She's good for poking fun at, if that's what you call liking, and we may be here months yet . . . years. Things like Australia are not fixed in a minute. I'm telling you, Mum, and I've told you afore, she'll stop me coming in altogether. I'll go to Birtley or Chester-le-Street for I just can't stand the sight of her in that

18

get-up. Look' – her voice took on a softer note – 'I've a couple of frocks, they're quite good – plain. Take all that lot of stuff of hers away and I'll fit her out. There, I can't say fairer, can I?'

Jinny turned and looked at her eldest daughter. She was sorry for Florence and she knew how she was feeling. At one time she had felt something like that herself when she first went courting. The fellow had been a bit uppish and hadn't taken to Lottie, and because of that she herself hadn't taken to him and had broken it off. But she felt bitter towards Lottie because of it. Then she had met Frank, and he had liked Lottie and said, 'Let her be; don't bother what she looks like, she's happy.' And so she had let her be, with regard to clothes anyway. But there were other things about which she couldn't let her be.

Jinny, shrugging these things off her mind, said, 'It's kind of you, lass, but it'd be no use. Lottie could turn a nun's garb into her own creation in five minutes, you know she could. You could rig her out up to the neck and then she'd come across some old hat and there she'd be, Lottie again. Don't worry' – Jinny smiled at her daughter – 'she's harmless.'

'Harmless!' Florence's voice became shrill. 'Harmless, did you say? I don't know so much. She wasn't so harmless with the fiddler, was she?'

Jinny's smile vanished and she answered tartly, 'Well, that's over and done with. She's promised Larry not to go near Bog's End again and she'll do what he says.'

'Perhaps, let's hope so.' There was a moment's

silence, then Florence, with a small wag of the head that spoke of the hopelessness of it all, said, 'Well, I suppose I'd better be going. I haven't got time to go to our Grace's now, I'll miss the bus. Will she be in this afternoon?'

'I expect so.'

'Will you tell her then that Sidney wants to see Harry? Ask her can they come over the morrow.'

Jinny's eyes narrowed, as she turned slowly about and looked at her daughter. 'What's afoot now? You're not putting them up to anything, are you? It's enough one family going.'

Florence's head jerked upwards again as she said primly, 'I know nothing about it. It's between Sidney and Harry.'

Jinny now glared angrily at her daughter for a moment before saying, 'Well, you can just tell Sidney not to get at Harry. Harry hasn't got the mind of a sparrow, he can be led. I'll get your father to see into this. I will.'

'See here, Mum. We're not still children, surely, and what's more . . .' Florence's voice stopped suddenly and her arm, unusual in its length, pointed towards the window, then in high indignation she cried, 'Look! Just look at her.'

The question of the moment forgotten, Jinny looked, and through the window she saw her sister Lottie running across the road towards the house; her cape was loose and she was holding it on to her shoulder with one hand, while with the other hand she held on to her large hat. As her high-heeled sandals, already over at the sides, were not made for running in, she had the appearance of someone well gone in drink.

And that's what several women in the street must have thought, for they turned from their various Saturday morning occupations of cleaning windows, polishing knockers, or lugging home great bags of groceries to stare at Lottie.

Mrs King from across the road went as far as to call 'What's up, Lottie?' but Lottie did not stop to make any answer.

'In the name of God!' said Jinny softly as she watched Lottie thrust open the garden gate, mount the three steps, then wobble up the path at a run.

The living-room window and front door faced the garden and the path led straight to the front door, but even in her distress Lottie knew better than to come in the front way over Jinny's clean step. But as she passed the window she gesticulated wildly to her sister before disappearing round the side of the house.

'In the name of God,' said Jinny again, 'what's got her now?' And she turned and faced the door but did not go towards it. Florence was standing in the middle of the room, and she too faced the door, and when her aunt stumbled in, her lip curled noticeably with her distaste.

'Oh! Jinny.' Lottie pressed her hand tightly against her ribs. 'Oh, Jinny, I've got the stitch.'

'What's up with you, woman?' cried Jinny. 'Have you gone mad?'

21

'Gone?' muttered Florence heavily.

'Oh! Jinny.'

'Sit down. What's the matter with you? Just look at you. Has somebody done something?' There was a note of fear in Jinny's voice. 'You haven't been down to Bog's End, have you?' Jinny reared to the extent of her five foot two inches, and her breadth, which gave the impression of equalling her height, seemed to expand still further.

'No. No, Jinny. I promised, and Larry said . . .'

'I know all about that. If you haven't been down there, what is it then?'

Lottie became suddenly calm. Under the balancing eye of her sister, who could cope with all things, her news did not now hold such ominous disaster. The family peace would be kept because Jinny would see to it; and Larry wouldn't be hurt, and he would cotton-on to Jessie again. Jinny would fix things. Sitting down like a slowly deflated balloon she said, 'Pam Turnbull's come back.'

Had Lottie consciously played for effect she would have been gratified at the result of her words.

'What!' Both Jinny and Florence spoke together; then Florence added, 'You're barmy, you've been seeing things.'

'No, I'm not; no I haven't, Florence, I saw her . . . she's back.'

'Where?' asked Jinny quietly.

'Bottom of Brampton Hill, in a big car, Jinny.'

'In a car?' said Florence. 'Who was driving it? What was he like?'

Jinny, casting an impatient glance at her daughter, said tersely, 'Does that matter?'

And Florence's look placed her mother in the category in which she held Lottie, as she said, 'Of course it does. If he was with her – her husband – there's nothing likely to start. Lord!' – she pulled at her glove with such energy that the cotton ripped – 'the things that people get up to in this family. If it isn't one thing it's another. You won't be able to show your face in the town next.'

'And why not, pray?' Jinny's face was red and her voice high. 'If you no longer want to own your family you know what you can do, lass.'

On this rebuke Florence's mouth became set and she looked again at Lottie, the question still in her eyes, and Lottie said, 'I didn't look at him, Florence, just at Pam. She was all dressed up and the car was red inside.'

'Suitable colour,' said Florence, turning towards the fire. Then on the sound of the back door opening and a voice bellowing 'Hello! hello! hello! where's everybody?' she closed her eyes. There followed the rattle of a bait tin being dropped on the scullery table, before the deep voice came up the passage crying, 'Where's that fat, old Jinny Broadhurst?'

Jinny, going quickly to the kitchen door, called to the youngest of her family, 'Stop making that row and come here a minute.'

Jack Broadhurst came into the room pulling off his coat. He was of short build, barely five foot five, and in appearance like his mother, but in comparison with her, because of his thin sparseness, he looked of moderate height. His face was square and inclined to ugliness, yet was saved by his eyes. They were the typical Broadhurst eyes. All the children of Frank Broadhurst had inherited his one good feature, deep-socketed, large, black-brown eyes. Yet no pair of eyes in the four children were alike, for each personality had individualized his own; whereas Florence's were surly, Jack's were merry.

'What's up?' He looked from one to the other; then his gaze settled on Lottie, and noticing her more than usually dishevelled appearance, he assumed a mock frown, nodded his head deeply at her and exclaimed in shocked tones, 'Lottie! What now, brown cow?'

'It's not me, Jack,' said Lottie.

'Stop your carry-on,' said Jinny. 'We have enough to think about – Pam Turnbull's back.'

Jack's brows drew together and his face sobered. 'Back? No!'

'Yes. Lottie says she saw her.'

'You sure, Aunt Lot?'

'Yes, Jack. Yes, I'm sure.'

'But she's in America. She wouldn't come back here, not so soon anyway after all that's happened.'

'It was her, Jack, and she looked at me an' all like she knew me.'

'Look,' said Jinny, turning to her son with the eagerness born of worry, 'if it's her, she'll be at her mother's, car an' all by now. Take a dander down to Powell's – you could be going for the paper or cigs

24

or anything – and if the car's outside the shop it's her all right. Lottie says the car's red inside.'

'Yes, Jack, it was.' Lottie moved her head in small nods.

Slowly Jack put on his coat again, his face looking older in its solemnity – he could have been forty-six instead of twenty-six. 'I hope you're wrong, Aunt Lot,' he said, and then went out.

He went down the back garden and into the lane, his step slow and heavy as if he were reluctant to reach the end and turn the corner. At the bottom of the lane was an open space and across it and bordering the straight main road that ran through the town were the backs of two shops, with flats above them. The buildings looked neat and compact. They were freshly painted and the windows of one of the flats were draped in fine lace curtains, hung cross-wise. This distinguished it from its neighbour, whose back window looked what it was, a kitchen window.

Jack walked round the right-hand side wall and to the front of the shops, and there opposite the grocery store stood the car as Aunt Lot had described it. His eyes just flickered over it before he entered the paper shop, where he immediately sensed that his entry was a little disconcerting to Mrs Powell and the customer for they were deep in earnest conversation; and he had no need to guess what the topic was. He picked up the newspaper, handed Mrs Powell the money and walked out. The fact that Mrs Powell had made no comment about the weather or the cost of living was further proof, if that had been needed, that Aunt Lot had not been mistaken.

As he came out again he stood for a moment and stared at the car . . . The bitch! The brazen bitch, for that's all she was.

On the spare land behind the shop once again, he stood and lighted a cigarette. There'd be hell to pay now. Even saying that Larry didn't go off the deep end, the whole place would be agog as it had been four months ago, when Pam Turnbull had walked out on him a week before the wedding. He stared at the ground and pulled his ear. How would Larry take it? The concern he felt for his brother was sincere and deep, for as opposite as they were in looks and temperament there existed between them a strong link of sympathy and an affectionate liking, which, as boys, in spite of the four years' difference in their age, had taken the form of constant sparring. With the years, the sparring had become verbal, which sometimes slipped into hot arguments, for although Jack privately acknowledged Larry's mental superiority, outwardly he scoffed at it. Yet all that touched his brother touched him.

He moved down the back lane, more briskly now. If he was in Larry's place, he told himself, he would ignore her, and when her name was mentioned, he'd say damn good riddance. But her name wouldn't be mentioned, not to Larry anyway – he had a good idea what the general opinion would be: Larry Broadhurst was getting a taste of his own medicine, they'd say. Hadn't he played the dirty on Jessie

Honeysett the minute young Pam Turnbull came on the scene? And had he thought of Jessie's feelings, and her living right opposite the door and seeing the palaver as the wedding day drew near? No, Jack knew that in a great many quarters there would be little sympathy for Larry now. That was something he had never been able fully to understand, Larry preferring that bitch to Jessie. Why, there was more goodness and soundness in Jessie's fingernail than in Pam Turnbull's body – yet who looked for goodness when he wanted a woman? He had only to take his own case and Lena's . . . Here, here. He gave a hitch to his trousers and a mental hitch to his thoughts. Lena was all right. A bit short now and then, but that was her condition. When the bairn was born she'd be OK again. Which reminded him, Peter Cox said there'd be a cottage going soon, off the Lowfell Road. The folks were moving. He'd take a dander with her over the fells this afternoon and see if there was any chance of getting it, that would please her. The very fact that he was making the attempt to find a place should convince her he was willing to make a move. Yet in the back of his mind he knew the chances of getting the cottage were almost nil, and to himself he made no secret of his relief, for he could not look forward to the day when he would have to leave his mother's table and ordered home for his wife's less than indifferent cooking and muddled management.

As he opened the back gate his father stepped out of the shed with a pigeon in his hand.

'Been indoors, Dad?' Jack asked.

'No, not yet.' Frank Broadhurst gently put the bird in the loft on the top of the shed. 'I've just come back from Grace's . . . grand mornin' for a walk.' He looked up at the sky, then brought his gaze down to his son. 'I've just had a talk with Joe. He says if we could raise the money now we could get Tilly's small-holding and those three greenhouses for a song. I wish your mother could see it that way and let us borrow a bit and take the risk. It would be better'n scraping and saving for another year or two, then starting from scratch. Life doesn't get no longer and I want to see the sky a bit.' He looked upwards again. And Jack, on the point of speaking, was silenced by his father jerking his head and beckoning him to the side of the shed and out of sight of the scullery window, where Frank rubbed his knuckles hard against his blue-veined cheek for a moment before saying in a conspiratorial whisper, 'I was wondering, least it's just an idea but I was wondering, do you think Larry would come in? He's always hated the pit, and he must have a bit put by, the way he's been working lately. He's picked up something these last few months alone. Do you think you could sound him for me? I don't want to ask him if he's not that way inclined. Tap 'im first, and let me know, will you?'

'Pam Turnbull's back, Dad.'

Frank's hand became motionless and his thin kindly face took on a look of comical surprise. 'Back! You're not joking, lad, about such a thing? She couldn't do that . . . not come back here after—'

'I'm not joking.'

'Have you seen her?'

'No, but Aunt Lot has.'

'Oh.' Frank sighed and gave a laugh, and his knuckles now rubbed at his neck as if he were shaving. 'Now you're talking . . . Lottie.'

'She's back all right, Dad. There's a swell car outside the shop, bigger than anything in this town, and in Powell's they're on about it already.'

Frank's eyes flickered to the sky again, then he looked at his son, his expression a deeply troubled one. 'What's to be done? There'll be hell to pay. Why has she come anyway? Look' – he took hold of Jack's arm – 'he mustn't see her, we've got to do something. Get him away for the day or something.'

'That would be no use, he'd see her sometime or other. She's here to be seen, judging by that car.'

'All that over again,' Frank said. 'My God, no.' He looked about him in a bewildered fashion for a moment, then slowly he walked up the path and into the house, Jack following him.

The kitchen was as quiet as if it had been empty. Jinny sat on the edge of a chair and her hands in her lap picked at each other intermittently. Lottie sat gazing from her sister to her niece, and occasionally her eyes would rest on Lena, only to drop away from the hard stare that met them. Lena, just returned from having a hair-do, had been told of the return of Pam Turnbull, and was now, while filled with a devilish glee, awaiting confirmation of the rumour. Anything that would tend to make her brother-in-law uncomfortable and take him down a peg found favour in her eyes. He was an upstart was Larry Broadhurst, a prig – there was nothing bad enough that she wouldn't like to see happen to him. Lena considered she had a way with men – a sly movement of her hips or a hitch to her bust could bring a man's hand out to her. Why, even old dad Broadhurst walloped her affectionately across the buttocks, but Larry Broadhurst, even before his wedding fiasco, had rarely opened his mouth to her. And to listen to Jack and the others talking about him you'd think he was God Almighty. He was a stuck-up nowt, that's all he was, and she hoped from the bottom of her heart that Pam Turnbull would stay and flaunt her money and her new man under his nose. She was no fool, was Pam Turnbull, and she had guts, too, to make the break at the last minute like she did. She had more sense than to tie herself to a pitman.

Lena now screwed herself back and forward on the chair and with her forefinger pressed the crinkled waves of her fair fuzzy hair into deeper grooves. She had been a fool; if she hadn't been so frightened at the time she would never have got herself tied up with this family. So deeply did she become engrossed in her personal regrets that when Jack did come into the kitchen she took no notice of him.

He touched her hair, saying, 'Come on, penny for them.'

'Stop it!' She turned on her husband. 'Don't be so

rough, I've just had it done. Did you see Pam Turnbull?'

'Listen to her.' Jack laughed down on her. 'She's been asleep.'

'Don't lark on,' said Jinny. 'This is no time for it.'

'I'm not,' said Jack in a slightly hurt voice, 'but if we all look like professional mourners when he comes in that's not going to help him, is it? We've got to put a good face on it.'

'Yes, Jack. You're right, Jack,' Lottie piped in. 'We should all be happy and pleasant.' She looked towards Lena, trying with all the power she knew to draw the surly young woman into agreeing with her. 'Shouldn't we, Lena?'

Lena, staring back at Lottie, thought, 'One of these days I'll hit her with a poker or something. I will, honest to God.'

She rose from the chair and went out without a word, and Lottie, blinking and bewildered, looked from one to another until Jinny's voice rapped at her. 'That cape and hat! I've told you, our Lot, time without number, I won't have them lying about in the room. Take them off that machine and upstairs with them. I'll put that cape in the fire, I will.'

As if Jinny's threat was imminent, Lottie grabbed up the cape and hat, and exclaiming, 'Oh Jinny!' went out. And Florence, pulling at her gloves once again, said, 'Well, I'll go if I can get through the streets for the gossip.'

Frank leaned forward and tapping his pipe on the hob, said quietly in the broad pitmatic which always irritated Florence, 'As long as it isn't about thoo, lass, thee's nee need to worrit.'

Florence stared at her father's back, her indignation swelling her slim figure; then muttering, 'Oh, what's the use!' she flung out of the room, banging the door behind her, while Jinny, after flinching and compressing her lips, turned and looking from her husband to her son, asked apprehensively, 'Do you think he'll make a shindy?'

Frank said nothing, but Jack answered, 'You never can tell. He might close up and ignore them, or he might get into a blaze and then anything could happen. Or he mightn't be able to stand it and go off.'

Jinny went to the table and attacked the cutlery, rearranged it with quite unnecessary energy. God forbid that should happen . . . she could stand anything but that Larry should go off.

2

LARRY

'I hate this bloody shift, don't you, Larry?'

Larry Broadhurst's answer was a grunt as he wriggled on his belly over the slack to the next prop.

'I don't mind working Sunday, Monday, or any other damned day but Saturday.'

A man pulling on a length of cable a few feet away laughed. 'United will change the day for you, you only have to ask them, Willie. And what have you to grumble about? You've got a ticket for the Cup, man!'

'Aye,' called another man further down the coal face. 'What I want to know is, how you got it, Willie. All those damn promises week after week, they'll be given oot the day, they said. And like hell they were, not a smell did we get. But you got one.'

'Aye, how did you bring it off, Willie?' asked the first man. 'There'd uv been no hanky-panky about tickets had it been Cardiff.'

'Aw, Taffy . . . Cardiff! Aw, don't make me laugh, man . . . Cardiff in the Cup Final! But I'll tell you how I got me ticket.' Willie Macintyre swung round on his belly and his tone became soft and confidential: 'It was like this. I was tipped the wink that I had only to subscribe a thoosand punds a year towards home comforts for the team and a ticket'd be mine . . . well, I did.'

'Aw, to hell with you!' said the Welshman. 'They'll lose anyway. Manchester will put them in their place, you'll see.'

'Manchester!' Willie spat into the dust before turning. 'I've bet ten-to-one on Newcastle. I've got ten punds on.'

'Thoo's a bloody fool.' This last came from an oldish man further along the face, and Willie shouted back goodnaturedly, 'All right, Jimmy, you won't say that if it comes off, but I'll stand you a bottle of the best if it does.'

'I'm likely to go dry,' said the man. 'Manchester'll wipe their backsides off the field. And I'll bet you two-to-one that you'll not get to Wembley with the rail strike coming off an' all.'

'For crying out loud!' said Willie. 'What a lot of supporters you are . . . you should go back to the Midlands, Jimmy. If I don't get the train, I'll take three days off and hitch-hike it.'

The man's answer was lost in a shouted order from the mother gate. There was a movement of men, a laugh here and there, muttered curses, and the work of moving the coal face went on. This was the back shift, and on this particular face, which was only a small section of the pit, there were thirty-four men employed. It was the shift that prepared for the night shift. The conveyor belt had to be moved towards the new face and the props withdrawn from the old face and the roof dropped. Some of the men were cleaning the conveyor structure; others were spreading stone dust to allay the danger of the coal dust; some hauled sections of the one-hundred-and-sixty-yard conveyor belt needed for the new face. Each man was absolutely conversant with his allotted task and well aware that a slight lapse or negligence on his part could jeopardise the lives, not only of his immediate companions, but of the thousand men hemmed in below millions of tons of rock, coal, and slate. But apparently this did not weigh heavily upon them; in the absence of the deputy, risks were taken lightly, for as some of them said, 'If we got the coal out by the book there'd be a lot more bloody talk of output going down.' The prevalent idea among these men was that not one of them could be done without, which was almost true – especially of the tried and tested old hands. Where would they be without hewers? thought the hewer; where would the hewers be without the shot-firers? What was the good of coal if there were no fillers, and no-one to see to that all-important item – air; and where would they be if they couldn't drop the roof?

Larry Broadhurst was no exception to this way of thinking, except in his case, there had of late intruded a further thought which became louder with each shift: 'One day somebody'll make a slip and I'll be flatter than the impression of the leaves on the coal.' And his reaction to this was: 'No bloody fear, it's not going to happen to me. I'm getting out while I'm whole.'

35

Willie Macintyre's voice suddenly rang out in song, 'Take thou this rose.' The deep baritone words shot to the roof and echoed along the face, and a laughing voice from the dim distance cried back, 'Ta, thank you very much. Don't it smell lovely!'

There was a gale of laughter, and the humorist shouted again, 'Take your black bullet, Willie, and get oot o' the team.'

Larry tried to close his mind to the chaffing and especially to Willie's voice. It was odd, he thought, how you grew away from people. Willie appeared to him now a gormless individual, yet at one time they had been inseparable. And Willie would say they still were. From schooldays to their time of call-up, which they had accepted, they had been pals. It was then for the first time they were forced along different ways, Willie into the Navy and himself into the Army, so that from the time they had returned home things had been different. He did not think that Willie sensed the difference . . . too dim, he thought. He supposed it was the war that had first brought about the change in himself, but whatever it was, it was a struggle now for him to act as Willie expected. He had to curb himself from snapping a dozen times a shift, 'For God's sake, man, shut up and talk sense.' He wondered if there had ever been days when they had laughed together, wrestled and boxed in the back garden with their Jack as referee, and it was hard to imagine himself, while still a lad, working like a maniac with tough and tested rescue men in order to relieve this same Willie trapped behind a heavy fall of rock. He would have worked until he dropped, as any man alive in a pit would do to save his fellows, but he would not have been spurred by the personal feeling that had permeated his being during those two days and nights. His heart was young and fresh then and he had been very fond of Willie; now he thought him gormless and daft, and this morning, dafter than ever, for his tongue had never ceased. There were only two things in Willie's life: Newcastle United and bull-terriers. And the liking for this particular breed of dog, Larry thought, was because Willie imagined it to have an affinity with the team.

'Our Joe picked up eighteen quid last week, do you know that, Larry? And he's working the night again . . . five bob an hour tonnage. It's not bloody fair, is it? It's the likes of him that makes the country think we're living like millionaires.'

'It's the luck of the kebble, and anyway you had your chance.' Larry's voice was terse and again it temporarily silenced Willie. As he wrenched at a prop without caution he muttered, 'Damn and blast it!' and he wasn't alluding to the stubbornness of the prop. He knew why Willie wouldn't go on the other shifts. He would work nowhere if he could help it but alongside him. But to compensate for his sharpness he made himself ask, 'What did they turn out?'

'Close on a hundred and thirty tons a shift.' Willie came like a dog to his side.

'Good,' said Larry.

'Aye, and they were on bonus: sixteen per cent on the top takings.'

'Good,' said Larry again.

'There's nowt good about it. It's not fair, Larry, man.'

God in Heaven! – Larry wriggled forward – why must he keep talking of things as if they were new. Every man jack in the pits knew what the other fellow was getting, or near enough to it. Talk about 'suffering fools gladly'. If he started on about the union now, he'd hit him. He wiped the running water and sweat from his face. It was this heat, humid, like a bath. The light from his lamp played on the roof. Grey, not black, here, and he found himself staring fixedly at it, and he had a sudden frightening desire to tear at it with his hands and rend it. His bowels seemed to be loose and shaking inside his stomach, he felt sick, as if he wanted to throw up. He steadied himself by bending his head towards the bottom again. Another dose like that and he'd run amok, like Tommy Scallen last year. The quicker he got out altogether, the better.

He turned to Willie and indicated that he wanted a chock, but Willie was heedless and laughing again. Back-pushing towards him with his foot Larry cried angrily, 'Look what you're up to! Throw that chock here. It'll be a damn good job when the Cup Tie's over, or you'll go barmy over that damn thing yet.'

Willie made no retort to this rebuke, but the little Welshman exclaimed to no-one in particular, 'Depity manager we have on the job, my God.'

Willie was quiet now and working in unusual

silence, and Larry thought, 'Hell, why must I go for him?'

If anyone had told him during the war that Willie Macintyre's company would irritate him beyond words, he would have called him a liar, for one of the two people he had really missed during those years was Willie. But now things were changed. Life was changed, the whole world was changed, so how could he expect to be the same. Willie's continued silence told on him as much as his chattering and brought him to a final decision. He couldn't stand any more. He'd tell Bradley on Monday that he was going, and a week today would be his last shift. He'd get his money out of the bank, buy a rucksack and go – he could be in San Lorenzo in a week.

He rested on his elbow and stared ahead into the black, speck-spangled light. San Lorenzo. He clutched at the memory to bring him respite. Perhaps they had rebuilt the bridge on the road to Pontesieve. It must have been a beautiful bridge. He'd go to Florence; he would walk and walk. Slowly, very slowly. There'd be no need to rush and tear. He'd see the galleries and palaces again, the baptistry, and then his thoughts would come clear, and the words would flow, and his sentences would be polished, and when that time came he would go into Margate, and write and write and write. Margate – it had been a silly name to give to an Italian village. A fellow from Margate had called it that because it held nothing that his home town could have held, for not even the war and the German feet had really touched it. Theirs was only a surface impression, they had not ripped away the charm of untroubled centuries that lay in its soil. The village stayed as it had always been. Except that it was empty of youth; there had remained only the aged, and the very young. But with the aged there was quietude, and that's what he wanted now, to be quiet. He could hope that no youth had returned to the village, he hated youth.

His mind was made up. Abruptly he went on to another prop and attacked it with controlled energy. Before him, he knew, lay a week of fighting and tears. His mother's tears would be hard to bear but he was prepared for them. It was a pity he had not left four months ago, but that would have looked too much like running away. He suddenly picked up an iron lever that was not in his way and flung it behind him.

'My God! Larry, look out. Do you want to brain me?'

'I'm sorry, man. I didn't think you were so near.'

They stared at each other in the dim light for a moment before returning to their work.

'Larry.'

'Aye.'

Willie crawled up and lay alongside him again.

'Larry.'

'Aye – I'm here. You're talkin' as if I was at the other end of the swing bridge.' There was an attempt now at jocularity in the tone, but Willie did not answer it in the same vein, but asked seriously, 'Is owt the matter?'

'No. What should be the matter?'

'Nowt, only I thought . . . But if you're all right.'

'I'm all right.'

'That's good.' There followed a pause, at the end of which Willie coughed and spat, then he added hesitantly, 'By the way, Larry, when I'm on I'd like a word with you about summat. I've been wantin' to get it off my chest for ages.'

Larry stopped his work on the prop and looked at him. His voice had been quiet and even possessed a worried note; it was as unlike Willie's usual approach as could possibly be imagined, and he was forced to ask, 'Something wrong? Have you got into a mess?'

'No, no.' Willie gave a sheepish grin. 'I'm not such a fool as I look. I don't put on more than I can afford.' He drew his forearm over his face. 'No, it's not like that.'

'Well, fire ahead, then.'

'Not here, man,' said Willie. 'If you'll wait for me up top.'

'But I thought you were scrambling to get to the match. The buses and the roads will be packed.'

'Joe Fowler's giving me a lift on his motor-bike. He's collecting some bait from me Ma and meetin' me outside. You don't mind, do you? You weren't thinkin' about comin' to the match?'

It was almost an appeal, and Larry knew he had only to show by the slightest sign that he did mind and Joe Fowler would go on his own.

'Don't be daft,' he said.

'I'll wait for you on top then, and mind,' he added with a faint return of his jocularity, 'don't go in for a beauty treatment or I won't see the match the day.'

Willie screwed round, and Larry paused and watched him. He had for a moment glimpsed the side he had liked about Willie, the quiet, tentative side. He had been mostly like that before the war, but not since. Sometimes he thought that the bullet that had passed through the surface of his neck had left its real mark in his brain. Well – he turned to the prop again – whatever was to be said couldn't be important, not when it was Willie who was saying it.

The morning passed rapidly. The road was driven forward; the mother-gate trunk conveyor belt brought up; the deputy made his second round of inspection; then the call came, 'Ride, lads.'

Larry, with Willie behind him, clambered over the stationary belts and hurried with the rest, like a colony of hunch-backs, up the mother-gate to the loading station, where, stooping still further, they crawled through the low doorways, past the winding machines and into the main roadway. Here with comparative ease and managing to walk part of the way two abreast (there being no wagons to give them an illegal ride today) they moved swiftly towards the cage.

The rush for the cage was greater than usual, for was it not Saturday and the match on. The buzz of talk centred on nothing else. Every man had something to say as regards the outcome of the game, except Willie – so whatever was on his mind must be of some import after all, thought Larry, for it was an unheard-of occurrence for Willie to keep his mouth shut when football was the topic.

Once above ground, their tallies and lamps given in, and in the bath house, Willie, by way of a reminder, said, 'You won't be long?'

'Give me ten or fifteen minutes,' said Larry.

'OK.'

As good as his word, he was washed and changed and in the pit yard within fifteen minutes, and there was Willie waiting for him. Neither spoke as they made their way to the main gates, but on the pavement outside which flanked the main road they paused.

'Well,' said Larry, half smiling, 'get it off your chest.'

Willie did not immediately begin, but after a moment of staring at his feet he raised his eyes and looked sheepishly at Larry. Then he opened his mouth, closed it again, and gnawed at his lower lip.

Larry laughed . . . it was a patronising laugh. 'Come on, man,' he said; 'Joe will be here in a minute with the bike, and Joe's not the fellow to hang about.'

Willie rubbed his hand tightly across his mouth. Then said quickly, 'It's about Jessie. Jessie Honeysett.'

A slow, dull, red creeping up from Larry's collar darkened further still the stubble that lay heavily on his cheeks and chin. His body stiffened and stretched. 'What about her?' His voice was gruff with reticence.

'I want to try me chance.'

'You want to—' Blank amazement showed on

Larry's face. This was the last thing in the world he had expected to hear. It was fantastic.

'I wouldn't butt in afore. You see, I thought after the other business . . . well, you might go back to her. I waited.'

The tautness went out of Larry's limbs and he gave a laughing 'Huh!' Then said, 'Why, man, I didn't know it was like that with you.'

Willie's head drooped and he looked at his feet again. 'Always has been, Larry, but she wouldn't look at any bloke with you in the offing.'

Larry stared at his friend, whom had he been describing in writing he would have labelled 'nondescript'. Here he had been for years now, looking down on this man, calling him soft because of his devotion to football and his dog, and yet in a matter of seconds this daft attitude had shown itself as merely a façade. He had been standing aside, as always, to make way for himself.

This knowledge of Willie's selflessness should have wiped the trying years of peace away and thrown him immediately back into the once happy state of friendship, but it didn't. Instead it brought up a feeling of uncomfortableness, of being put in the wrong. His inner self, which had no connection with his six foot one and which had suffered depletion badly these past four months, shrivelled still further, and for a moment he hated this smooth-faced, slap-happy individual who had caused a further shrinkage of his ego. And he had the grace to feel something of a hypocrite as he thrust out his hand and gripped

Willie's arm, saying, 'Why, man, you're daft. Go ahead and good luck. And mind, I'm telling you this' – with his other hand he punched Willie's chest – 'if you get her, you'll be getting a damn fine girl. And I should know. I'm a fool, but that's how it is – go on.' He gave him a push, and Willie, laughing now, said, 'Oh man, the relief. It's got between me and me sleep; it's even affected me football.'

They both laughed, loud, hearty laughter. 'You're a blasted fool, always were,' said Larry. Then pointing down the road to where a motor-cycle was weaving recklessly in and out of the traffic, he cried with forced heartiness, 'Here's Joe. Get going, and come back whole.'

Willie said no more, but with a look that had in it more than his vocabulary could express, he ran across the road to where the motor-cycle had come to a pulsing standstill.

Walking slowly now towards home, Larry thought, Well I'll be damned. It was unbelievable. Who would have guessed him wanting Jessie. He couldn't take it in. Anyway it was a relief . . . if she'd have Willie, he'd get her off his mind. And it should stop the innuendoes and the pushing too. His mother and them would give up now, surely. Yet would their reactions matter anyway? – he'd be gone soon. He paused in his walk and blinked into the sun. He couldn't really take it in . . . Willie sweet on Jessie and keeping it dark all these years.

The unselfishness, of which he would have been incapable, brought up a feeling of resentment against

Willie. The fellow was daft. He couldn't see himself willingly standing aside and letting someone else go in and walk off with a girl if he wanted her. He had wanted Jessie at one time, and he had seen he had got her. He could recall the day he had first noticed her. It was Maundy Thursday, Easter week, nineteen thirty-nine. He was singing in the choir – they were doing Stainer's 'Crucifixion' – and Mr Lombard had given him the solo, 'The Majesty of the Divine Humiliation,' for tenor. His mother and their Gracie and Florence were in the front row, and next to his mother sat Jessie. She was fifteen – he had known her since she was nine, from the time they themselves moved into the new council house. It was in the last row of the new estate and faced a lone block of pit cottages, twelve in all. The Honeysetts lived in number seven and right opposite to them, and in number ten lived the Macintyres: Willie, Joe, and their widowed mother. Willie and he had become pals right away, and although his mother had always referred to Jessie Honeysett as 'that poor little bairn', he had not noticed her until he stood in the back choir stalls and faced the congregation as he sang. She was staring at him with her lips apart and her eyes wide, and her face was full of light. It was a kind of light that the minister achieved when he placed electric bulbs just above the shoulder of the Virgin Mary in the crib scene at Christmas, and the light on Jessie's face was for him. He didn't know how he knew this, but he did, and it was that that made him see her, as if for the first time. She was tall and already her bust was high, and her dark brown hair was tied back, and he knew it would be in three long curls. He had pulled her hair once, a long time ago. He became aware, as he automatically sang:

'Here in abasement; Crownless, poor, disrobed, and bleeding:
There in glory interceding, Thou art the King, Thou art the King.
There in glory interceding, there in glory interceding,
Thou art the King, Thou art the King, Thou art the King!'

that there was nothing about Jessie Honeysett that he didn't know, for his mother had for years kept the whole house informed of her growing. He also knew in that moment that he wanted her for his girl, and that he'd get her. And he had. It had been easy, no effort on his part, no coyness, or come-hither tactics from her. She wasn't like the other girls about the place. You never saw her walk along the main road on a Sunday night after church. Of course, there was an easy explanation for that: she had always to go straight back home and look after her mother. Her mother! If ever he hated any living being it was Mrs Honeysett. Right from the first she had tried to put her spoke in. She'd said Jessie wasn't to go to church – it was wrong, as she had been brought up chapel. Then she had come into the open and said plainly she didn't want Jessie to take up with a pitman. If he'd had anything in him, she'd said, he would have stayed at the grammar school when he'd got the chance and not left when he was fifteen. She herself had married a pitman, and look where it had got her – nowhere. Worry, and worry alone, faced a pitman's wife, and that wasn't going to be for Jessie. He never knew how he had stopped himself from telling her what everybody knew, that it was the unpaid skivvy and nurse she was afraid of losing.

When he had been demobbed in 1947 he had been determined to marry Jessie in spite of her mother, but it would just happen that her father died and for once it looked as if Mrs Honeysett wasn't shamming and was really ill. Jessie was working, as she had been since leaving school, in Barrington's Flower Shop, and when she was finished there the remainder of her time was spent, as most of her life had been spent, cleaning and looking after the invalid, for now Mrs Honeysett became completely bed-ridden . . . and bed-ridden in an upstairs room, too. How many hours had he sat in that kitchen when his shifts allowed and watched Jessie, tired after a day of standing, trudging up and down the stairs in answer to the querulous calls. To him Mrs Honeysett was like a witch. If he went in without making a sound she knew of his presence. Perhaps, he had surmised, she gauged it from Jessie's eyes, for Jessie had never been able to hide her love. Recalling this now made him hot and shamefaced. God, what she must have gone through two years ago. Look what he himself had gone through since. It had been just retribution all right. If she had wanted her own back she had got it, with a vengeance.

His tread now was heavy and slow. He looked along the main road that cut straight through Fellburn and over to the right to where, in the far distance, towered the shaft of the Phoenix pit. Its accompanying pit heap had become the focal point of his hate lately. Each time he left his own pit, the Venus, he was faced by this one. Wherever you moved in this town you were confrontd by the evidence of a pit, and wedged between the two were straight rows of small houses – even the new estate had been pressed into the valley, leaving only Brampton Hill to escape and perch itself on the fells. Everywhere you looked in this town and everyone you looked at had pit written all over them. Well, he wouldn't be confronted by any of it for much longer. His shoulders went back and he pulled his cap closer on to his head. The quicker he got home and got it over the better. His pace quickened and then almost abruptly halted. In the distance and walking with her back towards him was Jessie Honeysett. There were others on the road but he could have picked out Jessie's walk in a million, not that she carried herself straight any longer, she didn't. Quickly he turned off left into Maple Avenue, round by Tomlinson's Garage and the new cinema, cutting through short streets of houses, some of which still retained half-section stable-type doors, and out again into the main road ahead of her, and right opposite the Turnbulls' shop. In his effort to avoid Jessie he had forgotten to avoid this part of the road. His face set, he crossed over, passing the big car standing near the kerb, and round the back on to the spare ground.

His teeth were set, and bitterness like alum was in his mouth . . . flashy cars, big business men. He knew what he'd like to do with all big business men . . . strangle them, the swine.

As he entered the scullery his mother came out of the kitchen.

'Hello, lad,' she said quietly.

'Hello,' he said.

He pulled a wet vest from his mackintosh pocket and threw it on top of the gas copper, and without having looked at her he said quietly, 'How much have I got in the store, Mother?'

When she didn't answer he turned and faced her. She was staring at him. 'About a hundred and fifty-six pounds, I think.' Then she added softly, 'Do you know, lad?'

'Know what?'

She saw that he didn't know, and she wetted her lips to ease the words off them. But they refused to come, she couldn't bear to see the look on his face when she should say, 'Pam Turnbull's back' – she had seen enough of that look when Pam Turnbull had gone away.

'Hello, Larry.'

Lottie came into the scullery, and Jinny's voice took on the form of a request, which was an unusual thing when speaking to her sister. 'Take the plates in,' she said. But habit told, and she cautioned sharply, 'And mind, don't drop them.'

'No, Jinny.'

'What's happened?' asked Larry.

'It can wait. Come and get your dinner. We're all in. Florence has been, she wouldn't stay. Sidney wants to see Harry tomorrow. I wonder what's afoot in that quarter?'

Chatting as she would have done on any other day when the tension on her son's face needed easing, she went into the kitchen, where her sweeping glance and quick shake of the head told the others to follow her lead.

'Sit up then, all of you,' she commanded; 'do you want to get this when it's clay cold?'

'Hello, there,' said Jack. 'Finished another?'

'Aye.'

'Goin' to the match the day?' asked his father.

'No.'

'I bet Willie's gone.'

'Yes, he went off with Joe Fowler.'

'Trust Willie. By the way, speaking of Joe Fowler, I met old man Fowler this morning on the way back from Grace's. He was on about you again. He says you're a fool, you could become a delegate, like that.' Frank snapped his bony fingers together. 'It's chaps like you they want. Pat Bingham is cocking his eye to that vacancy and he can hardly write his own name. He can talk all right, but that's not enough. Fowler says you could go along and have a word with him the night if you liked.'

Larry pulled his chair to the table and his head and shoulders moved impatiently. 'It's no good. I've told you, Dad. There's enough making a mess of the unions without me starting.'

'But they want fellows with head pieces,' put in Frank deferentially.

'There's plenty of them now, they've all got head pieces; that's the trouble, if you ask me. And I told you last night, Dad, you've got to believe in a thing before you can fight for it.'

'Unless you're called up,' said Jack, laughing.

'Ay.' Larry nodded and half smiled at his brother. 'Unless you're called up.'

'Never mind talking of calling up, sit up. Here, take that, Dad. Come on.' Jinny hustled her husband, and he, taking the plate from her hand, on which was heaped a huge section of meat pudding, enough for three normal helpings, said, 'Look at it! Are we on rations agen? You're not half gettin' stingy wi' the meat, lass. Look at that, our Lot.' He pushed the plate towards his sister-in-law. 'Not enough for a sparra, is it?'

'Eeh, Frank, you're awful. That would do me a week. Eeh, Frank.'

'Be quiet,' said Jinny, 'and get your dinners. All of you. Lena, will you serve the taties?'

As soon as they all started eating a silence fell on the room, making the clatter of the cutlery sound like a percussion band. The silence was not lost on Larry. It was as if they knew. And his father getting on about the union again. But they couldn't know. Not one of them would dream that he could leave home – the pit, yes, but never home. Had not his one cry for six years been to get back to it? What had his mother been going to tell him? He lifted his head to look at her, and his eyes were held by Lena's. And what he saw in them disturbed him. The half smile on her face told him she was amused by something, and when Lena was amused someone was nearly sure to be in trouble. He was in no doubt as to her feeling towards him – he knew he had asked for it, but he just couldn't stand her. He didn't know if she was more repulsive to him when she appeared happy or when she was indulging in one of her high-powered tempers to get her own way with Jack. What, in the name of God, had Jack been thinking about to take up with a great, fat, sexy piece like that . . . He wondered whose bairn she was carrying. Not Jack's, if the truth were told – she had rushed him too much. She had scarcely known him a couple of months before she had hooked him – a hole-in-corner affair in a register office by special licence. Their Jack must have been mad, stone mad. The house had never been the same since she came into it.

The look in her eyes deepened and her smile became a leer, and, challenging her, he asked her pointedly, 'What's on your mind, Lena?'

'Why do you ask that?'

'You're not amused about nothing.'

'Oh. Come on, all of you, if you're finished,' cried Jinny, getting up from the table. 'I want to clear away. Haven't you finished your afters yet, our Lot?' Then turning to Larry, and in an entirely different tone, she said, 'All your clean things are out. Are you going to change, or are you going to have a lie-down first?'

'I'll be going out shortly,' he said. He looked across the table towards Lena again, and after one straight hard stare he rose and went from the room. And as his steps were heard ascending the stairs Frank said quietly, 'Why didn't you tell him?'

'Why didn't you try it yourself,' said Jinny, ' 'stead of talking about union?'

'Aye.' Frank, gripping his lips between his fingers, pulled them, first one way and then the other. 'Aye,' he said again.

'Well, he's got to know,' said Jack. 'And he'd far better be told from inside the house than out. Somebody's got to tell him.'

'Well, why don't you go up and break it?' said Frank.

Jack said nothing for a moment, then muttered, 'It's going to be difficult. If he hadn't been so crazy on her . . . it wasn't ordinary.'

Lena made a noise like a gurgle. 'Is love ever?' she said skittishly.

This brought Jack's gaze on her, and his doting expression caused a boiling in Jinny's inside. Slush . . . they'd make you sick. What had come over their Jack? He'd always been the one in the family for joking, but nevertheless he had been sensible and cool-headed. What had come over everybody, for that matter, in the past two years? Her eyes moved to the window and to the cottage opposite. If only

54

Larry hadn't gone mad and thrown over a girl like Jessie, and their Jack hadn't gone soft in the head and been taken in by that fat piece.

'I could tell him.'

'What!'

All eyes were on Lottie. And she said again, 'I could tell him.'

'Huh!' Lena let out a laugh; and Jinny turned on her angrily. 'Be quiet, will you?'

'Well!' Deeply offended by the rebuke, Lena rose, and piloting the bulk of her fat and the added high bulk of her stomach with exaggerated dignity between the chairs, she sailed from the room.

'You shouldn't have spoke like that, Ma.' Jack's head moved from side to side.

'And you be quiet an' all,' said Jinny. 'I'll speak how I like in my own house. When you get one of your own you can do the same.'

'Well, if that's how you feel . . .'

Jack followed his wife, and Jinny called loudly after him, 'Yes; that's how I feel.' Then turning to her husband she said, 'You don't blame me, do you?'

'No, lass,' he said. 'I don't blame you.' Then they both looked at Lottie and she looked from one to the other and said eagerly, 'I can talk to Larry. You know I can, Jinny.'

'What'll you say?' asked Frank. 'How'll you go about it?'

'I don't know, Frank, but I'll just talk and tell him easy like. I can do it with Larry, I know I can. It's not like when I talk to other people. Can I, Jinny?'

After a moment, during which she looked at this sister whom she had mothered from the day she was born when her own mother had died and whose simpleness alternately aroused her anger and pity, she said, 'Go on then.'

There were some things that Jinny knew and understood in her mind but she had no words with which to express them, so when Frank said, 'I hope you've done the right thing,' she did not answer. There was a simplicity in Lottie, she knew, that had nothing to do with her simpleness; at times the simplicity seemed to erupt the muddled layers of her mind and express itself in words that were wise and whose meaning was beyond her ken. As Lottie went upstairs she sat down by the table and waited . . .

'Can I come in, Larry?' Lottie bent her head close to the door.

'Yes, come on.'

As she opened the door and saw him sitting at the little writing desk, set cross-wise in the corner, to the side of the window, she said, 'You writing, Larry?'

'No, clearing out,' he said. And he thought, There's truth in that all right.

'Well, I would have done it for you, Larry.'

He was forced to smile. She could not be trusted even to wash a cup without breaking it; as for dusting or tidying up, she created more chaos with her attempts than half a dozen children would have done. He let his smile linger on her and put out his hand and gave her a gentle push. It was odd, but of all of them it would be her he would miss most. His mother had tended to his wants and although he knew her love for him was strong it had always been guarded – no making flesh of one and fish of the other, had been her maxim. But Aunt Lot had openly poured her love and affection over him.

'Are you going to start on a new story, Larry?'

'Yes.' He paused. 'Just that, Aunt Lot – a new story.'

'Eeh, you're clever, Larry.'

He did not contradict her; it was nice for someone to think he was clever. But weren't they all under the illusion that he was clever? He had been under it once himself. At fifteen he had been so sure of his cleverness that he had left the grammar school. In his case, he could not blame his parents for urging him to go down the pit, for they had been dead against it, but he had wanted money and had convinced them that the school could teach him nothing more.

He had been a fool, a big-headed fool. And he hadn't to go down the pit to realise the mistake he had made – a week working up top had given him enough proof. The few years spent at the grammar school had apparently done little towards educating him – the benefit to be derived from it was generally felt only by the boy who stayed on until he was seventeen or eighteen – but there was one thing he had acquired, at least the elementary ingredients of it, and that was the questionable power of self-diagnosis, and through it he knew that his ignorance was abysmal. But more so was he aware of the ignorance around him, and particularly among those of his own family. Yet in spite of this knowledge with regard to himself he had attempted to write. He did not read in order to aid his writing, but wrote from the untutored pictures in his mind. And he got nowhere. But his self-analysis did not point the reason for this, until two years ago when life had suddenly blazed forth and showed him the reason for many things.

'There's Willie; he mustn't have gone to the match.'

'Willie!' Larry turned quickly to the window, and sure enough there was Willie hurrying down the street. What had brought him back? He was about to lift up the window and call, but the fact that he always kept clear of the window now checked him. At one time, the desk had been set right in front of the window so that he could keep an eye open for Jessie coming in from work, but now he kept the curtains almost closed, and although these would have been shield enough, he had moved the desk into the corner. It was likely Jessie that had brought Willie back; he must have done some thinking on the back of that bike. It said a lot for how he felt if he was foregoing a match to make a start on her.

'Larry – you know when you stopped me going down . . . you know where?'

'Yes.'

'I cried for nights. 'Cause I wasn't doing no harm.'

'Now, Aunt Lot.' His voice was stern and he thrust a finger towards her. 'Now, we don't want that again.'

'I know, Larry; I'm not asking anything.'

He bent over the desk. 'Is he back?'

'I don't know, Larry.'

'Then why are you on about him?'

'I was just saying – 'cause I was upset when you said I hadn't to go. I used to like to stand and watch him playin'. I didn't go in the bars, and I wasn't doin' no harm.'

'Perhaps not, but Bog's End's no place for you, inside or outside a bar, watching an old busker.'

'Aw, he's not old, Larry, and he talks nice . . . refined.'

Larry turned on her again. 'I thought you told me that he had never opened his mouth to you.'

'He didn't . . . he hadn't. It was when he was saying, "Thank you, Madam", or "Thank you, Sir". He never said Mister.'

Larry shook his head and smiled faintly. 'What's to be done with you, Aunt Lot? But don't you forget' – he again pointed at her – 'you promised me faithfully you wouldn't go near him.'

'I know, Larry. I know I did. And I won't. But it hurt, 'cause I wasn't doin' no harm.'

He smiled at her broadly now and put out his hand, and this time patted her arm. She didn't take advantage of this sign of affection as she usually did and grab hold of his hand, but turned and looked out of the window once more, and then in a muttering tone she exclaimed, 'There's Jessie goin' in. She looks tired, but she's still bonnie is Jessie. There's nobody like Jessie.'

There was no comment whatever on this from Larry, and Lottie continued her muttering. 'Her mother's very bad again. The doctor was there twice yesterday. She'll die this time, they think, Larry.' She turned from the window and came and stood near him. 'Larry, I don't want you to get upset, 'cause I know what it's like, and when you're doing no harm . . .'

Larry closed his eyes for a moment. He had found from experience that when Aunt Lot started to talk about Jessie the wisest plan was to say nothing, and then she would stop.

'And if you love somebody and they do something, it makes you feel awful. Jessie must have felt awful but she doesn't hold any spite. Some might. She's still got lovely hair, and she's still bonnie. I think she's bonnie.'

'Aunt Lot!'

The command made her jump, and she gasped and blinked down into his set face. 'Oh, Larry.'

'Now stop it.'

'But Lar . . .'

'Go on downstairs. Go on this minute.'

'No, no, Larry; I've something to tell you. Don't be mad.'

'I'm not listening.' He went to the door to open it, and she shambled after him crying, 'No, Larry, no. Not for a minute.'

At the urgency of her tone he turned to her and rasped, 'Well, no more of it mind.'

They looked at each other for a moment; then

noisily he banged the chair into place again opposite the desk, and sat down.

As Lottie stared at his back her fingers went to her mouth, and with the action of a child she bit at one nail after the other. Then in a whisper she said, 'I've been trying to tell you somethin', Larry, so it wouldn't hurt . . . Pam's back. She's in a big car, and it's red inside.'

He made no move, his head didn't lift, nor did his back straighten. Her words might have shut off his breathing and locked his body, so still did he appear.

Lottie's eyes began to run. Without puckering or moving the muscles on her face the tears spilled down her cheeks with the silent immobile crying which at times emphasised her oddness. She touched Larry's shoulder with the tips of her fingers, and after a long while, when he still made no response, she crept to the door and went out.

Larry, unlike the others, had not questioned Lottie. He knew what she had said was true. His mother's concern; the laughter in Lena's eyes; the restraint of Jack, and his father starting again about the union; and the car – red inside. After a long while he drew in a deep gulp of air. He was staring down on to the desk, his eyes fixed on a part where the veneer was chipped. With a sudden movement of his hands he inserted his nail under it. There was a sharp, thin, splitting sound, and almost a foot of the veneer leaped from the table into the air. As it fell noiselessly on to the bed-side mat he rose and went to the wardrobe, and wrenching open the door pulled down a suit. He undressed, flinging one article after another on to the bed, and when he stood clothed in his best, his tie adjusted and his trilby in his hand, he did not wrench open the door and with a step matching the dark fury on his face stride down the stairs and out of the house, but with a sudden heavy movement he turned and sat on the bed.

Fierce anger, mixed with pain and amazement and a reborn longing, were churning in him. He'd kill her. If he set eyes on her, he'd kill her. As sure as God was alive, he'd kill her, and the fellow with her. His hands, already clenched, tightened into knots, the bones straining through the skin. The fellow – he'd punch him to a pulp. Already he could see himself challenging the man to the quarry. There they could fight and only one of them would ever be able to walk up the steep bank again. The pain of his love coming uppermost for the moment relaxed his taut limbs, and his head drooped forward and his eyes looked into the mirror of the dressing-table and he asked of his image, as he had done a thousand times these past weeks, why she had done it. He was young, virile, a man with more about him than most, and she had loved him. Yes, she had loved him. The answer came to him as before . . . money, to which was added . . . her mother.

That Mrs Honeysett should have considered him unsuitable for Jessie had angered him, but Mrs Turnbull's attitude had been perfectly understandable to him, for hadn't she and her husband worked up an excellent business with one object – to give their daughter a chance in the world? He could remember the time, just after the war, when Mrs Turnbull's aspirations had aroused caustic comments, not untouched with envy, from the neighbourhood . . . sending her daughter to a boarding-school out of her war profits, the folks had said. What did they expect for her . . . that she should marry a lord or some such? You didn't make silk purses out of sows' ears.

There had never been anything resembling a sow's ear about Pamela Turnbull, but she was the daughter of a woman who had started a shop in her front-room window and who now not only owned a large store, but could buy property. Like the prophet who is never recognised in his own country, prosperity, even through hard work, aroused in Mrs Turnbull's neighbours nothing but envy. But in spite of the mother's attitude towards him, from the first he himself had felt nothing but admiration for her. It was she who had made Pam what she was, but it was precisely because she had done so that she was determined her efforts were not going to be buried in Fellburn. Pamela Turnbull had come to his horizon like a brilliant star appearing in day-time. At that period he had thought he was fully awake to life and that his days were bright, but the finished product of Pam Turnbull had showed up his days as dull and his life as commonplace, his brain mediocre and his ambitions without vigour.

It was on a New Year's Eve that he had met her, when he was playing first-foot. He had, to please his mother, been first-foot since he had come out of the

Forces. The darker the man, the better the luck. So on that particular New Year's Eve he had left the house just on twelve o'clock with a bottle of whisky in one pocket and a piece of coal in the other. There had been few people out in his street, for the custom was not kept rigorously nowadays, although most people held or went to parties. He had called a 'Hello' here and there to a voice in the darkness, and when he reached the top of the street and a car drove crazily off the main road and pulled up opposite the Campbells' doorway and the laughter bespoke of at least three of the Campbells being well away in their cups, he had moved on to the spare ground; for he didn't want to be dragged into the Campbells' house, which would have happened if they'd caught sight of him. They were a mad lot, the Campbells, harmless, but mad. Standing in the shelter of the Turnbulls' shop-yard wall, he had lit a cigarette, and stood for a moment out of the cutting wind, drawing on it. He'd had just enough drink in him to make him feel happy and at peace with the world. It had been a grand night and was only then just starting. He had laughed until he was sore. Willie was a fool. He had mimicked Norman Wisdom to a T. There was something not unlike Wisdom's fool character about Willie. He was a fumbler and a little pathetic at times, was Willie, but he could make you laugh. There had been no feeling of irritation towards Willie that night, for the whiskies had mellowed him. He had been about to move away from the door when a movement behind the wall made him pause. Someone was in the

Turnbulls' back-yard. The store room of the shop had been broken into only a week previous, so he stepped back quietly and glanced up at the windows of the flat. They were all in darkness. But Powell's, the paper shop, windows next door were ablaze with light. It was likely that the Turnbulls were seeing the New Year in with them. There came the sound of footsteps in the yard. They were distinct, yet quiet and seemingly cautious, and as the light from a torch streaked through a crack in the door he had thought, Someone's up to no good. Rotten trick to pick on this time. Yet it was the best time from a thief's point of view, for if a house was in darkness at twelve o'clock on a New Year's Eve in this town you could almost bet your life that house was empty.

When the figure stepped swiftly into the open he had grabbed at it and caught a handful of loose coat, and, before he could make any comment, the light from the torch was flashed full in his face and a throaty cultured voice had said, 'Let me go.'

He had not let go, but swiftly turned the hand that held the torch on to the speaker. And so he met Pam Turnbull.

In this first glimpse of the finished article he saw nothing of the Pam Turnbull that had been a bit of a lass of twelve in nineteen forty-seven, yet he recognised her. The close-fitting, shining black hair, that looked like wet sealskin; the pale transparent skin; the large oval of the eye-sockets tending downwards, from which all the lines of the face seemed to take their cue. It was an unusual face, striking in its contrasts of black and white, but in that moment he only took in the outline. He hadn't yet looked into the clear grey of the eyes. Nor had his gaze lingered on the mouth. He had laughed deeply in his throat and said, 'Sorry and all that; I thought you were a burglar.'

She hadn't answered for a moment, but had stood back from him shrugging her coat on to her shoulders, and when she said, 'You are Larry Broadhurst, aren't you?' he had laughed again, and replied, 'That's me. Larry Broadhurst.' And even a bit fuddled as he was, he had scorned himself for making such an answer. He should have used his best twang and said something polite in answer to a voice like hers . . . definitely la-di-da. That's what keeping a shop did for your bairns . . . culture. Oh, even in the darkness he knew that Miss Pamela Turnbull had it. He was amused at his thoughts, and when the church bells began to ring it was with a happy perverseness that his tone took on the pitmatic, as he said, 'A Happy New Yeer.'

'A Happy New Year,' she had said, then turning quickly from him had gone into the Powells' backyard.

Later, when he pulled Jessie behind the kitchen door and kissed her and felt her clinging to him, he had thought, This time next year we'll have a home of our own. Here I am thirty-one. Time's not standing still . . . look at that Turnbull girl.

He had next seen Pam Turnbull when he was coming home from work. You might have had a bath at the pit-head, there might be no trace of coal dust on you, you could be wearing a collar and tie and a decent mack over an equally decent suit, but you were still coming from the pit and everybody knew it. And yet he had never thought this before until he had seen the girl coming towards him. It was not only the boyish slimness of her figure, the lift of her chin, or yet her clothes which at first glance appeared to him plain and most ordinary until he came abreast of her that made him acutely aware that he was a pitman, an ordinary pitman, coming home from the pit, but the remembered tone of her voice. She was wearing a costume of dull grey. The rest of her attire was black, and it looked as if she was without a hat, so close-fitting and so akin to her hair was the tiny, black straw cap. Her whole attire looked as her voice had sounded . . . uppish.

Willie had started wise-cracking under his breath, 'Aye, aye! Who comes here? Me lady Turnbull. Bet you what you like she turns her nose up.'

He himself had not expected her to speak, but in an open, almost friendly manner, she had bidden them the time of day.

Gruffly, they had both returned the salute, and when she had passed, Willie, who in spite of his glibness was shy of all girls but who liked to appear knowledgeable in that direction, said, 'Whew! Don't tell me you've got to be born with blue blood . . . she's the lady of the manor all right. Fancy her speaking!'

Larry had not mentioned the New Year's Eve

incident to anyone, and as he listened to Willie's chatter the image of the girl stayed vividly in his mind and he found himself thinking sardonically, Unless she finds some bloke with money she's going to have a thin time. He couldn't see what she was going to get out of her years of polishing here; there was no-one in Fellburn for the likes of her, unless she hooked somebody from the Hill. He couldn't see her fitting permanently into a flat above the grocer's shop, no matter how posh the flat might be.

It was nearly six weeks later when he saw her for the third time. It was at the end of February. There had been a light fall of snow followed by a hard frost. He was on night shift at the time, and went down at five and rode just after midnight. It was a rotten shift, for he saw Jessie for only a few minutes at dinner-time. But it enabled him to get some sleep and yet left a reasonable part of the day free for his writing.

The sun, though, had been shining that day and lured him on to the fells. The air was thin and clear, the sky high, and he had tramped past Fatfield right to Lambton Castle, and it was there that he had met her. It was she who had stopped first. After an exchange of greeting which centred around the weather, they had walked on together. Not to have done so would have appeared stupid – the fells were as deserted as a barren desert, and who would expect two people to walk their separate ways while journeying across a desert? And before the walk had ended she had become for him a being apart, someone so far removed from Fellburn's women as they themselves were from the moon. The way she talked fascinated him; no long uncomfortable pauses; no waiting for openings; no pauses at all in fact, not like when he and Jessie tramped together. Her talking flowed from one topic to another, it was challenging and stimulating. He had told her that he wrote a bit, and he had felt immensely gratified at her interest, and in spite of the fact that her attitude, as she rattled off authors and their works, could have been that of a professional for an amateur, it inspired him with a warmth and a desire to do something big, which the blind adulation and open praise of his family had never done.

They had walked more slowly as they neared the town, and as if they both were aware that they must not be seen together, they parted while still on the fells, she to take a bus and he to walk the remaining two miles home with a step made buoyant by her parting words, 'It's the first time I've enjoyed myself since I came home.'

It snowed heavily the next day, but he had walked on the fells again, and she had walked there, too, and they had stood under the shelter of a barn wall out of the driving snow, quite close but not touching.

That night his output was down, and at seven o'clock the next morning he had been up and in Jessie's kitchen before she went out.

'Look here,' he had said, 'we've got to get married right away.'

She had been puzzled and definitely unhappy, and

had gazed at him long and hard before asking fearfully, 'What's the matter, Larry?'

'Nothing,' he had said; 'only we have waited long enough. Look, Jessie, let's fix it up now. Please.'

She had stared at him in silence, then she had said quietly, 'She's worse, much worse – it would kill her. I don't want her on my conscience for the remainder of my life. We have waited so long now, it can't hurt us a few more months. Imagine a wedding with her like this . . . I want to start our life clear. But I'll promise you this; if she's still here at Christmas, I'll do it. I promise you. I do, Larry.'

That day, lost in a desolate ice-bound world, he kissed Pam Turnbull. They clung together swaying like two drunks, straining to bury each in the other, and when they drew apart they were not exhausted by their efforts, but intensely alive and thirsting for more. He did not say 'I am sorry' – he knew there was only one person to be sorry for, and that was Jessie Honeysett. Jessie was twenty-seven and this girl was eighteen, yet Jessie appeared the younger now. It was as if her youth had never matured and therefore called up no fierce fire in him. Not the wealth of her bust nor the curve of her hips had ever excited him like the flat firm body of this girl. If at times, as he had done, he had felt the need for fulfilment with Jessie, some feeling akin to tenderness had checked him. And he had soothed himself with the thought that he did not wish to saddle her with anything, that she already had enough on her plate, for instinctively he knew that had he pressed his need, Jessie would

70

have met him and taken the consequences had they transpired. And that was the puzzle of the two natures he had never been able to work out: Jessie, good right through, would have done that for him, but Pam, having taken him to the point of madness, would shy away.

For a month he had kept up their secret meetings, then, almost on the point of illness, he had made a clean breast of things. The mental stress that followed had now a haze over it, for it would have been impossible to live remembering Jessie's face when he had told her. But the reactions of all the others put together had fallen far short of Mr and Mrs Turnbull's. They had threatened him; then used persuasion; then pleaded, appealing to his honesty, his manhood, and lastly his pride. Was he not a pitman and would always be a pitman? Had he wanted to be anything else he would surely have taken the opportunities offered when he was at school. How long did he think a girl with Pam's advantages would put up with his way of life? To which he had replied that he was not going to remain a pitman, that he had other ideas, he was going to write. He could still feel the hot humiliation that had suffused him when they actually laughed in his face. But this attitude on the part of her parents only made Pam the more determined that he should succeed. She kept his hopes high and made his confidence in himself boundless; she made him take a University correspondence course in English, and herself helped him with his studies. In fact, from that time, she tended to direct all the operations of his life.

And his love and wonder of her had grown each day, for through time she not only soothed her parents to some degree, but she conquered his own family. His mother received her in the house – she was not always very pleasant, but nevertheless she received her – and for one whole year life was ablaze with living, marred by only two things, Jessie's presence across the road, and Aunt Lot's chattering tongue.

But looking back now he could see that he had been deceived by everybody except Jessie and Aunt Lot, for when the smash came, although it upset weeks of preparation, relief ran through the house and could not be hidden from him, and he saw, too, that if the Turnbulls had appeared to accept him, that had been part of their cleverness, Mrs Turnbull's in particular. And how her cleverness had repaid her, even coming up to her own lifelong visions for her daughter. And the torturing part of it was that it had been he himself who had persuaded Pam to please her mother by going to the dinner in Newcastle with them and Mr Hinnery, the commercial traveller.

He had seen this traveller – a man of over fifty and safe. The dinner was being given for an old fogey from America, so Pam said, and would be dull and unbearable.

It was since the unbearable dinner that she had changed. There had been nothing to notice at first; then came the trips to Newcastle, to Carlisle, even to London – this last supposedly to meet a friend from

France – and all the time Mrs Turnbull getting nicer and nicer to him, more disarming. And then one evening, as he himself had told Jessie it was all over, so his mother told him . . . Pam had gone off with an American. An American! He wouldn't believe a word of it, but had torn up the street like someone mad. The shop was closed, and at first he was unable to get an answer at the house door, but he had banged until Mr Turnbull let him in. Both of them had pretended concern and said they had known nothing whatever about the matter. But they had been unable to hide their triumph. Pamela had made a catch beyond their wildest dreams, she had married the man who had been the honoured guest at the big dinner, the head of an American export firm.

She had gone, without leaving one word of explanation or regret, and he could obtain not the slightest clue to her whereabouts. But a week later, when he heard that the Turnbulls had both left the shop in care of a relative for two days, a madness had possessed him. He knew where they had spent the two days. And on their return he had stormed in on them. The shop had been full, and when neither of them would go upstairs with him he had, with two sweeps of his arms, scattered bottles and cartons right and left. Women customers had screamed and a crowd had gathered in the street.

Afterwards he had waited for the threatened summons, hoping it would come. But it had not, and he was forced to continue in the old routine of his life in a white heat of pain which filled his thoughts with a corroding hate. And his feelings were not eased by the knowledge that every man-jack who knew him was saying, 'Serves him right.'

The past recalled now brought with it a fear – what if, when he should see her, he could not keep his hate alive? He rose from the bed. He'd keep it alive all right. If nothing else would preserve it the knowledge that she had come back so soon to make another laughing stock of him should do it. He squared his shoulders. No-one was going to laugh up their sleeves at him. He'd see it out, he'd put a face on it. And he'd get even – by God, he would. How, he didn't know, but a way would be shown him. He looked towards the desk, where were stacked piles of his writing ready for burning. If he went off now they would say it was cold feet. Well, he wouldn't give them the chance. A week or so more would make no difference, he'd stay and face it. He looked in the mirror, and his eyes, almost black in his grey face, stared back at him and asked the question: 'How long was she here for?' There was an urgency in him to know. He picked up his hat, dragged open the door, and went out.

Across the landing, in the best bedroom, Lena checked the low rapid flow of her entreaty to listen to Larry's steps going down the stairs, but she made no comment on her brother-in-law, the time was not opportune. Later she'd get in a dig or two at the big-head. But about to resume the delicate subject of Aunt Lot she was forestalled by the look on her husband's face. To her, Jack was as soft as clarts, and equally as malleable. She had never questioned her power to make him do what she wanted . . . sulks, a little bit of temper, a wriggle of her body in the right places, and he would be all over her. But now his face looked set, he had the 'Stonewall Jackson' look. And why? Just because she had asked him to do something about Aunt Lot. That old wife would drive her barmy soon, and then there'd be two of them.

'You're not serious, Lena.'

The tone of her husband's voice was unlike any she had heard him use.

'I was never more serious.'

'But why?'

'Why? Are you daft an' all, or deaf? What have I been saying for the last half hour? She gets on me nerves, I want to scream.'

'Well, that's your condition. Women al—'

'All right, all right,' she cut him short. 'Say it's me condition. Well, in my condition I can't stand her. She's quite loopy, she's up the pole.'

'She's not up the pole.'

'What!' Lena rose from the bed. 'Do you mean to say you don't think she's barmy!'

'Yes I do. Of course I do. She's not barmy, she's a bit odd at times.'

'Oh my God!' Lena clapped her hands to her head. 'If she isn't barmy then I am.' Fiercely she turned on him. 'Are you going to ask your mother to send her away for a few weeks?'

'Where could she go?'

'She's got a brother in Hexham, hasn't she?'

'Yes, but he's never bothered about her.'

'Well, it's about time he did.'

Jack stared at his wife. There was an uneasy feeling in him that this attitude was not entirely due to her condition. This might be Lena, the real Lena, and he would have years of similar scenes, like Wally Mitcham two doors down. His ma and da had had their tiffs, too, but his ma had never nagged. They had been a happy family, a jolly family, and the funny thing was, he thought, it was Aunt Lot who had gone a long way towards making it so. You couldn't help laughing with Aunt Lot, or at her. And now Lena wanted him to ask his mother to send her away. He knew the reception he would get should he dare make such a suggestion. His mother might for ever be on at Lot for one thing or another, but she was fond of her nevertheless.

Lena, seeing no signs of softening on her husband's face, changed her tactics. She sank on to the bed again, her hand pressed to her breast, her body slumped, and as her face crinkled ready for tears her voice came in a small whimper, 'I've given in to you all ways. Look at the nursing home. Peggy Robson, that cheap slut, can go to one, but not me. Private one an' all.'

Jack's response was as anticipated. He sat beside her and put his arms about her, saying, 'Well, you know why that was, honey. It's because . . . well, I explained it all. I think a fellow should see and hear his bairn right away, especially the first. Look' – he lifted her face to his – 'I'll tell you what I'll do. You can have seven out of the next fifteen in the nursing home. How about that?'

She sniffed and smiled weakly, saying, 'You've got a hope.' Then laying her head on his shoulder, she whispered, 'Will you ask her, Jack?'

'No, lass. I'm sorry, I can't do that.' His voice was gentle but his tone was final.

'No!' It was almost a scream. 'You'll do anything for any other sod in this house but me. I'll ask her meself.'

She was up, out of his arms and out of the door before his expression had time to resume its former stiffness, and as she cried 'Out of me way, you, you barmy bastard!' he saw through the open door Aunt Lot staggering back against the wall, and from the frightened and bewildered look on her face he knew she had been listening. And he went slowly to her saying, 'It's all right; it's all right.'

But Lottie was not to be reassured, and she fled from him down the stairs, her face full of terror.

3

JESSIE

Born with a different temperament Jessie Honeysett could have been glamorous. She had the build that was acknowledged as being complementary to this difficult-to-define and elusive quality. She had a fine bust and broad hips. When in her teens, her straight firm body and upright carriage could have been likened to that of a Negro girl, an uncivilised one. Her face was large and inclined to squareness, the bone structure being prominent and too bold for beauty, yet with the magic transformation that rightly applied make-up can achieve, Jessie's attractions would undoubtedly have lifted her out of Fellburn had she possessed the necessary touch of personal vanity and selfishness. But it was only because Jessie's carriage was a natural and unrecognised part of her that she managed to keep it as long as she did, for from the time she could walk Jessie had been trained to fetch and carry. Even at four years of age, because she was a big child and looked more like seven, the duties that could have been given to a child of that age had been thrust on her. But for knowing and loving Larry Broadhurst, Jessie's life, large though it was within the frame of her body, would have been shrivelled to a dry kernel before she had reached twenty. It was her love acting like a spring which, without the aid of make-up, good clothes, or even normal rest, achieved for her, beauty. Now, although the love remained, the beauty was gone. At twenty-nine there was no spark of the girl left, nor yet of the young woman. The straightness had gone from her back – she could have been a woman of forty, tired with the burden of life and work; her body seemed to have given up, its slumping spoke of dead hope. Only in the far depths of her brown eyes could be glimpsed at times a look that puzzled those who knew her. It could have been the look in the worm's eyes, had it possessed them, before it turned. But no-one in his wildest surmise thought of Jessie Honeysett turning. She had, everyone knew, been a doormat too long. Her mother had made of her one kind, and she had made of herself another for Larry Broadhurst.

She stood now looking down on the dying woman who had sucked her life away. Mildred Honeysett lay against the hill of pillows gasping for breath. The water of the dropsy had swollen her once slim body to a great bag. With a thick stubby finger she now pointed to the floor and in between her gasps for breath she brought out the word . . . box.

Because obedience had become automatic and was not governed by her feelings Jessie immediately went down on to her hands and knees and pulled from below the high iron bed a brown tin trunk, such as would have been the proud property of a maid in the last century. She had over the course of years moved the trunk hundreds of times, but never had she seen inside it, for it was kept locked with a small padlock. She had always imagined that it contained the personal letters that had passed between her father and mother during the 1914–18 war, but her curiosity had never really been aroused. There were so few places in the house where one could keep anything private and so her mother, she thought, had resorted to the tin trunk for her letters.

Mrs Honeysett turned her head slowly and gazed down on the box. Her large, pale blue, glazed eyes moved over it then lifted to her daughter where she knelt by its side. She motioned with her hand, then slowly brought out, 'Promise . . . me . . . you'll . . .' A renewed fight for breath cut off her words and Jessie rose from her knees and eased the panting woman into a more upright position. And as she went to move back from the bed the hand, strong, even in its dying, clutched at her arm, and a clear penetrating light shone for a moment through the opaqueness of the eyes and into her.

'I'm . . . not going . . . yet.' The stare became fixed. 'Mr Dobson . . . get him. The box . . . the key.'

'Mr Dobson had to go away, he told you.' Jessie spoke quietly, flatly. There was no feeling in her voice, yet no sign of impatience.

'Get . . . him. Go on . . . send for him.'

It was the same kind of order that had sent Jessie scurrying up and down stairs since she could remember. There had never been such a thing as a request from her mother, always an order topped with 'go on'. Now as always she went, but more slowly than usual, and when she reached the kitchen she stood in the overcrowded stuffy little room and looked about her. Wherever her eyes alighted on the walls they were confronted by a scriptural text of some sort, large ones, small ones, framed and unframed: God is Love; I am the Way, the Truth and The Life; Repent Ye for the Hour is at Hand; This certificate is presented to Jessie Honeysett for regular attendance at Sunday School, Baptist Hall, Cromlin Street, Fellburn; This certificate is presented to Jessie Honeysett; This certificate is presented to Jessie Honeysett. Her gaze moved over them all. The largest of the selection was an illuminated text which hung above the mantelpiece. The words were wreathed by large white lilies and trailing ivy, and the ornamental script read, 'The Angel of Death is galloping on you to-day. Are you ready?' She sat down opposite to it. The Angel of Death had knocked at the door a number of times during the past years and Mrs Honeysett had stubbornly refused him admission, but now he had forced his way in and was upstairs standing by her bed. There was no denying him this time, yet a fear that even now he might leave the house alone brought Jessie's hands together, and gripping them between her knees, she spoke to the tract, appealing to it as if it had a life and power of its own.

'Take her,' she said. 'For God's sake take her this time. Take her before I do something.' She stared at the lilies and trailing ivy and whispered, 'If you don't take her something will happen. I can't bear it any longer. I can't! I can't! Not another day and night.'

Slowly her head drooped and her burning eyes looked down on her clenched hands. Then flinging herself from her chair she dropped on to her knees before it, and burying her face in her hands she implored of God, 'Keep my hands clean, O God. Don't let me have her on my conscience. Oh, keep my hands clean. What's coming over me, God? What's coming over me? I'm frightened. Don't let me do anything. Oh, don't let me do anything.'

A crash behind her brought her to her feet with a start, and she stared in actual terror at the text. It had fallen from the wall, knocking two brass candlesticks from the mantelpiece in its descent to the fender. Glass was sprayed all over the mat. The text itself was ripped right through the middle and the cord that had held it snapped clean in two. Yet she had replaced that cord only last year.

The fear still in her eyes, she cleared up the mess, and when some minutes later she mounted the stairs to the room above her heart was beating wildly, and although the fear was still on her her body seemed strangely light. She felt as she had done years ago when, for all her size, she used to run like a deer over the fells, with Larry Broadhurst after her. She paused on the landing and put her hand to her throat, then gulping for air as if she had actually been running she entered the room.

Her mother was lying in a twisted position, her body half out of the bed. Her arm was hanging limply down and on the lino and where it had dropped from her fingers lay the key to the trunk. Her mouth was wide open in what looked like a surprised gape, and on her face was no soft light such as death brings.

Rocking on her feet, Jessie walked to the bed and looked at the woman who had borne her, and as the realisation came that never again would she hear her voice she had the crazy desire to laugh, to sing, even to dance. For many years now she had rejected the idea of a devil, but it seemed to her in this moment that he had entered in, for it was an unholy joy that filled her. Turning, she fled into her own room and, throwing herself on her knees again, she begged of God to keep her sane; not to let her laugh; to take the strange, almost mad feeling away; to watch over her and help her.

A voice calling gently but urgently up the stairs brought her to her feet. She went across the little landing and down into the kitchen again, and saw Lottie standing there, and in spite of her own distress, she recognised Lottie's agitation and said, 'What is it – what's the matter?'

'Can you spare a minute, Jessie?'

Jessie sat down heavily before saying, 'As many as you like, Aunt Lot.'

'Oh. Is she asleep, Jessie?'

'Yes, Aunt Lot, she is asleep.'

'Well' – Lottie put her fingers to her lips and tapped them – 'it's about Lena, Jessie.'

'Lena? Is she ill or something?'

'No. But you know what she's trying on, Jessie?'

'No, Aunt Lot.'

'She's wanting Jack to get Jinny to send me away. Would you believe it? Send me away, mind.'

Jessie, resting her elbow on the table and dropping her head on to her hands, said wearily, 'She wouldn't do that. Why should she? You heard wrong.'

'But she is, Jessie. She's on about it now in the scullery. She says I'm up the pole. I'm not, am I? She said it in the bedroom to Jack. I heard her through the door. I'm not up the pole, am I, Jessie? Nobody's never said that afore, everybody likes me.'

'Of course you're not, Aunt Lot.'

'But, Jessie, suppose . . . 'cos she's havin' the baby she got me sent away. I'd die, Jessie. I couldn't leave home, Larry and Jinny and Frank an' all.'

'Don't worry. If they should want you out of the way because of the baby coming, you could come and stay here.'

'Jessie! Could I, Jessie? Oh, I'd like that. Oh Jessie, I wouldn't mind that. It's like home here, I've always come over here.' Lottie's face relaxed and spread into a smile. 'And I could help you, couldn't I? Look after your mother and that.'

Jessie gave no answer but smiled faintly, and Lottie, assuming her former troubled look as she went on, said, 'Why do they want me out of the way cos of the bairn coming? I'm good with bairns, everybody knows that. I've minded all the bairns in the street, and I minded all our bairns . . . Larry, Florence, Jack and Gracie an' all.'

'Don't worry, Aunt Lot. It'll be all right.' Jessie rose slowly from the chair.

'Will it, Jessie? Well, I'll go, cos you're busy. Everything's happened today. Pam Turnbull coming back and everything . . . Eeh!'

The look on Jessie's face brought the long-drawn exclamation from Lottie. 'I shouldn't have told you, but everybody knows now. She's in a posh car and it's all red inside. But she's married and she can't have Larry, can she?' She smiled weakly and then mumbled, 'Eeh! Jessie, I'm sorry. It's me tongue, it's as Jinny says. Yet she let me tell Larry, cos none of the others would. Eeh! I'll go. I'm sorry, Jessie.'

As the door closed on Lottie, Jessie sat down again. The magenta patch of wallpaper above the fireplace, standing out from its faded surround now that it had been relieved of the tract, gaped down on her as a symbol of her release, but as yet the release was so fresh that her mind had not erupted to the surface the buried hope that had grown steadily in the dark locked recesses of her being during the past four months, the hope that, once freed by the death of her mother, Larry would turn to her again, if not with the old love then with need. It had ceased to matter to her how he came as long as he came. Without him the spring of her life had dried up. Only the touch of his hand on hers and the passage of his eyes brushing roughly across her face could start its flow again . . . And now Pam Turnbull was back.

'No! no!' She brought out the protest loud and harsh, and again she cried, 'No!' Then, her voice sinking but still aloud she whispered, 'She couldn't. Not now; not just when . . .' Her eyes moved to the stairway that led directly from the room. Then, silently now, she said to herself, 'It doesn't matter. She's married, she can do nothing.' And because of her own experience of pain, she thought, Poor Larry. If only he had brought himself to speak to her before this happened and she could have gone to him now.

Impelled by the thought she moved into the front room and stood by the window. She could go over to the house now and break the long silence. She had an excuse, a good excuse – her mother would have to be laid out. Ma Broadhurst, together with Mrs King next door, usually did the laying-out for the street. She stared across the road, not conscious of the trend of her thoughts until her shoulders, slowly straightening, brought her carriage to a semblance of what it once was. No. She'd ask neither Ma Broadhurst nor Mrs King to do what was needed, she'd do it herself. She would be unable to believe that her mother was dead unless she herself did it. Moreover, as kind as the neighbours were, she did not want any of them in the house – there'd be enough talk soon when she stripped these rooms of the clutter and hypocrisy of years, for even if she should be left with only a table and a chair she meant to rid the house of its suffocating rubbish. And her mind, returning once more to the pain of her life, told her that if there was any move to be made with regard to Larry Broadhurst it must come from him, for she knew that all the moves in the world on her part would be useless. She turned from the window, went into the kitchen and taking a kettle of boiling water from the hob she went up the stairs, this time without a pause.

It was half an hour later when the tap came on the back door. Jessie let it be repeated three times before she went downstairs. With the empty kettle in one hand and a pile of dirty linen mounted on the other arm, she came into the kitchen, and through the window that looked on to the small square of backyard she saw Willie Macintyre, all dressed up.

The sight of him brought a swift aching fear – something was wrong with Larry. He had done something; the return of Pam Turnbull had made him do something. But when, depositing the clothes swiftly inside the copper in the corner of the scullery, she opened the door, Willie's approach did not suggest that his errand concerned Larry. He was both jovial and ill at ease.

'Hello, Jessie. Now don't have a fit at seeing me.'

'Hello, Willie.'

'How are you, Jessie?'

'I'm all right, Willie,' she said quietly.

He fidgeted and ran his hand up and down the door stanchion. 'Can I come in a minute?'

Jessie stared at him, then said, 'Yes, Willie. Come in.'

She had always liked Willie Macintyre because he had shared her adoration of Larry. Yet at times the adoration had irked her and she had thought, Why is he always hanging about? Why can't he get himself a girl and leave Larry be?

Now inside the house and standing in the kitchen, Willie's joviality suddenly left him, and twirling his best cap in his hands – he had never been able, like Larry, to rise to the heights of a trilby – he said seriously, 'I was wondering if I could help you in any way, Jessie, with your mother being bad an' all? Get the coal in an' things.'

More than bewildered now, she stared at him. There were two sides she knew to Willie Macintyre. She had seen the reverse of the clown when Larry had left her. His pity for her then had brought him to her door, but for the most part he had been wordless. The bewilderment suddenly lifted and she knew why he was here. He had heard of Pam Turnbull's return and once again he had come to offer his condolences, for like herself he may have imagined that, the way being clear, Larry and her would eventually come together once again.

She said, 'It's all right, Willie.'

'But I could do something, surely . . . an errand or something. Could I go for your mother's medicine?'

'She's dead, Willie.'

'What!' He seemed to leave the ground with surprise. 'Eeh! lass, I'm sorry, I didn't know. When?'

Jessie looked at the clock. 'Twenty-seven minutes to three.'

'Twenty-seven minutes to three?' he repeated. Then screwing his eyes up, he too looked at the clock. 'That's nearly an hour ago, Jessie. Is . . . Mrs King upstairs? I'm sorry I came, Jessie, at this time.'

'It's all right, Willie. I didn't send for Mrs King. I've done it myself.'

'What!' Again he started. 'You laid your mother out?'

If the words had implied that she had achieved this with the aid of a sledge-hammer he could not have registered more surprise.

'I had to do it myself, Willie.'

'Have you had the doctor . . . the undertaker?'

'The doctor was here at twelve. He gave her forty-eight hours. But you could do something for me, Willie, if you wouldn't mind. You could drop a note in to Farrows the undertakers and ask them to come. And you could tell the doctor.'

'I'll do anything, Jessie, anything. I'll go now. And you must have company. There's nobody in our house, me ma's gone off to Birtley to see my Aunt Flo, but I'll get Mrs King and Ma Broadhurst.'

'No, no, Willie, don't bother; I'm all right.'

Thrusting his cap on to his head he looked at her. All right, was she? She wasn't if he knew owt . . . she had just laid out her own mother. My God! What a thing to do. And – he glanced swiftly at the windows – the blinds weren't down. The years of strain had told at last. 'Sit down,' he said; 'you must have somebody here. Now sit quiet.'

She did as he bid her. When he had gone she sat quiet with her thoughts. They would come pouring in now; there would be knocks on the door and flowers; there would be condolences – the harsh things that had been said about the woman who had made herself into an invalid would be forgotten; she would be spoken of as Poor Mildred, and people would remember nice things about her. But it would soon be over. A week, then she would have the place to herself, clear and stark. It would take perhaps years to refurbish out of her meagre earnings the four little rooms, but no matter how long it took, she would do it. She put her hand to her head. It was odd, but the clearing of the house, the ridding it of every semblance of her mother, seemed at this moment about to take precedence over everything; the thought of it even was balm over the pain that was always in her heart. She felt nothing, no ache for Larry, no sweating fear of Pam Turnbull and burning jealousy of her elegance, and realising this, she thought, Perhaps I am ill. This numbness . . . I don't feel anything any more. Well, if this was being ill she wouldn't mind it; it could last for ever if it kept the pain of living away.

As the back door and the front door opened simultaneously, and Mrs King came in one way and Jinny Broadhurst in the other, she knew the ritual had begun.

It was half-past nine when Mr Dobson, the minister, came into the kitchen. He had just returned from Newcastle, he said, and his wife had told him the news. Poor, dear Mrs Honeysett, how she had suffered. And her patience . . . well, she would now be reaping her reward. She had been a good,

God-fearing woman. Hadn't her life proved that? And her home. Well, in a way he was glad she was gone while he was still in harness to minister to her needs, for now, although his spirit was still young, his flesh was getting old, and he would be glad to rest. Yet, he was glad he had been able to see so much of her. They had been great friends. Great friends. How had she been at the end? Peaceful, he was sure; peaceful. Had she left any word for him, any last message? Oh, how he wished he could have been with her in her last moments, but he had been forced to attend the Church Conference. Yet he wouldn't have left her had he known the end was so near.

Jessie looked down on the rotund, smooth-faced minister as he talked. She had always disliked Mr Dobson; she had come as near to hating him as she could hate anyone. At first, because, following his visits, life in the house had become more difficult for her father and herself; and these latter years because of his constant ranting. Rarely could he speak without reverting to the Old Testament. Hell-fire and brimstone were his preventive medicines for sin, and it sickened her when, during his long visits to her mother, the droning of his prophecies would float down to the kitchen. But even then she had supposed he was good at heart, to give up so much time to sitting with the moaning invalid. It had been within the past few hours that her hate had really escaped into life. Her eyes hard now with knowledge, she stared at him. She knew now why he had spent so much of his time upstairs, and she had a strong desire to cry out at him 'You crafty, scheming old scoundrel!' But she restrained her desire. He imagined that she was as dense as her mother had no doubt made her out to be, and with that denseness now she would match his craftiness. So, keeping her voice as calm as she could, she said, 'No. She left no word.'

Mr Dobson did not take his eyes from her face. 'Was she conscious to the last?'

'Yes.'

'And she left no word – no message for me?'

Jessie made herself appear puzzled. 'Message?' she said. 'No. What kind of a message were you expecting? What about?'

'Nothing . . . nothing. Just a word to an old friend. Ah . . . er . . .' He moved the length of the hearth rug and back. 'What are your plans, my dear? You know I am here to help you. You know you just have to call on me. I am used to deaths. Births, marriages, and deaths, and all the trouble they entail. Now, will I see to the business side for you? The undertaker and the insurance people?'

Jessie found it difficult to speak quietly. 'Thank you all the same, but Mr Macintyre along the street is seeing to things.' Her tone gave to Willie's name the dignity of a city business man. 'And the insurance won't take much seeing to. There are two policies and together they come to £38.'

Mr Dobson's eyes were now boring into hers, and during the silence which he seemed to enforce she stood their scrutiny without blinking. Then with a sharp movement he took his glance from her, and turning his back on her, he picked up his hat and went through the front room to the door. But there he stopped, and this time, without looking at her, he asked, 'Did your mother leave a will as regards her property?'

At this Jessie was quite unable to hide her resentment and indignation. 'Will!' she cried. 'What for?'

He turned and faced her from the street, as, flinging her arms wide and taking in the room and its furniture, she said, 'If this is what you call property, it won't need a will to dispose of it – anyone can have it for the taking. As regards a will, what had my mother to leave? I have worked to keep her and this house going for years.' Her voice rose. 'Years! Every penny I have ever earned has gone to keep her. A will!'

'Ssh! ssh!' Glancing up and down the street, Mr Dobson cautioned again, 'Ssh; ssh! Now, now, don't get upset. I know, I know.' His voice was soothing. 'You have been a good girl . . . woman,' he substituted. 'I just wondered. And I thought if there were legal matters to be dealt with I'd be able to help you. It's very difficult at such times for a woman, especially a woman all on her own. Anyway, I am always here to help you; you have just to call on me as did your dear mother. I will look in tomorrow after the service, Jessie, there may be something I can do. Good night. Good night, my dear, and the good Lord strengthen you.'

Unable to speak a word in farewell, Jessie closed the door and stood for a moment with her back pressed tight against it. An anger, new to her placid nature, was flaring through her. The scheming old hypocrite! But for his being away for the past few days she would never have known what was in that box. Quickly she went through the kitchen and up the stairs, and once in her own narrow room she took the precaution of putting the bolt on the door – Ma Broadhurst would be over any minute, for she had insisted on sleeping in the house with her, and with the privilege of an old neighbour she might walk in on her even here.

Pulling the tin trunk from the corner to where the dim bulb of the centre light shone down on it, she took from the top drawer of the stained wooden chest the key, and for the sixth time in as many hours she knelt by the trunk and opened it. First she took out a small wooden box, and moved with her finger a number of golden sovereigns. They looked dull and naked out of their wrappings – each one had been carefully wrapped against its rattling. Seventy-eight, there were. They must have lain in this box for the last thirty years, and likely many years before that. She knew from where they had originally come, for her father had often said that her grandmother, who was an old skinflint, had left a bit, even though when he had tackled her mother she had always protested that there had been only sufficient to bury the old lady.

Once again Jessie lifted out the old clothes, vests, knickers, petticoats and woolly things, all heavy with the smell of camphor, and there beneath them lay the notes, rows of them. The one-pounds neatly stacked in tens; the ten-shillings also in bundles of ten. Twenty-two bundles of one-pound notes and thirty-four bundles of ten-shilling notes. Three hundred and ninety pounds in notes, and seventy-eight pounds in gold. Four hundred and sixty-eight pounds. And the sovereigns were worth double.

Where the notes had come from she could only guess – the pinching and saving of a lifetime, for there had been no compensation when her father died, only the money that the pitmen themselves had subscribed and the bit from the lodge. Together, they had come to nearly two hundred pounds, and she remembered having almost to fight to make her mother use it towards the housekeeping. Always she herself had turned her earnings over to her mother, who would then begrudgingly dole out a few shillings to her. And right up to the last six weeks Mrs Honeysett herself had seen to the paying of bills and the ordering of food. Everything except food was bought from the store through clubs. Jessie had never been able, during any part of her life, to walk into the shop and buy herself an article of clothing, and had it not been for Larry Broadhurst, never would she have been able, even if she had had the time, to move outside the town. And all the time her mother was hoarding this money. Her father, for years and years after leaving the pit, had gone without his baccy, and rarely, like other men, would he have a shilling in his pocket, except when a mate would slip him something.

In this moment it was anger for her father that was tightening Jessie's muscles. Her hands clenched on the bundles of notes – her mother would have given every penny of this to that fawning little hypocrite. 'Promise,' she had said. Well, she hadn't promised. But even if she had, she knew she would not have kept the promise.

It was evident now that Mr Dobson hadn't known what to expect. Her mother had likely held him attentively to her over the years with promises and hints of benefiting the church and incidentally himself. Before she would allow him to touch a penny of it, she would put the whole lot in the fire. She took the money out of the trunk and locked it in the top drawer. Out on the landing she stopped for a moment and looked towards the closed door behind which lay the trimmed, bloated remains of her mother.

Then on a deep intake of breath she turned away and went downstairs.

4

PAM

'You don't mind me talking about Jessie, do you, Larry?'

'No,' said Larry, banging the door of his clean locker shut. 'Carry on.'

He spoke truly when he said he didn't mind hearing Jessie's name mentioned. Now that Willie was in the running for her the burden on his own conscience was eased a little, and the longer Willie talked, the less time it gave him to think. It was six days since Pam Turnbull had come back, and there was no immediate sign of her going. Willie had tentatively informed him that Mrs Turnbull was bad . . . something wrong with her inside, she was going to have an operation. And he had added, 'I know how you feel, but that girl's not worth a second thought. She's no good, not to you or anybody else.'

Now Willie went on talking of Jessie. 'She's not the same, if you know what I mean. I think she should see a doctor. Me ma says so an' all. All the pictures are down, every damn one of them . . . and she's given a mountain of stuff to the rag man. Old-fashioned, but good. And the coffin was hardly out of the house, me ma said, when Sam Collet from

Bog's End came with his lorry and loaded all kinds on it. The cottage looks as bare as a coot's backside.'

They entered the lamp house and picked up their lamps and tallies, and when they were in the yard again and making for the steep iron steps that led to the cage, Larry, knowing that some remark was expected and awaited of him, muttered, 'Seems a damn good job to my mind, ridding the house of that clutter.'

'Aye,' said Willie, eagerly picking up the threads again. 'Some of the stuff should have gone, I'll admit, but she's clearing everything out. I called in on me way down the day, and the minister was there. I don't like that old fella, I nearly give him a mouthful. You wouldn't believe it, man, but he was almost cursing her because she had got rid of the texts. But the funny thing about it was, she didn't act a bit like you would expect, she wasn't nervous or anything. She didn't give in like she usually did to her mother. No, she looked him in the eye and stood her ground. It was fair surprising to see her standing up to him. There was another bloke with him, the new minister or some such. He's taking Dobson's place. He looked a decent enough fellow . . . youngish. He didn't open his mouth.'

Sitting on their hunkers, knee to knee, their bait tins swinging from their hands, they took the swift and sickening descent of the cage in silence, and when they stepped out into the narrow roadway their silence continued, for all about them were men, silent, too, for the most part, and all hurrying with the eagerness of lovers towards the coalface. Only when the shift had actually begun would the tongues become released.

The talk today was divided between two subjects – the strike and the cup-tie. Twenty-six thousand miners in the Doncaster area had come out on strike three days previously in support of the strikers in the Markham main colliery – and the fight for the Cup was two days ahead. The only man on the shift who had a ticket was Willie, and his answers to the others' chaffing were today unusually erratic, for his mind was on Jessie. When he'd discovered how he stood with Larry last Saturday, things had seemed plain sailing – he had even given the match the slip to come back and start 'getting in' with her. But from when he had seen her, all kinds of difficulties had come his way – her mother dying like that, then the funeral – he hadn't been able to give her an inkling of what he was after. Well, the way was clear now, and if Newcastle won, every penny would go on the ring. It would that. Last Saturday he had intended asking her to come up to London with him to see the cup-tie. By, he had thought, I'll give her a day . . . she'll enjoy herself. But now, although his interest was still with Newcastle, the great day could not monopolise his mind entirely; and this Willie found disturbing. He wanted to go on talking to Larry about Jessie, but Larry's face looked tight and his eyes were narrowed to slits, as if to shut out the dark world about him.

Unable to find release in listening to the others, Larry was endeavouring to shut the sound of their voices from his mind, and as the shift went on and on the minutes became eternities filled with anger and questioning and pain, and when at ten past five he saw the light of day slashing at the rough walls as the cage rose to the surface, he sincerely thanked God for the release. This particular shift, more than any other this week, had been pure hell. It was hard to say which was more tired, his mind or his body; his body was aching inside and out, but the fever in his mind overlaid the aching. He wasn't saying now as he had been saying with every blow he had struck during the last seven hours, 'I've got to see her', but he was saying grimly, 'What good will come out of it if I do? It's done . . . and if I don't watch meself I'm going to crack. I should have gone as I intended last week . . . But it's not too late even yet. I could tell Bradley tomorrow, and tell them at home tonight.'

Parting as usual at the top of the street, Willie went down one back lane and Larry branched down the other. There were women here and there at their gates. Some said, 'Hello there, Larry'; some said, 'Another over?'; some said nothing. Among the latter group were three Podger women, mother, daughter, and daughter-in-law. They lived a little way below on the opposite side of the lane, and their back garden was railless and had the appearance of a miniature rubbish dump, covered with weeds. These self-same weeds had caused his father to make a strong protest last year, for his garden-loving soul had been outraged at the neglect and the flying weed seeds. The protest had been verbal and strong, and had been answered more strongly still by the Podger men. Larry and Jack coming to their father's defence, had evened the affair, with the result that the two families no longer hailed each other. Larry, passing the fixed stare of the women, knew exactly what they were thinking, and when he got inside the house he thought, Damn them. Laughing up their sleeves. And their malicious glances seemed to set the seal on his decision, for when Jinny, coming into the scullery to meet him, said 'Hello, there,' he replied 'Hello,' and added, 'Is there anybody in, Mother?'

'Lena and your da,' she said. 'Why?'

He took off his coat and hung it on the back of the door before saying, 'About the money in the store – you remember I asked you on Saturday – can you get it out for me by the week-end? I'm leaving.'

'Leaving!' The word sprang out and left her lips vibrating like a tweaked wire.

'I've got to go.' He turned his back on her.

'Oh! lad . . . don't. She'll be gone soon . . . she can't stay. Emily King says she thinks they're flying back Monday. It's only a day or so more . . . don't go, Larry.'

'I've got to go. I was going in any case.'

She watched him go out, and her eyes followed him as he went up the stairs, then bringing her pinny to her mouth she bit on it.

'Is that Larry come in?' Lottie, in a red jumper and an old-fashioned green skirt, came laughing into the scullery. Jinny had not included her when Larry had asked who was in . . . Lottie in or out was of little consequence.

'Be quiet you,' Jinny barked at her. And Lottie, apologising with word, look, and manner, said, 'Oh, all right, Jinny. I'm sorry.' And blinking rapidly, she went into the kitchen again to continue talking to Lena in an endeavour to make Lena like her, so she wouldn't ever again ask for her to be sent away.

Jinny, following her into the kitchen, took a buff-coloured envelope off the mantelpiece and going up the stairs to Larry's door she said softly, 'There's a letter here for you.' Then turning the handle she went in.

'Thanks.'

He was pulling a clean shirt over his head, and she put the letter on the desk. While still buttoning the shirt he looked down on it. The address was typed, that meant it was from the correspondence school. Well, that was finished.

'Won't you wait, Larry?'

'I can't. I'm telling Bradley tomorrow. I'll be off next week. I've had it in mind for some time.'

She stood quiet for a moment before saying, 'Where do you think of going?'

He tucked his shirt into his trousers. 'Italy.'

'Italy!' She stared at him for a moment longer, then went out.

She had yelled a lot in her time about making them all alike, but in her heart she knew that when Larry left home, and this time of his own accord, he would never come back, and the breach made in the family circle, which covered a radius of six miles, to Hylton on one side and Birtley on the other, would be such that not one of the others would be able to close it. For in a secret recess of her heart, into whose chamber she allowed herself only infrequent visits, was locked a passionate love for this son. The only clever one of her brood; the only fine set-up one of her brood; the only one of her brood who at odd times ever thought of her as a woman, like that time when he had torn up Frank's old top coat which she wore around her when sitting waiting for their coming in from the night shift or getting up to see them out on the fore shift. Three Christmases ago it was, when he had bought her that blue dressing-gown, padded all over and fit for a queen, and she had almost cried when she had had to cut nearly a foot off the bottom. Yet she rarely wore it, thinking it much too good and that it would be a shame to muck it up for everyday wear. She did, however, wear it for him, but for her husband's and younger son's reception she went to the trouble of putting on all her clothes.

Dressed now for outdoors, Larry was about to leave the room when he remembered the letter. He reached for it on his way to the door and, having ripped the end off, he pulled out a single sheet of paper which bore the date and two words: The Barn.

Once, many years ago, he had taken cramp while swimming in the river below Durham. It had been a frightening experience. The cramp had attacked his legs, and the pain had brought fear with it, and the fear had caused heat to flood his body even though his leg felt dead and cold. Somehow he had reached the bank and lain for what seemed to him hours, face downwards, gasping for breath. Now he felt like that again, as if he were drowning, and the fear was on him, and he gasped as he stood staring at the sheet of paper.

When he went downstairs he did not go into the kitchen but into the scullery. Jinny was taking a covered dish from the gas oven, and he said, his voice steady, ordinary and low, 'I won't have it now. You can leave it out . . . I'll warm it up when I come in. Don't wait up . . . so long.'

She made no protest. 'So long,' she said and watched him walk down the garden path to the back gate and into the lane, upwards towards the fells, not downwards towards the town, and she said to herself, 'Now why?'

The barn was derelict; holes gaped in its roof, and the timbers at the sides had been torn off here and there by wood hunters. It stood within a few yards of an even more derelict cottage. Roofless, with only its outer walls standing, it gaped starkly to the heavens. Both buildings showed signs of target practice, and both appeared as a scar on the bright budding green of the copse under which they sheltered. They were a good three miles' walk from Fellburn and a mile from the nearest main road, which touched Fatfield and led to Chester-le-Street.

Sometimes the barn was invaded by a scrounging party of boys, but mostly it was the haunt of lovers in the evening, and men of the road at night. As regards the tenancy of the courting couples, it was first come first served. But in the afternoon or early evening, on any day except Sundays or holidays, you could almost be sure of finding the barn deserted. It was here that Larry and Pam had met during the first secret weeks of their love-making, and it had remained a rendezvous through their courtship.

The sweat running in his oxters and his shirt clammy on his back, he now approached the place which he had thought never to see again except in the torment of his dreams, and as he came to the copse his pace slowed until it stopped. The thud of his heart pounded against his ribs and reverberated through his ears until he could hear nothing but the agitated beats. He passed his hand over his mouth, then pulled at his collar, stretching his neck out of it. There was no anger in him, only a longing and a feeling of excitement, but as he moved on, more slowly now, he endeavoured to work up his fury, telling himself that at the sight of her he would become mad, he would kill her. He moved round the back of the barn. There were gaps in the wood on that side and if he could see her before she saw him it would, he hoped, give him something of an advantage. But he could see no sign of anyone through the holes. With a weighed step as if walking through snow he made his way to the front, and to the big doorless gap, and here he paused a moment before stepping over the threshold. The beats of his heart were all converging in his neck, swelling it and pressing out the sinews like muscles. He made a small movement forward, and there she was, standing in the far corner. The blood in his veins was no longer blood but water. His body was without support, he had to grab wildly at his anger, forcing it into his eyes and his thrusting lower lip. And as she came slowly towards him he found it easier to hold it, and thrashed himself into a state of vituperation. The nerve of her, daring to send for him. She'd be sorry she had made that mistake, by God she would, when he had finished with her. She had walked right into his hands, miles away from anyone. He'd spoil that polish, that complacency. He took in the fact that she was dressed plainly as usual, but he knew that it was a more expensive plainness than ever before. Her face looked paler, smaller, and her eyes larger, and altogether she looked older, much older. Thirty, not twenty.

Within a few feet of him, she stopped, and when the silence between them screamed in his head, he ground out between his teeth, 'You! You! Well, what do you want?'

'Oh, Larry.' Her voice was a mere whisper but the inflection was as soft and clear as usual, and the sound of its polished tone really did madden him . . . it wiped away all pretence of anger. The pain and humiliation of the past months suddenly erupted and, boiling together, brought his forearm up with a swing. But before the back of his hand descended on her face he checked it, and it wavered a moment before dropping heavily back to his side.

'You should have done it – I would have felt better.'

Her eyes passed in turn to each of his features. They lingered for a moment on the scornful, thrusting curve of his lips, then returned and met his eyes and the dark anger glinting from the narrowed lids.

His maleness had drawn her from their first meeting, that New Year's Eve night in the dark, and now she was aching with its loss. She said again, 'Oh, Larry.' And he replied harshly, 'Drop that. What do you want?'

Like a child, she said, 'Just to see you, to hear you.'

'You're a bit late in the day, aren't you, with that line.' He was talking the broad, rough idiom used in the pits, to which sound he had never before treated her. Always he had tried to match her polish, being so careful of his grammar that at times his speech had become stilted. But now there was no need to keep up with her, and only in his natural tongue could his anger flow. 'You've got all you want, money . . . a car. What more can you want?'

She gazed silently up into his face. And the pain he saw there cut into him, but he would not recognise its thrust. Instead, he added brutally, 'And an old bloke to supply the romance.'

After a long moment her eyes dropped from his and she turned from him and made for the opening, saying, 'I shouldn't have come, but I wanted to tell you . . . I'm sorry.'

As she moved past him towards the door his hand went out and gripping her arm he swung her round towards him again. 'You're going . . . just like that?

You're walking out, just as easy as you did afore? You brought me here to say "I'm sorry Larry" ' – he mimicked her voice – 'and you've said it. And you're going – at least you think you are.' His grip tightened on her arm. 'You little swine! You dirty, double-crossing, money-grabbing little swine! To think that you could walk out on me without a word, not a word, and you dare come back here.' A twist of his hand and he sent her reeling against the barn wall. Then advancing on her, he cried, 'For two pins I'd throttle you . . . I'd swing for you.'

She stayed where he had flung her, tight pressed against the timbers, and the utter dejection of her, the hand gripping the arm that had almost cracked under his fingers, her head drooping, and her lower lip held tightly between her teeth, combined into such a poignant weapon that he fell beneath it.

'Pam' – he was standing over her – 'Pam.' Another moment and his arms were about her, lifting her up again. 'I'm mad. Oh my God! I don't care what you've done. I don't. I don't.' As she turned to him, flinging herself on to his breast, he said again, 'I don't. Oh, my God!'

'Larry. Larry . . . Oh, Larry.' Like someone in a fever her face moved against his neck while his arms crushed her to him, and when without further words she lifted her mouth to his, they kissed as at their first meeting, madly, drunkenly, on and on. But unlike that first time, they were not exhilarated with their exertions but spent. Quietly they leant upon each other, his fingers moving through her hair as he gazed over her head out through the door to where the shadows lay long in the twilight. And he remembered an evening they had sat here watching the magic pattern made by the shadows. It was the first time he remembered hearing the word penumbra. He hadn't let on he didn't know what it meant, but had looked it up when he got home . . . partly shaded region round shadow of opaque body. Shadow crossing shadow, she had explained it . . . She had opened the door to many things.

He asked quietly now, 'Tell me why you did it.'

She moved her head against him, and it was some moments before she answered, 'Mother keeping on and on . . . and Arlett, you know, from France. Her brother Jacques . . . he had tried to make a living at writing but hadn't succeeded. And he had influence. I didn't tell you, it would have depressed you, and . . . and, I had a horror of living all my life in Fellburn. Then I met Ron.'

His hands slackened about her, and she pulled them around her again, pressing them to her, crying, 'Don't . . . he's got to be mentioned. And anyway, I'm not going to blame anyone. It was me. And yet it wasn't.'

She grew limp in his arms and her voice became weary. 'If I'd been left to myself, to grow up being myself and not sent away to school. Your values change; it's impossible not to feel the influence of those around you, all good-class people. Don't you see, Larry? Part of me wants to live ordinary, and part of me never can now. I'm always at war with myself. If I could have remained like Jessie Honeysett, loving you . . .'

'Leave her out of it.' His face was stiff and his mouth hard again.

'But why? We must talk and face up to things. You hurt her, and I hurt you. And now I'm hurting Ron.'

At this second mention of the man's name he pulled sharply away from her, and thrusting his hands into his pockets he moved towards the door, and stood looking out.

'Larry . . . please.'

She came and stood before him again.

'Tell me one thing,' he cut in. 'Are you going to leave him?' He watched her eyes widen and then slowly droop and cover their expression, and he muttered between his teeth, 'So that's it. Why did you send for me? You want a husband to supply your toggery and a lover to supply your needs . . . is that it?'

The brutality of his words and tone brought her head up, and she said, 'This is a new side of you, a side I never guessed at.'

'No, by God!' He laughed harshly at her primness. 'But you should, it's your own creation. And whatever you do don't call a spade a spade . . . remember your education. Ron . . . Ron.' He spat out the name. 'It's all Ron now. An old man, old enough to be your grandfather.'

'He's not.' The protest was hot and indignant.

'No? Not at sixty?'

'He's not sixty, he's fifty-one.'

'Fifty-one!' Slowly he shook his head. 'You married a man of fifty-one. Your mother egged you on to do that, and because I was thirteen years older than you she tried to make out it wouldn't be quite decent. Fifty-one! Before you are forty, he'll be a doddering, slobbery . . .'

'Be quiet!' She was the madam now, haughty, commanding. And his lip curled at her.

'I'll be quiet all right. You're not making a fool out of me twice . . . oh, no. Goodbye, and I wish you luck of him. And you can go down on your knees and thank God you've got back to him whole. If I did what you deserve I'd make a mess of you.'

'Larry.' Swiftly she clung to him, pleading now. 'Don't go. Please don't go. Can't you see? I'm so unhappy, I'm only defending him because . . . He's not to blame, it's me and my mother.'

'Take your hands off.'

'No, no I won't. I got him to bring me over so I could see you again. I made Mother's illness the excuse. Each day I've watched you coming from work – the sight of you has torn my heart out. I didn't know how much I loved you until it was too late . . . He's flying back on Monday without me – I'm to stay until my mother has the operation. But before God, what happens to her doesn't matter; it's only you that matters. There, now you know how bad I am. I've manoeuvred everything to be near you again.'

'But you won't leave him?'

'Not just like that, I can't. It'll have to come slowly. He's been so good, so kind.'

Making a deep sound in his throat, he tore himself from her hands and with such force that she overbalanced and catching her heel in a pocket made by the dry, churned mud outside the door she fell headlong to the ground.

He gazed down on her for a moment, and when she made no effort to rise he stood over her. 'Get up,' he commanded roughly. 'Come on.' But still she made no move to get to her feet. Only her shoulders began to shake.

Tears in the ordinary way would have had no effect on him – tears were a woman's outlet. He had seen his sisters cry, his Aunt Lot and his mother, and Jessie . . . but Pam, never. Her poise had always seemed to forbid tears. He could never imagine her crying. He had always felt that she possessed some quality that would rise and aid her on all occasions – he did not call it a hard core. But now she was sobbing helplessly.

Bending and gathering her roughly up, he carried her back into the barn. There was a heap of last year's bracken in the corner, which they had never used because of its suspected livestock. But now he laid her on it, and taking off his overcoat he spread it on the bare floor in another corner. Then having lifted her, still sobbing, on to the coat, he lay beside her and pulled her sharply into his arms.

5

THE FIDDLER

'Jessie, can I come in?'

Jessie, calling through the window, said, 'Yes, Aunt Lot.'

Lottie came slowly into the kitchen, exclaiming in awe and admiration as she did so, 'Eeh! Jessie, it's lovely.' Then she looked around at the walls, her eyes widening. 'But aren't you going to hang no pictures?'

'No, Aunt Lot.'

'None at all?'

'No. Well, not yet. When I see one I like, I'll put it up.'

'Eeh.' Lottie shook her head. 'Your blue wallpaper looks lovely, but if you had a picture on it . . . Oh, and your new suite. Isn't it little!' She patted the G-plan settee. 'But why did you get a wooden-armed one, Jessie? Don't you like them like Jinny's one in the front room? That one's lovely and padded. Eeh, but Jessie.' Lottie stopped and gazed about her in evident bewilderment. 'It all looks . . . well, I don't know.'

And Lottie didn't know how to express the effect the room was having on her. For all its niceness and newness, it appeared very bare to her.

'And Willie's done your top pink, Jessie. Did you want him to do it pink, Jessie?'

'Yes, Aunt Lot.'

'Eeh, I've never seen a pink ceiling.'

Further comments seemed to be beyond Lottie for the moment, and she shook her head a number of times before concluding, 'Willie's kind . . . he's nice and kind and jolly. He makes you laugh. You know what he said about me yesterday? He said I was the star in his sky, and he dreamed about me at nights, and if Jinny would only let him he'd marry me like a shot. Jinny hit him with a dish cloth and pushed him out of the scullery. Oh, he makes you laugh. He was pleased that Larry's not going away now, not yet anyway. Jinny drew all his money out of the store, and he had some in the bank an' all.'

The object of Lottie's visit had been to impart this news and she did it in the best way she knew how. Jessie went on poking the fire. She took up the shovel and brush from the brand-new companion set and swept a cinder from the new sheet of blue painted tin that covered the hearth. What did it matter? This week, next week . . . he would go – his mother had said he'd had it in his mind for some time now. And there she had been, for the past few months, like the big fool she was, hoping against hope that he would take up the threads where he had snapped them, unconsciously praying, daily, hourly, waiting for a move. And now he had put off his going. Why? But need she ask? And yet she did ask herself for the hundredth time, how could Pam Turnbull affect him now? She was married, and happily, it was said. Mrs King had made it her business to see the man; she had even spoken to him when he was passing through the shop. A fine man, had been her verdict, a real gentleman, and she knew a real gentleman from a copy. And he didn't look old a bit, not more than forty, and if anybody asked her, Pam Turnbull had fallen on her feet, and she was damn lucky. Not that she had anything against Larry Broadhurst, Mrs King had added hastily, but a gentleman was a gentleman, and when all was said and done, Larry, but for the war, had been no farther than the pit, and she had never been able to see Pam Turnbull as a pitman's wife.

It saddened Jessie to realise that there was little or no sympathy for Larry, and almost no condemnation of Pam Turnbull. The verdict was that she had done well for herself. She had, after all, got herself a fine man, and a rich one, and hadn't she come back to see her mother when she knew she was ill, although she must have realised that she might be laying herself open to censure, or even something stronger from the Broadhursts. And yet speculation was rife as to whether the two main parties had met, and deep in her heart, curiosity began to gnaw at Jessie about the same question. Last week he was going, now he wasn't. Why?

'Lena had a pain in the night, Jessie, and Jack had to get up. But it's not due for five weeks yet. You should see the pram she's bought. Eeh! it's big. Jinny didn't half go on about it. She said it would hold quads. There's nowhere to put it except in the front room. And it's got a great big canopy. All cream it is, all of it, pram an' all. Twenty-eight pounds it cost. Eeh, you should have heard Jinny. And a satin quilt. She won't let me near her, Jessie, and when I tried to talk to her the other day she told me to shut me mouth. You don't think she'd try to get me . . .'

'No, no.' The fear in Lottie's voice brought Jessie round to her. 'Don't worry about that. Would you like a cup of tea?'

'If you're making one, Jessie. Can I sit in your new little chair?'

'Of course.'

'Eeh, it's soft. Is it that Dunlop-o stuff?'

'Yes.'

'Lena says she wants a mattress of that. Jinny says her wants would sink a pontoon. Lena's mad the day 'cos Jack didn't get that house. She's made him go to Washington – she'd heard tell of one there – and he wanted to go down to the club and see the cup-tie on the telly. They had a row, and she had a pain and she went to bed. Eeh, Jessie, fancy Willie being in London and seeing the match. Do you think Jack would have seen him on the telly? . . . Oh, ta, Jessie.' Lottie took the cup from Jessie, exclaiming further, 'Is this new china an' all? Eeh, the things you've bought. Are you going to buy new for all the house?'

'Yes, gradually.'

'Is it all empty upstairs?'

'Nearly.'

'What do you want to go and do it for, Jessie?'

'You wouldn't understand, Aunt Lot.'

'No, likely I wouldn't. Frank says I'm dimmer than a peasouper.' Lottie laughed, and there was a touch of sorrow in the admission. And Jessie said pityingly, 'You're not, Aunt Lot.'

'Oh, I don't mind what Frank says, Frank's all right. He's nice, is Frank. Can I stay here a bit? There's nobody in except Lena – Jinny had to go to Florence's. She went like a gale of wind with Frank when she heard they were all going to Australia.'

'To Australia . . . who?' asked Jessie.

'Florence and Sidney and Grace and Harry, and all the bairns. Eeh, she's up in arms. It's Florence's Sidney has done it. Florence came in this morning. She says they can all start a business over there and make a fortune building. Jinny made Frank go over with her and try and talk them out of it. And he wanted to see the telly an' all. He says they'll do what they like anyway, 'cos people do. Do you know?' – she leant towards Jessie and whispered – 'Sidney's cute. He's had all the papers and things for weeks, everything's cut and dried, except to persuade Harry. And now he's done that.'

Lottie rattled on, and Jessie, sipping at her tea, ceased to listen. Soon it would seem all the Broad-hursts would be gone: the girls she had occasionally played with, Jack who had teased her, Larry she had loved. Had? Would she ever be able to stop loving him? Perhaps one day, when she could no longer see his shadow in the room across the road, when she no longer stood at the side of the curtain in the front room to watch his coming and going, when there was no longer the fear in her that the sight of his striding figure would cause her heart to leap, nor deep humiliation fill her when in the distance he would cut down a side street to avoid her. When that day came, perhaps the wound would close. She would rather the wound gaped for ever.

'Would you like to come for a walk, Jessie?'

'No thanks, Aunt Lot, I'm going to do some shopping. I'm starting work again on Monday, and there's some things I want to see to. I'm slipping into Newcastle . . . I should be away now.'

'Oh, all right then, Jessie. It's a lovely day to go to Newcastle, and it will be quiet an' all. Look at all the train-loads that have gone to London. And it will be nice an' all on the fells. Jinny says I haven't got to go into the town but I could go a little walk on the fells if I didn't go far. Just to Knott's Corner. And if I didn't jabber to nobody. She doesn't like me talking to people.' Lottie gave this information to Jessie as if it was something new she was imparting; then added, 'Well, I'll be off. Enjoy yourself, Jessie.'

In her own room, Lottie donned her fur cape, picked out from the bottom of the cupboard a large straw hat with faded streamers, drew carefully on to her hands a pair of washed-out white gloves, discarded a torn leather bag for a red raffia one to match her dress, and so attired walked out the back way and up the lane and on to the fells.

Once on high ground where the wind was fresh, she had her work cut out to keep the skirt of her dress down and her hat on her head. But there was no-one about to laugh at her efforts today. It was safe to say at this moment that ninety per cent of the community of the Tyne had their eyes glued to the television sets, or their ears to the wireless, but tomorrow, weather permitting, the fells would be like a park with strollers.

Knott's Corner was about twenty minutes' walk from the house . . . where the main road touched the fells. From it was a good view of the town sprawling in the valley between its two grim guardian pits, and to the right, as if rearing its head out of the mire, was Brampton Hill, its large houses clearly visible from this point in their wooded surroundings. A hawthorn-hedged lane led from the main road at Knott's Corner on to the fell top. It formed a breakwater to the wind. But gaps showed in it here and there as if to afford the strollers a quicker access to the open ground. It was when nearing one such gap that Lottie saw the car. Its interior seemed to light up the narrow lane, and she stopped dead. The wind making a fresh attempt to dislodge her hat at that moment caused her to totter sideways in an effort to hold it on, and in doing so she found herself looking into the front of the car, where sat Pam Turnbull, and she was smoking.

Lottie stared, her mouth slightly open. Jinny didn't hold with women who smoked. She wouldn't let Lena smoke in the kitchen where there was food about, or cook with a cigarette in her mouth. But eeh! didn't Pam Turnbull look lovely . . . smart, like the pictures that were in the books in Doctor Kent's surgery.

When Lottie saw Pam suddenly open the door and step out into the road she moved quickly out of sight away from the gap. She didn't want Pam to see her – Pam would think she was spying on her. Then as Pam's voice came to her, she felt herself stretching. Her head went up and back, and her ears seemed to extend in an effort to make sure she was hearing aright. Pam was saying, 'Larry. Larry.'

Lottie's hand went to her mouth, and she tried to stop herself from breathing. The voice from behind the hedge said, 'I thought . . . Oh, it doesn't matter – you're here. Darling, I've been waiting an hour all but five minutes.'

Lottie pressed her mouth tightly to still the loud sound of surprise that jumped to her lips when Larry's voice said, 'I got involved. I had to go over with Mum and Dad to Florence's. Oh, my God, it was awful . . . the bickering. Why don't they let people do what they like? They're going to Australia, the whole lot of them. I'm sorry you had to wait. Oh, my darling.' There was a pause. Then Larry's voice, different now, was saying, 'Come on.'

Lottie's amazement would have been comical to an onlooker, for her widened eyes and mouth were stretching her long features still further, until her whole face looked like an elongated 'O'. That was Larry. With extreme caution she turned slowly and looked through the hedge, and there they were not two feet away from her. If either of them had turned and glanced sideways, they couldn't have but seen her through the thin sprinkling of green on the bushes. With startled eyes she watched Pam Turnbull look swiftly up and down the road, then press herself close to Larry saying: 'Kiss me again – quick.'

She watched Larry's arms swiftly round her, and when she saw his mouth cover the lips held up to his as if he would devour them, her head drooped as if she were witnessing an indecent action, and shame that such an action would have aroused went through her, until from her goose-pimpled neck to the rim of her hair she looked aflame. Not until she heard the car move did she raise her eyes – and then it was gone. She stood peering through the hedge for a long while before turning and retracing her steps, and with each she thought, 'Eeh, Larry. And she's married.'

Stopping suddenly and staring in her perplexity towards the town, she muttered, 'It's wrong. Mrs King says the man's nice. Larry can't have her, he's doing a bad thing.' Her mind became clouded and her thoughts fuzzy, and she could quite easily have let the matter slip and be lost in the confused jumble that formed the greater part of her thinking, but she hung on to it, trying to straighten this bad thing out. Larry was her world. She had gone to her room and laughed and cried her relief when she knew he wasn't going away; she had done it quietly so's Jinny wouldn't hear, for Jinny had been short all the week, and was making on Larry's going was just like anyone else's. Yet she knew that Jinny was upset . . . but not so upset, she imagined, as she herself was, for hadn't Jinny all the others, while she had only

Larry. No-one was as kind to her as Larry, and she was afraid of no-one's displeasure as she was of his. Larry never said sharp or hurtful things to her, yet all the combined upbraiding of the family could not touch her as did a reproving glance from his eyes or his voice saying 'Aunt Lot', like that. If Larry had gone away today, as he said he was going to do, she would have been upset and in a state, but it wouldn't have felt like this.

She was incapable of describing to herself how she felt. She could not say that because her god was a god no longer, but as other men, she had been deprived of a standard wherewith to judge within the limits of her mentality. When he had deserted Jessie her world had rocked, but had steadied itself again as the sanctity of the approaching marriage had shone a purifying light around him. That it wasn't to Jessie he was to be married had remained a constant ache, yet because it concerned Larry, the wonder that all marriages held for her was magnified a thousandfold. But now he was carrying on, and with this same Pam Turnbull after all she had done . . . and her married, and to a nice man.

She moved on, slowly now – there was no joy left in the day. The nice walk was ended. She was not thinking as she had done on the outward journey, I wonder what Jinny'll bring back? Perhaps some prawns – the bus stopped opposite Tiffley's in the market place and they always had piles of prawns. Or perhaps she'd bring tripe, and they'd have it done in the oven for their supper. Tripe and onions and new oven-bottom cake! Her mouth had watered and she had given a little skip. Then remembering Jinny's caution that outside she must behave herself, she had given a hitch to her cape, and walked for a dozen or so steps with studied, sedate primness . . . But that had been before she had reached Knott's Corner.

She was now within five minutes' walk of home and at the juncture of the paths that led, one to her own quarter, one straight down to the market place and the centre of the town, and one going directly left to the disreputable Bog's End, when she stopped again. She didn't want to go home, not yet anyway, until she could be sure she wouldn't split on Larry. She mustn't do that or there would be murder in the house. And Jinny would go mad and Frank wouldn't stand for it. He'd have no nonsense like that, would Frank. But she knew that her tongue had dominion over her, and that she had no power to check her words once they started flowing, and she was worried.

A dog barked on the Bog's End path and she saw it in the distance coming racing towards her. She liked dogs, little ones . . . not like Willie's Bill. Oh, he was a holy terror was Willie's Bill. But this one was little and brown and soft.

As the spaniel puppy came panting and yapping to her feet she stooped down unafraid and patted it, whereupon it went into a frenzy and rolled on to its back with joy. She looked down on it laughing gaily – the effervescence of the puppy seemed to have the power to sweep away her trouble for the moment –

and like a mother with a child, she lifted it up and hugged the wriggling, squirming animal to her, laughing gleefully when it licked at her face.

'Now, mam, you mustn't let her mess you up.'

Trying to control the capers of the dog she turned to where the voice came from, and as she saw its owner her hold on the puppy slackened, and the dog, for its own preservation, clung to her cape, and in a moment both were on the grass.

'Here! here!' The man silenced the yapping animal with a sharp slap, and picking up the cape, he handed it to Lottie.

'It's sorry I am, mam . . . I hope she hasn't done it no harm.'

'No, no.' Lottie's voice was high. 'It's only an old thing. Jinny's been going to burn it for years.'

'It maybe is, mam, but it becomes you.' The man's eyes held covert laughter, and he screwed them up in appearing to consider her before continuing: 'I've seen you before, haven't I?'

For the second time that afternoon, Lottie blushed; not only her face but the whole of her body felt the surge of blood. She said softly, 'I like to listen to you.'

'That's nice of you, mam, very nice of you. You appreciate good music; it isn't everybody that does.'

Emotion engulfing her, Lottie let her gaze dwell on the dog. It was running round in circles now. Perhaps it was the remembered feel of the fur or the attraction of the stale mixture of cheap scent that had emanated from it that checked its galloping, but stop it did, and giving a surprising leap for so small an animal it snapped at the cape dangling from Lottie's agitated hands.

'Away wi' you!' cried the man. 'Drop it, you divil! Drop it, I say.'

But it was Lottie who dropped the cape, not the dog, and before the man could lay his hands on it the puppy was away, scrambling down the path dragging the bedraggled fur after it.

Her hands held to her mouth, in great distress, Lottie watched her precious garment being trailed over the dirt and the frantic efforts of the man to retrieve it, and not until the dog, the cape, and the man disappeared from her sight did she give a startled, agitated cry. Taking to her heels with the agility of a girl, only slightly more erratic, she fled after them down the pathway, running the whole length of its twisting five hundred feet until she reached the bottom.

Gasping and panting, she came upon the man. He had the cape in his hands, and she could see that it was rent its full length in at least two places. The man's polite, easy-going manner was gone; he began stamping around, crying, 'I'll murder you! I will. Come here, you damn brat.'

Then, on seemingly catching sight of Lottie, he came to her, and his manner was soft again. 'I'm sorry to the heart, I am, mam. But look. Look' – he pointed to her – 'don't you worry, I'm a dab hand with me fingers – it isn't only the fiddle I can play. Let me get a needle and thread into me hands and I'll make it as good as new for you.'

Lottie lifted her distressed eyes from the garment that was, for her, the epitome of gentility. It lay across the man's hands, not only moth-eaten now, but a lacerated thing. Her face crumpled pitifully. 'Could you?' she asked in a small voice.

'I can, I can; I'm as good as me word in all things. Don't distress yourself, mam. And I'll kill that animal stone dead before your eyes.'

'No, no! Oh, no, please. Oh, don't hurt it. But if you could do something to me cape . . . mend it.'

'I can, I can. Would you care to step in a minute . . . look, over there.' He pointed past the allotments to where an old gipsy caravan stood on the railway embankment. 'And while I'm doing it you'll have a cup of tea, for all the trouble me and mine have caused you this beautiful afternoon. Come on, come on. I was never so happy as at this moment to know I've rented this fine place to entertain you in your distress.'

For a moment even the thought of the cape was wiped from Lottie's mind. She was being asked to have tea with the fiddler in his house, and he spoke so beautifully to her, and treated her as nobody else had ever done, not even Larry. With each moment she was feeling more like her idea of a lady. Perhaps he'd even play to her.

The joy of being a recipient of any great honour comes only once in a lifetime. All the events of the day were forgotten; Lottie's being became alight and the reflection was seen on her face. It was the fiddler's answer. As if he were escorting unexpected royalty, he walked deferentially a little to the front and to the side of her with one arm outstretched towards the caravan, the other hugging the cape. And with the air of royalty, Lottie followed.

Jessie had looked in Binns' and countless other shops in Newcastle and decided against getting herself anything today. On leaving Fellburn her resolve had been high and forceful – she was going to buy herself a complete rig-out. Let them think it was out of the insurance money or what they liked. It had already been prophesied, she knew, that she would run herself into so much debt she wouldn't get out of it in a hurry. Seeing the new things coming in yesterday, Mrs King had said, with the licence she thought her motherliness and age permitted, 'I'd go steady, lass. It's all right getting a bit on the hire, but you can overdo it. And don't I know it.' No-one had suspected that she had paid outright for the furniture in the kitchen – that is, no-one except Mr Dobson. If he had dared Mr Dobson would have attacked her openly. He knew there had been money in that box, but he knew he was helpless to prove it. How could he prove that a woman who had for years accepted charity from her neighbours in the way of meals, and very often money, had been storing up a hoard, and had used it as a power to draw his attention and prayers? He would come out of it badly if he tried, and he knew it.

Although, because of her sufferings at her mother's hands, Jessie would have fought him to the last breath for the money that was rightly hers, she was glad and relieved that he was leaving Fellburn, for beneath her new-found courage she was nevertheless afraid of him and what his hate of her might give rise to.

But now her earlier high resolve had dwindled to 'There's always another day; I'll come and look round again; I'll find something that I want.'

It was while these thoughts were occupying her mind that she cut through a side street towards the bus stop and came upon 'Madame Fonyer's'. In Madame Fonyer's window reposed a suit, with a long coat to match, together with the hat, gloves, bag, and rolled umbrella. There was no price attached to any of these articles, nor was there anything else in the window. Jessie stood staring at the symphony of browns. That was the kind of thing she would like, the kind of clothes she had dreamed of. But they wouldn't fit her, at least, she didn't think so.

Her doubting eyes lifted over the curtain that was hanging from a shining brass rail around the window, and she could see that the shop was empty. Half her indecision not to buy anything today had been because she was afraid to face the smart pressing saleswomen in the big shops. But this was a small shop, tiny almost . . . but good class – too good class for her, she could see that. She just wanted something a bit out of the ordinary, away from the store type. But that was a lovely brown.

Before she had allowed herself to think further, she had tentatively opened the door and stepped on to the deep pile carpet, and as she did so a woman emerged from a curtained doorway.

She was a small woman, fat and dark, and dressed in black, and she resembled Mrs Broadhurst so closely as to be her sister – that is, until she opened her mouth.

'Good afternoon, madam. Can I help you?'

The broken English made Jessie regret her impulsive entry. She would never be able to afford anything here – she wasn't going to throw the money away. 'The suit in the window,' she said. 'Could I price it please?'

'Oh that.' The woman looked Jessie over, her small bright eyes playing on her shoulders, her bust, and her hips. 'It would never fit you, madam, it is only a thirty-eight hip.' She shook her head. 'It is such a pity. You have a fine figure, allow me to say so . . . you would dress well.' She lifted her finger as one would to a child, and continued, 'And I have the very thing that would fit you. The very thing, fortunately.'

'But I only wanted . . .'

'All right, all right.' The little woman raised both of her hands shoulder high. 'Look at it, madam, that is all. If you do not like it there will be no harm done. None . . . none.' Madame's smile broadened. 'None in the wide world. I like my clients to return, and all of them return, year following year . . . the people who like to look well without having their pockets drained. Will you step this way?'

As in a daze, Jessie stepped that way, and beyond the curtain Madame pointed to a Louis XIV armchair in gilt and faded rose. 'Be comfortable,' she said. 'Let us enjoy ourselves, eh?' Whereupon she pushed open the sliding door of a cupboard which took up the complete side of one wall, and her hand went straight to a dark, dove-coloured costume, its lapels edged with gunmetal grey, and bringing it to Jessie she laid it across her knees. 'Feel,' she said, pushing the material into her hands. 'Beautiful, yes?'

'Yes. Yes it is.' Jessie gazed hungrily down on the suit, and Madame Fonyer gazed at her.

Jessie's eyes lifted to the Frenchwoman, and she said softly, 'But the price?'

The Frenchwoman stared into the face before her – part of her life's work had been to study people. Certainly she owed her exclusive and very successful business to her capacity to judge and judge correctly. Before her she saw a woman with a figure modelled on the old Greek proportion, and clothed horribly. Certainly some women could get clothes off the peg to fit them; this one, never, unless it was an exclusive and expensive peg. And the woman's face . . . it was intriguing in that it showed so much purity and pain. Madame Fonyer had lost her husband in the first war and two sons in the second. She knew what pain was. But there were varying kinds of pain. This woman's face recalled the child they had brought to her house in Marseilles. She was fifteen and had been in the hands of a German soldier; the same look was here. She leaned forward until her eyes were on a level with Jessie's. She did not mean her pocket to suffer through sentimentality, but she decided to be kind, and she smiled into Jessie's face. 'I would like to dress you, madam. Try what I will show you. If it is too much for your pocket, then' – she shrugged her shoulders – 'I will have enjoyed myself, and so will you.'

Never before in Jessie's narrow life had she come across anyone of Madame Fonyer's personality. Suddenly she was filled with a recklessness. Her whole body relaxed, and she returned the smile, and Madame Fonyer's plump white hands shot out, and she touched both of Jessie's cheeks with a sharp uplifting tap. Whereon both women laughed, and Jessie thought a surprising thought, There were others kinds of living. You could get over and forget lots of things if your days were filled with people like this one here.

Madame closed at four on a Saturday. Jessie had entered the shop at half-past three. At five thirty she was still there, sitting in a dressing-gown much too small for her and drinking tea and eating cake at a delicate Cabriole-legged table. She had talked during the past two hours as she had never talked before. For the life of her, she couldn't tell what had made her do it. She had told this little fat stranger all kinds of things; but of course, not everything, not the important things.

But Madame Fonyer had filled in the gaps in Jessie's narrative, not at all inaccurately. She had taken to this big, soft-voiced, tender woman, who had been used and hurt, and who was on the point of fighting back. Madame Fonyer did not often get people like Jessie in her shop. Most of her clientele were forceful, sturdy and bumptious, made so, she surmised, by the harsh Northern environment. Part of her religion was that for a woman there was no morale builder to compare with clothes. But not always did she go out of her way as she was doing today to press this point. She was intrigued by this big gauche woman who had crept into her shop on a very slack afternoon, so much so that she had called in her fitter from the work room, not to take measurements and let the alterations take their turn, but to do what was necessary now, such as letting out the waist of the skirt and dropping the hem on the matching coat. Madame, biting deep into a piece of cream-filled sponge, said playfully, 'Don't let this be the last time you pay me a visit.'

'Oh, no,' said Jessie, 'I won't.' Then she added naïvely, 'I haven't enjoyed myself so much for years . . . I don't think ever, not like this. I never thought buying clothes could be like this.'

'Well' – Madame wiped her fingers – 'see that you repeat it . . . this enjoyment.'

'Oh, I'll come back again,' said Jessie, and she meant it. She had parted with forty-nine pounds as if they were shillings, and for it she had received a costume, a coat, a hat, and a pair of gloves. Twenty-five pounds the costume had cost. She knew she was mad, but it was a wonderful madness, as the mirror had shown her. The colour of the costume had made her skin look so different, and Madame Fonyer had taken a lipstick and with a few strokes made her mouth look different, too. But she'd rub that off, once she was outside, for in make-up she had never gone beyond cream and powder. Her mouth was large, and she thought that lipstick would certainly not enhance it. She only hoped it was dark when she left the shop.

But it was still light when Madame saw her to the door, and there she looked down at her shoes. 'Now, don't forget, plain navy colour . . . but plain. Half heel, and fine leather. And a new blouse too you must have; soft, mossy-pink, very pale. And come and see me when you have them, yes? Goodbye, my dear.' She shook her hand. 'You go out a different woman . . . and keep that back straight. And don't forget to come and see me again.'

'Oh, yes, yes, I will, and thank you, thank you for a wonderful afternoon. I'll never forget it . . . it was such a surprise. Goodbye, goodbye.'

'Au revoir,' said Madame.

Like a ship being launched from the stocks, Jessie moved into the street, and like a ship when it first contacts the water, she rocked a little. She was exalted and frightened at the same time. She had to go to the bus stop and she'd have to stand in the queue, and there'd be sure to be someone who knew her.

On the pavement a man made way for her, and as he did so, his eyes moved over her, and she became hot. It was the lipstick, she'd rub it off. She moved the striped box that housed her old clothes to enable her to get to her handbag. Then with her handkerchief to her lips she hesitated, for before her mind's

133

eye there had flashed a picture of Pam Turnbull, poised and painted. Her chin jerked, and with a definite movement she returned the handkerchief to her bag, and remembering the wonderful woman's injunction as to her shoulders she kept them back as she neared the bus station.

Self-consciously she took her place in the queue, and she had not been standing long when from behind her came two well-known voices. If she had been recognised, their owners, she knew, would have hailed her immediately. But it wasn't until they boarded the bus and were seated on the opposite side to her and she smiled at them that one of them exclaimed, 'Why, it's you, Jessie. Why, lass, I didn't know you. And yet I thought I recognised that build and that hair. Well, well.' She nudged her companion. 'It's Jessie.'

'Jessie?' The woman leant forward and said, 'It is an' all. Why, lass, we didn't know you.'

That was all. Jessie sat back, and time and again during the journey she felt their covert glances upon her. There would be talk. Well, let them talk. When they were on about her, they'd be leaving someone else alone.

It was dark when she reached home, and as she turned the key in the lock Mrs King came out of her own door.

'Is that you, Jessie?'

'Yes, Mrs King.'

'She's not with you then. Have you seen owt of Lottie?'

'Lottie? No. Why?'

'She hasn't turned up from being out, and Jinny's nearly bats. She got back at five and Lottie wasn't in then, and there's been no sign of her, and Lena's bairn's coming. I'm just on me way over. They're in a right pickle over there. She had to get the doctor straight away, and there's a nurse there an' all. It looks like a hospital job if they can move her.'

'Oh, I'm sorry.'

'Troubles never come singly. I'll tell Jinny you haven't seen Lottie. It was her last hope that she'd be along with you . . . Been gettin' some new things?' By the light of the street lamp she peered at Jessie. 'Not black . . . well, nobody goes in for black these days. You're wise. I can't see very well in this light, I'll have a look at them the morrow. If you hear owt of Lottie, let Jinny know, won't you?'

'Yes, of course.'

Inside the house, Jessie switched on the light, and she paused with her hand on the switch. It was funny about Aunt Lot. Where could she have got to? She was such a gullible creature. Anyway, there was one thing certain: she'd get it when she came in.

She drew the blinds, then took off her coat and laid it gently over the settee. And she was making to remove her hat when she muttered aloud with a gesture almost gay, 'I'll go up and see what they look like.' She picked up her coat again and was at the foot of the stairs when she heard a scraping on the scullery door, and a voice calling her name. Startled, she stood still. No-one could get into her yard unless they climbed the wall – the yard door was locked and bolted. Stiffly and quietly she moved into the scullery.

'Who's there?' she asked.

'It's me, Jessie.'

'Oh . . . Aunt Lot.' Jessie gave a relieved laugh and quickly unlocked the door. And almost immediately Lottie fell into her arms.

'Aunt Lot! What is it? Look, stand up. Stand up.' But Lottie wouldn't stand up, and practically dragging her, Jessie got her to the couch. She had forgotten about her coat, and when she released Lottie, it dropped to the floor. She snatched it up quickly, shook it, and laid it over a chair; then she turned to Lottie saying, 'What's the matter, Aunt Lot? Where have you been? How did you get into the yard?'

Lottie was panting as if she had been running, and she reached out and clung on to Jessie's hands, and she mouthed at her words before they came out. 'Oh, Jessie, I'm frightened . . . I am, I am. Jinny'll kill me.'

'No, no, she won't. Be quiet now. How did you get into the yard? I didn't lock you in, did I, as I went out?'

'I got over the wall from Kings' side. There's boxes in their corner, but I fell on this side and hurt me leg, me foot. It's paining, Jessie, something awful, and I'm frightened. Oh, Jessie, what'll Jinny say? And me frock all torn . . . and me other things. Look . . . look. Eeh!'

The long, tear-stained face twisted up still further, and she cried, 'She'll put me away now, like Lena said.' And she let out a wail and clapped her hands over her mouth, so that Jessie said sharply, 'Now, now, stop it, Aunt Lot.'

Lottie made no reply, but with her hands still held to her mouth she rocked herself. That something was terribly wrong was quite evident. Lottie was without her hat, her dress was torn, and a strip of embroidery from an old-fashioned white petticoat was dangling from below her dress. But in her face was the greatest evidence of her trouble – her eyes were terror-stricken. She began to moan and whimper through her fingers, 'She'll send me away . . . she'll have me locked up. She said she would . . . if ever I . . . Eeh!' She turned to Jessie, clutching at her. 'You won't let her do it, will you, Jessie? You said I could come and live with you.'

'And you can, Aunt Lot, you can. Look, sit quiet for a minute, and I'll go and see if Willie's in. He'll tell Jinny, for she's worried about you.'

'No, no, Jessie, don't leave me, I'm frightened.'

'But what about? Where have you been? I thought you were going for a nice walk on the fells.'

Slowly Lottie leaned back; then she slumped sideways, and Jessie, thinking she was going to faint, cried, 'Put your head down and I'll get you a drink.'

'I don't want none,' Lottie whispered. 'I did go on the fells, Jessie.'

'Well, tell me,' said Jessie soothingly, 'did something happen there? Come on now, tell me what happened.' She stroked the tangled hair from Lottie's wet brow.

It was some time before Lottie spoke again, but when she did it was not in her usual disjointed way, but almost coherently clear, as if the incidents of the afternoon were passing before her mind as a series of pictures which were plain to see and equally easy to describe. And the first part of her disclosure struck Jessie like a blow between the eyes.

'It was after I saw Pam Turnbull . . . she was waiting for Larry. And he came, and they got into the big red car and went off.'

Gone was the armour of the new clothes; ripped away was the uplifting pleasure of the past few hours. It couldn't be starting again . . . it couldn't. He wasn't . . . he wasn't . . . He wouldn't look at her after what she had done to him . . . and she married. What could she be to him now?

In answer to this question a feeling, new and almost terrifying in itself, reared up in her. The rage filled her head as if it were a white heat . . . it pressed on her eyes, misting them. He would sell his soul for her. The knowledge was so bitter that for a moment she forgot Lottie and her plight and made to rise, but was stayed by Lottie's hands plucking at her again.

'Let me tell you, Jessie, so's you can tell Jinny . . . tell her for me, Jessie. It was when I was upset 'cause of Larry, and was standing looking over Quarry Hill saying to meself, "I mustn't let on to Jinny about them, about them kissing and that", when the dog came. It was a nice little dog and I stroked it. And then he came up, the fiddler.'

At the mention of the fiddler, Jessie's attention was

138

dragged from herself and she said dully, 'Go on.'

'Well, the dog got me cape, Jessie, and dashed off with it, and he went after it. And when I found them at the bottom of the lane it was right near where he lived, and me cape was all torn.'

'But he lives in Bog's End, Aunt Lot,' said Jessie.

'No, Jessie, not now. Behind it, this side, near the allotments, in a caravan. He rented it off the stall woman in the market.'

'Go on.'

'Well, me cape was all torn and he said he would mend it. And he did . . . look.' She unfastened the cape and went to pull it off her shoulders when Jessie said harshly, 'Never mind that, go on.'

'Well, he sewed the cape, and he made me some tea, and then he played the fiddle. He played lovely, Jessie; it was beautiful sitting and listening to him, and the caravan was lovely and clean. He showed me the cupboards and everything. Oh, Jessie.' Her hands clutched again on the sleeves of the new costume. They were dirty and sweaty, but it didn't matter – the hope that the clothes had inspired was dead.

'I'm not bad, Jessie, am I? I'm not, Jessie . . . say I'm not bad. Jinny'll say I'm bad.'

'No, no she won't. Go on.'

'He kissed me, Jessie, the fiddler kissed me . . . I forgot about Jinny and everything. And then I remembered Jinny and what she'd do if I didn't behave meself, and I was coming home – I was, Jessie, I was. Honest to God, I was. And . . . and' – her eyes fell to her torn dress and petticoat and her head moved pathetically from side to side – 'I cried Jessie . . . after . . . I cried and carried on. I was frightened to come home, and he hit me, and when it was dark he pushed me out. And I came to you, and I got over the wall and hid in your shed, waiting for you.'

Jessie herself was trembling now. The pity of it . . . the poor, lovable creature who wouldn't hurt a worm and who had for years been a source of anxiety to her sister had now brought Jinny's fear to fruition. The very thing that Jinny had dreaded for her from a young girl had happened. And she was forty-two. Yet for a fleeting second Jessie found it in her heart to envy this simple creature. Her own mother had repeatedly warned her against sin, but she need not have worried, Larry had been firm for them both. But would he be firm with Pam Turnbull? No. No, he wouldn't – she was married and safe. The words suddenly screamed in her head, bringing her to her feet.

'Where you goin', Jessie?'

She was unable to reply for a moment, and Lottie begged again, 'Where you goin', Jessie?'

'For Willie. He'll bring Jinny over, and I'll tell her. Don't worry, only sit quiet.'

She pushed Lottie back on to the couch and went into the front room, and there paused a moment, and she said what she had thought she could never bring herself to say, no matter what he might do. 'I hate him! I do, I do.' Savagely, she pulled open the front door and went into the street, and she had moved only a few steps towards the Macintyres' door when she became aware of Larry. He was stepping off the road on to the kerb, making for the same place as herself.

This was the first time they had come face to face for over two years. Jessie stopped within the range of the street lamp, Larry was on the fringe of it. The revolt had brought her head up and she was no longer conscious of her clothes. They were now secondary to her figure, gaining from it, not it from them, and the effect was startling.

For a moment Larry could not believe that he was looking at Jessie Honeysett. Jessie had never had any dress sense – even his mother had said, 'Well, anyway, there'll be one thing sure, Jessie will never ruin you with what she'll spend on clothes. Her mother's laid that foundation.'

Now, side by side with the feeling his conscience was creating and which he thought of as terrible, was a feeling of actual amazement. Jessie in this new guise was a creature he had no knowledge of, yet this was the woman he had cast off. And as he stared at her the terrible feeling increased.

'Hello, Jessie,' he said gently.

She did not reply but looked straight into the eyes that had held the world for her and whose caress could melt her bones, and she refused to be torn to shreds by the sight of them again . . . or of those arms, fleshless under the coat like steel bands. Even in this moment she could feel them still. But they had been round Pam Turnbull today, holding her,

141

crushing her. Her fixed stare nonplussed him, and he said haltingly, 'Aunt Lot's missing. Dad's out looking for her . . . I've just come in.'

'Aunt Lot's with me, she's got a sprained ankle.'

'Well' – he sighed, then gave an uneasy laugh – 'thank God for that.'

'You needn't be so quick in thanking God,' said Jessie. Even to her own ears her voice was foreign, for it was harsh and hard and belonged to this new being struggling painfully to birth.

Its brusqueness, so unlike her quiet, rather lazy tones, made his brows gather as much as did the significance of her words, and he stared at her through narrowing eyes, waiting for her to go on.

And she kept him waiting, extending her own torture, before saying, 'She's been with the fiddler . . . in his caravan. Her clothes are torn off her back, and as far as I can gather, she was there two hours.'

'God Almighty!' Quick anger flooded his face now, and his hand went to his chin, gripping it, and he brought out between his teeth, 'She promised.'

'Promised!' The low clear word held so much scorn that she saw him flinch, and slowly and with deep emphasis she added the next words: 'She went with the fiddler after she had witnessed the meeting between you and your lady friend on the fells.'

Never had she seen a look such as was now on his face. Amazement, shame . . . yes, and fear were there. Her head went higher. For once during their association she was on top, the situation was in her hands. She wanted to hurt him, cut him to the heart as she had been cut. She wanted to lay some burden on his conscience, for she felt that the hurt he had done her had made no impression on it.

'If she hadn't been standing worrying about how she could keep what she had seen to herself, it's likely the fiddler would never have come across her; and even if he had, her fear of your august displeasure would have checked her.'

As she spat the words out she was more and more surprised at their sound. It was as if the old, meek, acquiescent individual was standing aside listening to this being who looked and sounded as if it knew no fear. Certainly the fear of displeasing this god had fallen from her, and as she watched the creature that had come to life under the fingers of Madame Fonyer she realised that in her love for this man had been a great element of fear – fear of displeasing him, fear of not being good enough for him, or clever enough – oh, certainly not clever enough. And what she had feared had come upon her.

Her thoughts came back to Jinny and Aunt Lot and brought pity into her being again, and after one long look at his shamed face she turned on her heel, and keeping her head up and her back straight, she marched to the door and entered the house.

When the door of Jessie's cottage closed behind her, without a bang, Larry stared towards it for a moment before turning and walking heavily towards his gate. Of all the things that could happen this was about one of the worst – not that Lottie had been with the fiddler, and God knew that was bad enough, but that the first person to confront him about Pam should be Jessie. Once again he felt himself a swine, and entering the house he thought, God, what a mess! And he knew that the mess must get worse, it couldn't get better. And yet he would have it no other way.

Frank stood before the couch, his face turkey-red and his whole manner terrifying, and Lottie, gazing up at him through running eyes, whimpered, 'Don't be mad at me, I meant no harm.'

'No harm!' Frank almost exploded. 'No harm. You're not so daft, Lot, you knew what you were doing. What if you have a bairn, eh?'

'Eeh, no, Frank; I won't have a bairn, I'm too old.'

'I wish to God I could think so, and for your sake I hope you are. Jinny'll kill you when she hears. All the trouble in the house the night, and now this. For two pins I'd bray you. I would, so help me God. All these years you've been looked after, worried after, and now this. Well, there's something I can do . . . I can make him marry you just in case you shouldn't be old enough. I'll make him pay dearly for his entertainment.'

'No, Frank.' Lottie tried to rise. 'Eeh, no, I don't want to leave home. What could I do? I'd die without you all. I don't want to see the fiddler no more. Oh, Frank . . . Oh, I don't.'

Her voice was lost in her crying, and Frank, although knowing that his threat was idle, continued to use it until Jessie put in quietly, 'About getting her across, Dad, there's no need; she can stay here . . . it would be easier.'

He turned to her, wiping his face with his handkerchief. 'It's kind of you, lass, but you shouldn't have to put up with our troubles, you have had enough of your own through us. My God! For this to happen.'

He dabbed at his neck and Jessie said, 'It would be better if Mam didn't see her until tomorrow.'

'Aye, it would that. What she'll do . . .' There were no words to describe his wife's reactions and he shook his head. 'Hell'll be let loose. All these years, Jessie, you know how she's taken care of her, and if anything further should come of it . . . ' He checked his tongue at this point – Jessie to him was a young, unmarried lass. 'Larry and me's going down there now, and God help him if I get my hands on him. You'll let her stay the night then, Jessie?' He was ignoring Lottie now and speaking as if she was not in the room.

'She can stay as long as she wants to.' Jessie patted Lottie's shoulder.

'It's more than she deserves, but she'll need some comfort with what's coming to her. She will that.'

With this soothing, parting shot, Frank went out, and Jessie, looking towards the door, thought, Yet even this will be put in the shade when you know what your son's up to. Like a mask that had been worn for an evening the new defence suddenly slipped, and the old self emerged fully again and saw the trouble and shame this latest development would bring on the house across the road. The reactions of

145

the girls and of Jack and Lena did not seem to matter. It was the effect on Mam and Dad Broadhurst that stood out, and of the two, Jinny would be the one to suffer most. Jessie had always been aware that Jinny's secret ambition was respectability for her family, high respectability. Her aim had been to bring them up a cut above the rest of the folks around the place; and behind her restrained, rather taciturn front was a sensitiveness always keyed to respond to the doings, good or bad, of her children. But the sin of her beloved son, when it should come to her ears, would bear her down. Yet in some strange, twisted way it might be a Godsend, Jessie thought, for it would divert some of the storm from this poor creature. And feeling that she must try and prevent Aunt Lot from precipitating the storm that she knew was about to burst over her she sat down slowly on the couch beside Aunt Lot, and taking her hand said haltingly, 'It will be best for everybody, Aunt Lot, if . . . if you don't tell Jinny or anyone else that you saw Larry with – ' she could not bear to speak the hated name, so substituted, 'with anyone else on the fells; it would only upset Jinny more. You understand, don't you, especially now?'

'Yes, Jessie. I'll try and not let on . . . I will, honest. I'll try and stop it coming out.'

'That's right. Come on, I'll help you to bed and get you a hot drink.'

'Oh, Jessie, you're good. I always knew you were good. I said to Larry – Eeh! there I go again. Do I go upstairs to the front room?'

'Yes. And I'll strap your ankle up, and you can stay in bed tomorrow.'

With some difficulty she got Lottie upstairs and settled for the night; and she was in her own room before she realized that the whole evening had passed and she had not taken off the costume. She looked down at it. There were Lottie's dirty finger marks on the sleeve and a splash of milk on the skirt. But she made no comment on them to herself as she undressed.

Before getting into bed, she went to the bottom drawer of the chest and took out an imitation-leather wallet from which she extracted a sheet of much-thumbed paper. She looked down on it for a while. On it was the only piece of writing she had attempted in her life.

When Larry had first impressed her with his cleverness and poured into her willing ears the results of his efforts, she had asked God why He had so favoured her in bestowing on her the love of this clever man – brilliant had been the word she'd used. It was only after months of secret effort on her own part that the few lines on this paper had evolved. They were the total essence of her feeling which had been squeezed from her soul. She did not know if they were good or bad, and she had been too humble to show them to her lord, but she had promised herself that when they were married and everything there was to know about her was made known to him, then she would show him these lines. For the last time now she read them:

Love I can bring you only faith;
No money, no power, no deep wisdom;
No beauty, no brains; no tongue to charm,
No voice to sing. But to you I come not empty,
I bring no wrath, I bring you faith.

Spurn me not for lack of all the charms
You see in others, but compare them with me.
Without grace I stand; but no empty hands
Do I hold forth, but full they are
Overflowing from my heart's core
To bind you ever more . . . with my faith.

Slowly now she tore the paper into tiny scraps and put the heap on top of the drawers, and when she got into bed she lay staring up at the ceiling, seeing there what she imagined Lottie had seen in the meeting on the fells.

'Spurn me not for lack of all the charms you see in others!' Turning her face into the pillows she pressed it tight, trying to check the flood of tears. But they gushed from the well of pain in which her whole being was submerged.

6

THE WILL OF GOD

Jinny's house had always been well ordered. Holidays, strikes, births or deaths: on a Monday she washed; Tuesday she ironed; Wednesday she allotted her spare time to the upstairs rooms; Thursday she did her front room and the inside of her windows; Friday she spent on her kitchen and back, and shopping; and on Saturday she did her big baking. But now, eleven o'clock on Monday morning, she was sitting in the front room by the empty fireplace, staring at the big jar of wilting daffodils that Gracie had brought in last Wednesday. They covered the whole of the opening between the curtains and were an effective shield from the garden path. She was staring at them in troubled, probing perplexity, as if from their dying she hoped to draw some clue to explain her own fading and suddenly troubled life.

She was fifty-nine, and she had protested silently these past few days that it wasn't fair, she shouldn't be called upon at her age to bear such troubles. Not all in a heap anyway. If these things had happened when she was younger then she could, she felt, have stood up to them. But now, they upset her something terrible. They made her head swim and her heart not only sore but beat so rapidly that at times she became frightened and worried, so that all she wanted to do was to sit and cry. This last troubled her most of all, for she had never been given to crying. Everything, she thought, had happened on that black Saturday. Her two girls contemplating going to the other end of the earth had seemed bad enough until late that night, holding Jack's child in her arms, had come the awful premonition, which was to grow into certainty not only within herself but in the telling silence of others when they looked down on it. Then Lottie . . . Lottie. Her small, tightly compact body moved in quick jerks expressing her feelings more clearly than words. If she'd got her hands on her sister that night she would surely have killed her. It was as well that Jessie had kept her over there for the following week, too. But now the anxiety of waiting to see if there were to be results of this escapade were so nerve-racking that she felt that just another week or so like these past few days and she'd go off her head. The dread of Lottie having a child kept her awake at night, and into her waking nightmares would come the thought of the child across the landing, and that would lead to the troubled perplexity on Jack's face and her growing dislike of Lena, whose constant nagging was upsetting the house still further, and, as always, her thoughts would lead her to her elder son. As they did now, and she asked herself why he hadn't gone when he'd intended. But, as usual, before she could give herself any answer to this question, she bounced up, saying aloud, 'The washing . . . I'll never get a start . . . and the dinner an' all.'

But before Jinny went into the scullery to begin on the washing she turned up the passage and went to the open front door, and from the steps she looked down on the pram. The pram itself was an irritation to her, for it dominated not only the garden and the house but the whole of the street. There was scarcely a woman in the road who hadn't examined the pram from inside or outside the gate. It was the talk of the place, and more so because of what it carried.

In the soft shadow of the high silvery fawn canopy lay the child. The child who rarely cried and who only showed evidence of life when sucking at Lena's breast. It looked a healthy child, fat and chubby. It showed no definite deformity; it had two eyes, and a nose and a mouth, but the mouth had a sort of shapelessness, and the nose was too small to be a nose. But it was the eyes that drew other eyes. They were not lying in soft valleys, hemmed in with cheeks like blush-coloured mountains, but were lying level with the brow and cheek bone. They looked almost as if they were painted on the flat surface. They were without expression; they looked – what was the word Larry had used? – non-existent. As she stood gazing down at her grandchild the back door opened and Lottie came along the passage to her side.

In a persistent endeavour to obliterate the trouble she had caused, Lottie's mind led her to act as if nothing had happened, or if it had, as if it was over. All Jinny's nagging and scolding could not touch her persistence to be happy like she used to be. With the knowledge that the fiddler had 'done a bunk', the memory of the latter part of the time she had spent with him quickly faded, and apparently the only thing that marred her happiness was Lena's attitude towards her, for Lena would not let her touch her child, not even look at it.

'Can I bring her in, Jinny?'

'No; you've been told.'

Jinny kept her back towards Lottie as she spoke. She had never once looked her full in the face since she had come back from Jessie's.

'It's spitting on, and the pram'll get wet.'

'Get in!' cried Jinny, digging backwards with her elbow. 'And shut up.'

As it was beginning to rain Jinny went down the two front steps, pushed the pram around to the back, in through the scullery and into the kitchen.

Lottie was waiting, and she pulled a chair out of the way so that the pram could go partly into the corner of the room, and as Jinny pushed it past her, she exclaimed, 'Oh, she's smellin', Jinny. Can I clean her?'

Gripping the handle of the pram, which almost reached her bust, Jinny's eyes stared blankly before her for a moment before she barked, 'If you don't stop it, our Lot, I'll hammer you. Before God I'll hammer you! Lena says you're not to go near her. Hundreds of times she's said it, and that's going to be enough . . . it's her bairn.'

'But why should she, Jinny? I minded all our

bairns. You know I did. Didn't I take Florrie and Gracie out on the fells when you were working half days at Mrs Peel's? Now didn't I? And you've always said the only thing I could do was mind bairns.'

'Shut up, will you!'

Mistaking the strained quietness of Jinny's voice for softening, Lottie went on, 'Ah, Jinny, there's no harm in me wantin' to nurse the bairn, is there? Mrs Wilson used to pay me, you remember? A shillin' she paid me for looking after her Basil. Why won't Lena? I don't want nothin' off her.'

'Lottie Broadhurst' – Jinny's voice was terrible with threat – 'I'm warning you something dreadful'll happen if you don't give over. I'm telling you . . . if you don't give over. I want peace in this house, and if you start pestering Lena when she comes in, before God, I tell you, I'll bray you. She isn't too good yet and if you upset her any more . . .'

Jinny left the threat unfinished. Within herself she knew that she really didn't care how upset Lena was. She was a fat, lazy hulk, and although she'd had time enough to get really on her feet again, she was playing up. This morning's walk to the store was the first move she had made out of the house, and then she'd had to be asked to go. She expected both herself and the bairn to be waited on. Well, it wasn't coming off. She was past looking after bairns . . . she'd looked after enough in her time.

Lottie, temporarily silenced, gazed at her sister; then her head began to move with short staccato swings, like the pointer of a metronome, an indication of her bewilderment; when something was beyond her, her head would swing. Suddenly it became still, and looking over her shoulder she gazed down into the pram, and after a moment, as if fascinated by the child, her whole body was drawn round towards it, and as she stared down at the baby, pity swam from her eyes. It was as if the odd seam in her own composition recognised a similar something in the child. Then with deep, soft gentleness she spoke words that set blaze to the tinder of tempers that had been smouldering in the house for weeks.

'Poor thing,' she said. 'She's just like little Mary Tollet. Mary looked just like that. I remember seeing her . . .'

Suddenly Lottie's words were cut off and drowned by a scream, which preceded a flow of vitriolic language such as no Broadhurst man or woman had used in the house before. Lena, filling the doorway, appeared like someone suddenly caught in a frenzy of madness. She was carrying a handbag in one hand and a shopping bag in the other. The shopping bag she flung to one side of the room, and her handbag, with the heavy metal clasp, she aimed straight at Lottie's face.

The bag hit Lottie on the neck, and gasping in terror and hugging it to her she backed towards the fireplace as Lena advanced on her, crying, 'You! I'll do for you.'

'Here, here, hold on!'

Jinny, grabbing at Lena's arms with a strength out of all proportion to her size, managed to push her

154

into a chair. And now she too began to shout, trying to drown Lena's hysterical flow. 'Be quiet, woman! Have you gone mad? Stop it! Do you hear!'

No-one heard the quick footsteps coming down the stairs, nor did they seem to take any notice when Larry appeared at the kitchen door. 'What in Heaven's name's up?' he cried as he came in, pulling the braces of his trousers over his pyjama coat. His feet were bare, his hair on end, and his eyes full of sleep.

'What's the matter with her?' He stood at his mother's side looking at Lena, but her answer was lost under Lena's cries, and he cast a swift glance to where Lottie was cowering in the corner of the room, and part of the situation was made clear to him. Pushing his mother aside, he grabbed hold of Lena's shoulders and shook her vigorously, commanding as he did so, 'Stop it! Do you hear – stop it!'

Slowly Lena's screaming gabble subsided, and she leant back gasping. Her mouth hung open and her tongue lay over her teeth like someone who had been choking. Her face was running in sweat and through her open coat the top of her breasts lay bare where the buttons of her dress had been burst asunder with her fury.

The kitchen was quiet now but for the sound of her laboured breathing, and Larry, stepping back from her and reaching for a pair of his father's slippers from the corner of the fireplace, thrust his feet into them, saying, 'This house is getting more like a mad house every day.'

His words seemed to revive Lena's frenzy.

'Mad house!' She sat up. 'Aye, it is like a mad house. It always has been with her in it. And now she says me bairn's mad.'

'I didn't. Oh, Lena, I didn't.' Lottie's voice was choked with her crying.

'You did, you . . . !' She made to rise from her chair.

'Ssh! Be quiet.' Jinny put a soothing hand on her shoulder. 'There now, it's all over. Come on upstairs and lie down.'

Lena shrugged Jinny's hand away and looked at Larry. 'She did. She said . . . she said it was like Mary Tollet.'

Larry turned and looked at Lottie. Poor Aunt Lot. 'Out of the mouths of babes and fools.' She would have to be the one who would voice the fear of the house. Well, it had to come sooner or later. And poor Jack. It was him he was sorry for, not this fat, sexy bundle of conceit.

Little Mary Tollet lived in the next street. He had passed her hundreds of times without giving her much thought. She was shapeless, with tight, vacant eyes, a gaping mouth and, more often than not, a running nose. Sometimes she played with the more kindly of the children, but even they laughed when, talking through her nose and with wild gestures of her arms, she'd try to make herself articulate.

The thought that Lena was to be saddled with such another as Mary Tollet aroused a spark of pity in him, and he said, 'She didn't mean that. And who

156

can tell anyway at this stage what a child's going to turn out like? Come on, take a pull at yourself.'

Larry's words were meant to be soothing, but being unable to hide his real feelings for her they conveyed little sympathy and quite a lot of censure. And Lena was quick to sense this. Dragging herself up out of the chair, she faced him, and her voice, although controlled now, still held fury. 'Take a pull at myself! Be calm, and ape the head of the house! You are calm, aren't you? Two-bloody-faced, I'd call it, but you, Lord Almighty, would call it calm. We must all breathe, eat and sleep when our Larry says we've got to.' She cast a malicious glance at Jinny, then went on, staring hard into Larry's set face, 'And now our Larry says I've got to take a pull at myself. Well, here's one who doesn't take orders from you. I don't need to take a pull at meself. And why? Because I know that she, that mad bitch there' – she pointed to Lottie's shrinking figure – 'isn't far out. Yes, I know; I know.' She turned on Jinny now, throwing the truth at her. 'I'm not daft. And do you wonder at it if the bairn's not right, looking and listening to that!' Her arm was thrust out towards Lottie but her eyes still held Jinny's now pitying gaze. 'Looking and listening to her every day I was carrying. And what's more I know all about everything. Yes, everything. How can you expect my bairn to be all right when your father was in the asylum – there's no madness on our side. Aye, you can stare' – she nodded at Jinny – 'I know. You kept it dark, and I got to know.'

'My father in the asylum?' Jinny's short figure was

stretched taut now. 'My father in the asylum? You've got hold of the wrong end of the stick, lass. My father was badly shell-shocked when a bomb dropped on Palmer's shipyard in Jarrow in the 1914 war and he was away for some time having treatment, but as for being mad, he was no more mad than you are.'

'No? He had her!' Again Lena's arm was thrust out. 'He had her before there was any war on, and do you mean to stand there and tell me that she's all there?'

It was Larry who answered this question, and angrily. 'If you were half as wise as she is you'd be twice as intelligent as you are. And babies like Betty can happen to anyone, it's got nothing to do with heredity.'

'Oh, the clever bugger talking again!'

The audible gasp from Jinny was more at the use of a bad word in front of a man than at Lena's attitude towards Larry.

'Lena!' she said, stern dignity over-riding her pity of the moment. 'I'm having no language like that in this house. You've used enough these last few minutes to do for the day. The men don't use it, and as long as I'm here the women won't.'

Lena stared back at Jinny, and a slow sarcastic smile touched her lips. 'No bad language? Not in front of your gentleman son?' Her voice was mocking. 'My God! It's laughable. He can pinch another man's wife as soon as his back's turned and go whoring with her. No swearing! Why, I wouldn't waste me spit on him, never mind me swearing.'

Turning her gaze from Jinny's tightly pressed lips

158

to Larry's blanched face, she laughed openly at him. 'One at home and one away, Pam has. Good luck to her. You think you're a clever pup, but what are you? A nowt . . . a sucker, a big sucker.'

Slowly Lena left the kitchen and a silence behind her, a silence that tore at Larry, shrinking his manhood and reducing him inwardly to the lad who was always being pulled up on the carpet before the little Trojan who was his mother. Under the startled stare of her eyes he was forced to push back his shoulders. Well, it had to come out sometime. It was a wonder, knowing Lottie's tongue, it had remained in the dark so long – he'd never had any fear of Jessie splitting. He turned to the window, saying, 'Don't take it like that, it can't be helped.'

'Don't say that.' Jinny brought out the words painfully. 'It's wrong, you know it's wrong. What can come of it anyway? And your father, he'll go mad, he won't let it go on.'

'How can he stop it?' Larry's voice sounded flat and empty of emotion. 'It's nobody's business but my own.'

'You're a fool . . . a fool! Do you hear!' Her tone held half anger, half pain.

'Doubtless.'

'She took the other man because of his money. Do you think she'll give that up?'

Larry swung round from the window, and she was shocked at the glare in his eyes. It was a ferocious glare that would, she knew, not respond to reason, and as he passed her she did not try to detain him but looked after him, the lined skin of her face quivering. Then with a plop she sat down, and stared at the shining, scaly backs of her podgy hands. They were lying in the hollow of her lap, and she continued to stare at them until Lottie moved from the corner and stood near the fireplace. Then she lifted her gaze from them, and the sight of her sister seemed to galvanise her into life. Springing out of the chair, she advanced towards Lottie, who shrank back as she had done when a child, crying, 'Aw! Jinny . . . aw, don't.' For answer, Jinny's hand came up and caught her a blow alongside the face that sent her staggering back against the mantelpiece.

'I told you I'd hammer you, didn't I? Take that.' Her hand descended on her sister again, on the other side of her face this time. 'And that. All the trouble you've caused, you big, useless lump. By! I'll make you remember this day.'

As her hand caught Lottie another blow across the head, Frank and Jack appeared in the doorway. They both stood for a moment as if mesmerised, then Frank exclaimed, 'Here, hold your hand a bit, woman. What's up?'

Jinny's raised arm hovered, then dropped to her side, and she turned to her husband; and to his utter amazement she burst into tears.

Jack looked from his mother to his aunt; then he raised his eyes to the ceiling. Directly above was his and Lena's bedroom, and if he could believe the evidence of his ears there was the sound of muffled sobbing coming from there, too. Throwing his bait tin on to the table, he took the stairs two at a time and burst in on Lena, saying, 'What's up, honey? What's it all about?'

Lena was lying across the bed, still in her outdoor things, and at his touch she turned and clung to him, crying, 'It's her! It's her! I've always told you. And now she says Betty's like . . . like Mary Tollet.' There was no admitting now that she knew this to be the truth. She lifted her tear-ravished face to her husband's. 'That's what she said.'

Jack, after gazing into her swimming eyes for a moment, pressed her head into his shoulder. He made no comment whatsoever, nor did his face show any surprise; but it bore a stretched look, as if his mouth was determined to pull itself away from the rest of his features. After a while he began talking, but kept his hand pressed firmly on the back of her head so that he could not see her face. 'We had better take it to the doctor.'

'I'll not go to the clinic.'

'There's nobody asking you to go to the clinic; we'll go to the doctor. They can do wonders these days.' He did not add that he had no hope at all that his child would benefit from any modern wonder.

'Jack.'

'Yes, honey?'

'I can't stay here no more, we must get away.'

'All right, all right, love. I'll go down to the housing office as soon as I get me dinner, not that I want any. Come on now.' He kissed her and dried her face. 'We'll face this thing together, eh?'

'You think if there's anything wrong it can be put right?'

'Why woman – certainly.' His voice was almost jocular. 'Look, you lie down. Get your coat off, and I'll bring you something up.'

'Will you bring her up for her feed?'

'Yes. Come on.'

With the gentleness of a mother, he took off her shoes and drew the eiderdown over her, then went downstairs.

His father was in the kitchen having his dinner; his mother was in the scullery; Lottie and Larry were nowhere to be seen. He went and stood near his mother, but she did not look up at him, only continued to scrub the collars of the shirts before throwing them into the gas copper. Twice he made an effort to speak but seemed unable; and after a moment he walked slowly into the kitchen. His father went on eating as if he were unaware of his son's presence, and Jack in his turn acted as if he, too, were not there. Stooping, he picked up the child. She gave off a strong smell of sick, and her napkin was soaked. He clutched at two clean napkins hanging from the brass rod, then went out of the room.

Frank, laying down his knife and fork, rose from the table, and going to the fireplace took his pipe from the mantelpiece and knocked it on the bars, and the sound rang through the house with a hollow empty ring, as if it were vibrating in a place devoid of life.

7

EMANCIPATION

'There's something fishy about it all.' Mrs Macintyre spoke quietly but pointedly as she took the spare needle from the heel she was turning and stuck it through her thick grey hair.

'There's nowt fishy about it.' Willie, sitting at the corner of the table, his back half turned to his mother, bit on the thumb-nail of one hand, while with the other he fondled his dog's head.

'No?'

This monosyllable did not draw her son, but was followed by what she imagined was a telling silence, which forced her to continue. 'Where's she got the money from then? New furniture, new clothes – she didn't get them all out of the insurance money. And she paid ready for the furniture. Young Ted Baker in Bygraves' told his mother she paid cash for every article she got, and is still buying more. Ask yourself' – she turned to him – 'if you're not supplying her with money, who is?'

Willie's fingers joined his thumb, and he bit savagely at them in rotation. That's what he would like to know. As his mother said, there was something fishy – not about Jessie. No! his mind defended loudly

– but there was something fishy somewhere. Yet he could see no way of getting to the bottom of it. It didn't really matter so much to himself, but he had to satisfy his mother. Yet it did matter, because since she had got those new things Jessie was changed. Just how, he couldn't say. He had nothing really to grumble about; things were going swimmingly. Wasn't she going out with him the night? He had got himself worked up over asking her, but she had accepted like a shot, quiet like, and with no humming or harring.

'You've always given me your money to put by for you.' Mrs Macintyre took the needle from her hair and concentrated her gaze upon it as she picked up the loops on the heel, but went quietly on: 'Why couldn't the cup-tie winnings go along with the rest? You don't carry sixty-eight pounds around in your pocket.'

Willie turned swiftly about. 'How do you know what I got?'

'I made it me business to find out. You've always told me what you got afore. Now you have a big win and you don't.'

'I gave you ten pounds,' said Willie reproachfully.

'That doesn't matter, lad – not that I wasn't thankful. But I knew you had money, and Jessie stocking up like that – well, I'm no fool, and I'm too old a cat to be hoodwinked by a kitten. If you're going to set up a new house for her and buy her clothes like she's getting and dress her up to the eyes, then I say, marry her. There's enough scandal about the place without you causing any more.'

It should have been perfectly easy for Willie to say, 'I want to marry her. What do you think I'm going after her for? And I'm going to spend every penny of those winnings on a ring,' but he knew where that would lead, for the fact that he was going to spend over fifty pounds on a ring would drive his mother frantic – the years of counting pennies had made her careful of even the farthings. He hadn't bought the ring yet, for although Jessie was nicer to him than he had dared to imagine, he was more unsure of her now than he had been four weeks ago.

The answer he gave to his mother was, 'That'll come in good time. I don't want to rush things, her mother just dead, an' all.'

'Huh!' Mrs Macintyre gave a derisive laugh. 'Her mother dead. That certainly hasn't affected Jessie. Only in one way. It's given her scope. She's going clean 'long to hell with show and pride.'

'She's not. I thought you liked Jessie. You always said she was too good to be treated like she was, with' – he added hesitantly, naming no names – 'one after another of them.'

'She was. I did like her, but I've never seen such a quick change in anybody in the whole of my life. Look.' She stood up, and folding up the sock, put it in the knitting bag hanging from the arm of the chair, and then facing her son determinedly, she went on, 'You say you haven't bought her those things?'

'I've told you,' snapped Willie.

'You swear on it?'

'Talk sense, Ma. Could I have bought her all that stuff for sixty pounds?'

'No, you couldn't. But you've had five pounds clear a week for yourself since you were demobbed, and that's nearly nine years ago. And you don't bet all that away, and there's hardly a week passes but you have a win of some kind. I know' – she pressed her hand out towards him – 'I get me share, but you can't spend all you've got left.'

Can't I? thought Willie, turning and looking down at the table once more. That's all you know. He had never dared tell her what he put on horses, dogs, and pools during the course of a week.

'And you swear you haven't bought her those things?'

'Yes. I've told you.' His placid features were screwed up in annoyance.

'Then' – Mrs Macintyre brought her hands together, and held them tightly against her waist line – 'it's as Emily King says.'

Willie waited, but when his mother did not immediately divulge what Mrs King had said, he turned to her, saying, 'Well, come on out with it. What does Ma King says now?'

'Well, you'd better know sooner than later – somebody's sure to tell you. That new parson fellow, Mr Ramsey from the chapel, he's been in there twice every week since her mother died.'

Willie stared for some moments at his mother in dumbfounded surprise, then he cried, 'My God! Trust women! Why, Mr Dobson was never off the door-step and nobody accused him of keeping Mrs Honeysett.'

'This one's not like Mr Dobson. Old Dobson was like a professional beggar – he went where he could get a free meal, or a back-hander. This one's got money, they say, and he's all la-di-da. He's making arrangements to send the bairns from six Bog's End families to Shields for a week in the summer holidays, and standing all the expenses. But in spite of that he's finding he can't buy the members. Some of them are getting their backs up . . . Mrs King for one. She says it's like listening to blasphemy to hear him preaching. And tell me this: why, when Jessie's never been inside the chapel door for years, should she be going now, all in her fine toggery? Tell me that. No, lad, there's something fishy, and you'd better find it out now.' As she turned away from the sight of his troubled face, she left one final weight on his mind: 'If it isn't you, it's him, and you know best which it is.'

Some minutes later the clatter of dishes in the kitchen brought Willie to himself, and as if awakening from sleep he shook his head. It was fantastic. What would they concoct next? Women were terrible creatures – they turned on their own like wild animals. Jessie being kept! Why, it was almost laughable. Now if it had been one of the Podger girls, or Rene Fenton, or anyone else about the place . . . but Jessie. Women! He moved his head slowly, and as he did so the dog nuzzled his hand, currying for his attention, and he said, 'Aye, all right' and rose and took the lead from a hook by the corner of the mantelpiece. It was now ten minutes to six, and he reckoned if he walked for half an hour he'd feel better.

With the dog pulling on the lead, he went through the scullery, but said no word to his mother, nor she to him – she had, as she said to herself, given him enough to set him thinking.

Out in the lane, he was walking past Jessie's back door when he pulled Bill to a stop. The door was ajar, which was odd, for she never left her door open. Tugging at the dog, he went towards it, and pushing it further open still he looked up the yard, and there, within the kitchen, he saw her, standing with her back to the window.

It took some little persuasion and force to get Bill into the yard, for he was not going to be deprived of his walk without making a protest, and the scuffling he made brought Jessie to the door.

'Hello, Willie,' she said. 'I got in early; Miss Barrington let me off. Poor Bill.' She stooped and patted the dog. 'Were you taking him for his walk?'

'Yes; and I saw your door open.' He looked at her questioningly.

'Oh, Mrs Noakes came the back way for the National Savings. I forgot to close it after her. Come on in . . . come on in, Bill.' She urged the dog over the threshold, and, as she closed the door behind him and Willie, she added, 'I'm having all my visitors at once . . . Mr Ramsey's just called.'

Willie moved slowly into the kitchen, and a tall,

thin young man put a half-empty cup of tea on the table and rose from his chair. 'Hello,' he said.

'Hello,' said Willie.

'So this is Bill . . . I've heard of Bill. Hello boy.' With both hands he rumpled the dog's head, and Bill, as was most unusual with strangers, responded by grabbing the minister's cuff in his great teeth and playfully growling.

'You would, would you?' As the minister ruffled his ears Bill became more excited, until Willie said sharply, 'Stop it! Sit.' Whereupon the dog ceased its playing and reluctantly sat down on the hearthrug. The young man straightened up and looked at Willie. 'He's a fine beast. They're my favourite dogs, bull terriers. I had one when I was a boy, but it developed mange and my father had it put to sleep. Has he had mange?'

'No,' said Willie flatly.

'They say that all bull terriers are born with it in their blood, but in the case of pedigree puppies they drain off the blood when they are born. Wonderful things they do now, don't they?'

When Willie made no reply to this, the minister turned to Jessie, smiling at her, saying, 'Well, Jessie, I'll have to be on my way. I'll see you in the morning, then?'

'Yes.'

'Come to the vestry after the service and I'll give you those books. Being my own, I don't put them on the shelves.'

'Thanks. I will.'

'And thank you for the tea, Jessie; it was a Godsend. Goodbye.' The minister nodded to Willie, then added, 'Is there any hope of seeing you to-morrow, too?'

'No,' said Willie definitely.

The young man's laugh filled the room. 'Well, that's straight anyway. That's how I like it. Good-bye. Goodbye, Jessie. And you too, Bill.' He patted the dog's head as it sat by Willie's feet. Then laying a detaining hand on Jessie's arm, he said, 'No; don't come; I can let myself out the back way. Goodbye.'

As Jessie watched the minister walk down the back yard, Willie watched her, and when she turned to him and said, 'He's a wonderful young fellow, a sight different from Mr Dobson,' he said, 'Aye, I can see that.'

'Will you have a cup of tea, Willie?'

'No; I've just had me tea. Thanks all the same.'

'Well' – she paused and rubbed her upper arm with the palm of her hand – 'I won't be long.'

'Oh, it's all right,' he said. 'Jessie . . .'

'Yes?'

He looked for a moment at a small gilt-framed picture on the wall, which he hadn't seen before. 'Dutch Interior', it said, 'by Pieter De Hooch'. It was all reds and browns and seemed dull to him, but when his eyes once more alighted on her face, he couldn't for the life of him say, 'Look, Jessie, it's for your own good. I wouldn't say anything, but you know what women are.' And so on. Instead, he said, with a motion of his head towards the wall, 'A new picture?'

'Yes. Do you like it? Mr Ramsey told me of them. There's a number. I'll get them gradually. It looks like a real painting, doesn't it, but it's only a print.'

He went towards the door, and she said, 'I won't be long, Willie . . . about twenty minutes.'

He did not turn and smile, nor was there a usual chirpy word from him; all he said was, and then dully, 'All right.'

His manner caused her too to stand and watch him as he went down the yard. What was the matter with him? Something was wrong. Perhaps he'd had words with his mother. Yet he rarely, or never, had words with anyone, and not with his mother.

She went upstairs and into the front room, which had become so changed in the past four weeks as to be unrecognisable. It was now papered in green, and the woodwork painted cream. It held a small, dark-oak bedroom suite and a single divan bed, and these stood on a russet-coloured carpet. She had done the room entirely herself, which had added greatly to her satisfaction. It had taken her nearly three weeks of nights to complete, but the self-imposed task had a two-fold mission: she had begun to make the house fit to live in, and in doing so, she was giving herself no time to sit down and think. She worked until the early hours of the morning, and when, almost dozing on her feet, she went to bed, sleep soon came to her. Even when her mind, escaping from her hold, wandered down the pain-filled channels again, her physical weariness would come to her aid. And in the mornings too, there was no time to think – it was only in moments like the present, when she was donning her new clothes, that her heart cried pitifully for what might have been. But before the cry could reach her lips, the new Jessie would take control and the longing be pressed down, and she would say, 'That's over and done with. You were a fool long enough, and just look at what's happened since you took a pull at yourself.'

Willie was courting her. She was, even now, not quite over the surprise that he should want to. When he had asked her on Wednesday if she would go to Newcastle with him tonight, she had replied, 'It's all right, Willie, there's no need to be sorry for me. I'm not worrying any more.' 'Sorry?' he had said. 'Sorry? I'm not sorry in that way. I've been wanting to ask you out for years, but I wasn't in the running.'

This knowledge had given her a strange feeling and brought comfort to the self that she was endeavouring to displace. It was odd, but with Willie she felt she could be nothing but the old Jessie, while with the minister she could be nothing but her new self.

Two days after Mr Ramsey had called with Mr Dobson and stood silent while that enraged man had told her just a few of the calamities that were going to befall her for stripping the house, particularly the walls of its tracts, he returned. He had been awkward at first; then said in a boyish fashion that suited his face and manner, 'I think you were right, you know, about scrapping those pictures and things. Clutter. It's no use, inside or out of you. Do you read much?' he had ended.

'I've never had the time,' she had replied, 'but I've always wanted to.'

'Good,' he said. 'I'm starting a library in the church hall, and I want customers.'

'But I don't come to church any more. I haven't done for years.'

He had looked at her, his smile gone and his face showing the seriousness with which he took his vocation and, which was more evident to her, the unsureness of himself.

'By what I have gathered in the short time I've been here, I'm going to need new customers very badly soon. If I'm to be true to myself, things are going to be pretty awkward for me from a number of quarters.' He had paused and stared, half shyly, half frankly, at her. 'I'd like to think of you as one of my staunch supporters. When I saw how you made that stand the other day, I thought, I'll be all right if there's only a few like her to back me. Will you come?'

Never had Jessie been given credit for firmness; never had anyone suggested that they would be better having her behind them. But at that moment, the man standing before her, who had held a parish in the south for nearly three years, had appeared like a young lad, a young lad who somehow, she sensed, was as lonely as herself.

That was the beginning. The following Sunday she had gone to listen to him, and each Sunday since. In fact, twice last Sunday. It was, she felt, as if God had sent her a source of strength, making, in the new minister, a spring from where she could draw the antidote with which to inject the humiliation that had bowed and beaten her these past two years. He had a way of making her – she was even now still hesitant in allowing herself to think such a term – like herself a little bit. Larry had never encouraged her to imagine herself intelligent, but the minister did, and she found that she not only liked the books he loaned her but that she was able to discuss them with him. Just a few minutes ago, before Willie had come in, she had experienced the same feeling which had first come to her when drinking tea with Madame Fonyer . . . there were different ways of living. Different people opened up new avenues for you. They might be just escape avenues, but better that than no escape at all.

Would she feel like this if she married Willie?

She was staring into the mirror, buttoning the delicate, moss-coloured-pink blouse, and she did not give herself an answer, but thought, I'll pop in next Saturday, and show her the blouse. I think she really meant that I should go back. Then with her finger on the top button, she stopped and said, 'No, Willie could never make me feel like this.' Willie could never make her feel other than she was; he could open up no new avenues.

There came a knocking on the back door and the sound of voices coming from the back yard, and she went down the stairs putting on her costume coat as she did so and thinking, I hope it isn't Aunt Lot. I'd hate to have to push her off. But to her surprise it was Mrs Macintyre at the door, and Willie. Willie's face looked grim, and he was standing in the scullery barring his mother's entry.

'What is it?' asked Jessie in perplexity.

'I want to have a word with you, that's all,' said Mrs Macintyre over her son's shoulder.

'I've told you,' said Willie, 'it's none of your business. I'm telling you, Ma, if you go on I'll walk out. I'm telling you.'

'I'll chance that,' said Mrs Macintyre stolidly. 'Can I come in?' She looked past her son to Jessie.

'Yes, yes, of course. But what is it?'

'Look, Jessie,' begged Willie over his shoulder, 'go on upstairs, or come on out, and don't listen to her.'

'Be quiet a minute, Willie. What's the matter? If it concerns me, I must know.'

With a sigh and a shrug, Willie gave up and let his mother pass. Then before going out, he turned to Jessie, saying, 'Mind, I've got nowt to do with this. Don't hold it against me, mind, Jessie.'

Bewildered, Jessie said, 'Hold what?' then turning to Mrs Macintyre, she asked, 'Will you sit down?'

'No,' said Mrs Macintyre. 'What I've got to say had better be said standing up, lass.'

'Well, go on.' Jessie's voice was now flat; she knew the symptoms, she'd seen other mothers fighting because their sons were showing signs of leaving them. But, nevertheless, she was surprised, for she had always thought that Mrs Macintyre liked her, or, to put it more correctly, was sorry for her.

175

'It's just this, lass . . . there's talk. I know Willie's old enough to take care of himself, but I'm his mother. I want you to answer me one question. Is he buying your stuff for you?'

Mrs Macintyre's small bright eyes took in the room.

So that was it. She should, she supposed, get on her dignity and cry, 'How dare you!' but instead she said dully, 'No; he's not.'

'Well' – now Mrs Macintyre sighed a long significant sigh – 'if he's not, who is, then, lass? I think Willie and me's got a right to know – you know how things are with him. He should have asked you himself, but he's too blooming soft.'

Jessie stared at the woman. 'Who is?' she repeated. 'Nobody . . . I'm buying it myself.'

'All this?' Mrs Macintyre's voice lost its conciliatory tone as her arms swept about the room. 'And upstairs an' all? And all ready cash? Oh, yes, I know. It's funny how things get about. Look, lass, I wasn't born yesterday, so don't think you've got a fool on. You never bought nearly two hundred pounds' worth of stuff yourself. You get four-fifteen a week and you've only had that for a little over a year. And don't tell me you've saved it either.'

'Then where,' asked Jessie slowly, 'do you think I got it?' Staring the older woman in the eye, Jessie waited.

'I'm waiting for you to tell me that.'

'I've told you.'

'I don't believe you, lass.'

'Well, where, Mrs Macintyre,' Jessie repeated, 'do you think I got the money?'

There was quite a pause before Mrs Macintyre spoke again. 'You hadn't any money before your mother died, and the insurance money only covered the funeral.'

There was another pause.

'That's right,' said Jessie.

'Oh—' Mrs Macintyre turned away. 'You make this hard for me, Jessie. But I don't want to see my lad made a fool of, he's a good lad.'

'Where do you think I'm getting the money then?' Jessie's voice was low and flat, but persistent.

'Well, since you won't speak up and you force me to, that young minister. It's the talk of the place the number of times he's in here, and you neither daft, sick nor dying. It wouldn't have mattered how many times he came, if you hadn't suddenly got all decked out in new things, expensive things. And the house an' all. Don't you see, lass, two and two go together. And to see him go out just now and the look on my lad's face, I just couldn't stand it.'

Jessie slowly sat down. Her face was drained of its colour. She looked up at Mrs Macintyre, her mouth opening and shutting, but she made no sound.

These past two weeks, when she had continued with her buying, she had ceased even to wonder what the neighbours were thinking. Previously she had thought they would, like Mrs King, think she was getting them on the instalment plan. But now her heart began to race. That young lad. She did not actually look old enough to be his mother, but inside herself she felt old enough. It may be there was a matter of only two or three years' difference in their ages, but their worlds were on widely separated planets. And the folks were thinking, and not only thinking but saying – Oh, my God – she felt she was going to be sick – if he should hear. Oh, anything but that. She'd tell them about the tin box and even give Mr Dobson what was left.

'Mrs Macintyre' – she leaned forward, appealing with her whole body – 'I'll tell you where I got the money. From . . . from my mother. She left it . . . she had been saving.'

There had been a reluctant sympathy in Mrs Macintyre's eyes for this lass she had known since she was born, but in a flash it was gone, and indignation was in its place. It was Mrs Macintyre's proud boast that it was impossible for anyone to hoodwink her, and now Jessie Honeysett was about to try it on. Well, let her take what she got.

'Your mother! Jessie Honeysett, do you think you're talking to somebody from Sedgefield? Your mother! Why, I never thought it of you. Let the dead rest, lass, and be what she was, good, bad or indifferent. It's wicked of you to try and pin something on her. Do you want me to believe that she was saving, pounds, hundreds, when you often had hardly a bite to put in your bellies? You were only getting three pounds a week all during the war, and your mother told me with her own lips, after your Da died, that she had to spend every penny of the bit she got on keeping the house going, as you wanted to save up for your wedding. She said she had to eke it out.' Mrs Macintyre stood back from Jessie. 'I hate to have to throw this up to you, Jessie, but there's hardly a house on this side of the street that hasn't kept you both going with meals one time or another.'

'I tell you, Mrs Macintyre, she did. Pounds and pounds.'

'Be quiet, Jessie! Don't sin your soul. Earn your money which way you like – you're not the only one these days – but don't smirk the dead.'

Jessie looked into the small, hard eyes, and what she saw there brought fear back into her life. Not so much for herself, but for that kind, young fellow. No-one would believe her about the money in the box, she had left the telling too long. But, but he was a minister . . . they wouldn't dare to say such things about him! She stood up, crying, 'You daren't say such things about him! He's a minister. He's young and kind. That's his only fault, he's kind.'

'A minister? He's a man, isn't he? A minister! Remember old Conway, the deacon . . . the dirtiest old swine alive. And I'll grant you he's kind' – her eyes indicated the room again – 'but if you want him to keep down his job, then keep him out of your house.'

Like a stone Jessie dropped back on to the chair, and bowing her head, she began to cry. And Mrs Macintyre, seeing in the fast-flowing tears the confession of guilt, turned and went out, convincing herself she had acted for the best and stopping her ears to the voice of her conscience, which was saying, If it had been Joe after her you wouldn't have troubled your head. Joe was never free with his cash like Willie.

8

DECISION

As fast as her rotund body would allow, Jinny bustled up the stairs. Half-past eight here and neither of those two lazy lumps out of bed yet, and she herself been up since five, with the kitchen all cleaned and the ironing half done. Pausing on the landing for breath, she looked first towards Lena's door and then to Lottie's; then making her way to her daughter-in-law's room, she knocked and opened the door in one movement, and on the sight of Lena's great, relaxed body lying sprawled across the bed, she sucked in her lips. Then, casting her eyes towards the cot, she exclaimed angrily, 'Whew! the smell. Lena!' she called.

There was only a wriggle from Lena.

'Lena, get yourself up. Come on.' She shook her by the shoulder.

'Here, who you pushing? What you think you're doing on?'

'It's after eight o'clock, and that child stinking to high heaven.'

Lena pulled herself up on the bed, pushed back her hair, and rubbed the sleep out of her eyes. 'If you don't like the smell, why don't you clean her?'

This last remark deprived Jinny of speech. After one long stare, she marched to the door, and there, regaining her tongue, she cried, 'Well, if that isn't the limit. And it's the end . . . do you hear?' She did not wait for Lena's reply, but went out, banging the door after her.

Of all the cheek . . . the brazen piece! Well, something would have to be done; things were going from bad to worse. Since they had taken the child to the doctor's, Lena had neglected it shamefully. But she had put up with a lot because of her son. He was in a bad way about the bairn, and oddly enough he made more of it now, since he knew there was no hope for it. The doctor had said he was afraid it was a mongol type – it was early days yet, but they had to be prepared to see her always as she was now. If she had been a cretin they could have tried iodine or thyroid. There had been fair successes with cretins, but he was deeply sorry and could hold out no false hope.

Mongols and cretins . . . Jinny had never heard of such names, but she had known, as well as the doctor, from the start that the child wasn't right. And she had known, before they took the bairn to him, what his verdict would be.

Well – she pulled at a busk in her corset that was probing her breast – it was their responsibility, and they would have to shoulder it. And in a place of their own, too, for she couldn't stand it any more. One thing on top of another.

She did not knock on Lottie's door but thrust it

open, and in her present frame of mind she was prepared to haul her sister out of bed. But Lottie was already up. She was sitting on the edge of the bed, dressed, and she looked apprehensively at Jinny, and said apologetically, 'I'm sorry I'm not down, Jinny, but I feel sick.'

The words almost caused Jinny to collapse. She gripped at the door stanchion and stared at the thin angular body of this woman, whom she had sheltered and protected in her own brusque way for forty-odd years. She raised her eyes to the long grotesque face. No, no; God wouldn't allow such a thing to come about. Women, good married women, would give their souls for a child . . . and been married years, and never seen the sign of one. But her! Only once with that dirty little fiddler and she was going . . . No, no; it was something she had eaten.

'Have you eaten something?' The question was so low as almost to be a whisper.

'No, Jinny . . . I've been sick all the week. I didn't tell you 'cause you were upset about the bairn.'

Being unable to look at her sister a moment longer without doing something she would later be sorry for, Jinny turned quickly away and went down the stairs, and sitting by the kitchen table she began to pick wildly at her apron. Her world had gone mad, absolutely mad. A mental bairn upstairs, her own son's bairn; Gracie and Florence on their way to Australia; Larry skulking like a thief after another man's wife, and the whole place alive with the scandal of it; and now, the crowning . . . Lottie carrying a bairn. The house would be like a menagerie.

Years ago her Granny had told her that, as a child, she had paid a ha-penny to go into a menagerie, and had there seen a boy with a head so large that it had to be supported with a built-up framework, and he was being taunted by a great, tall, thin man, whose arms were so small that his hands appeared to sprout from his armpits. But the boy with the big head had laughed all the time. She had been dreaming about her Granny last night and of the times she used to tell her stories, and this morning she had woken up thinking of the one about the menagerie. And now she felt that her dream had been broken, for she could see her own house becoming a menagerie. The thought terrified her, and made the thumping come into her head again. She moved her eyes about the room, taking in every article of furniture. There was nothing that did not gleam. These past weeks she had put double her effort into the house. If her furniture shone and her windows gleamed and her curtains were fresh, then she had vainly imagined nothing could go far wrong. But all the time they were going wrong, her whole world had gone wrong; it had indeed turned into a menagerie. She looked down the garden and across the road. Even Jessie . . . Jessie, above all people, having an affair, not with Willie – she could have understood that perfectly – but with a minister, who looked like a lad compared to her. But nevertheless, for all his young looks, he was a quick worker; he hadn't been in the place five minutes. But who was to blame anyway for Jessie going to the bad? Nobody but her own son. He was to blame . . . What was she talking about? She roused herself . . . Jessie going to the bad . . . she didn't believe a word of it, and she had told Emily King so. Old Dobson had called three times a week on Mrs. Honeysett and the Catholic priest was for ever going into the Connellys, and there'd been nowt said about them. It was because of the furniture and the new clothes the tongues had wagged. She was supposed to have said that her mother had left the money. Well, it was like Jessie to say a simple thing like that, there wasn't enough badness in her to concoct a better story. But where had she got the money from? Oh, what did it matter? Why worry about Jessie? Hadn't she enough to think about with her own house as it was? She put her hands to her head. Perhaps, she thought, this pain in me head'll drive me barmy, and I'll laugh like the lad in the menagerie. Eeh! dear God, what thoughts. She got to her feet, and as she did so the click of the garden gate brought her eyes to the window again, and she saw Frank standing, his hand on the gate, staring down at the pavement. She watched him for a moment, then went to the scullery and put the kettle on one gas-ring and the frying-pan on the other; and she was placing two gammon rashers in the pan when the door opened. She glanced round as usual to say, 'Hello there', but she did not give her husband the greeting, for before she could speak, he said, 'Where is he?'

'Who?' she asked.

'Larry.'

'Why, he's in bed. You know he's in bed.'

'How should I know? Can you count on owt he does?'

'What's the matter now? Dear God, what's the matter now?'

Frank gave her no answer but pushed past her, and up the stairs.

Pulling the frying-pan to one side, she went to the foot of the stairs and listened. Frank's voice was raised, but she could not hear what he was saying. And when he came down again, she said, 'Tell me, what is it?'

'It's nowt,' he said.

'Nowt?' she replied. 'You don't go on like that for nowt.'

'Let's have something to eat,' he said.

She was still staring at him and demanding to know what was wrong when she heard Larry's unmistakable tread on the stairs, and she was at the scullery door as he came into the passage. He did not speak to her, but went past her, thrusting his shirt into his trousers. She watched him wrench open the front door and go down the path and stand, as she had seen Frank do, looking down on the pavement. When he again came into the house the skin round his mouth showed a pasty white against the dark stubble on his cheeks.

Frank, standing in the kitchen doorway, said, 'Things have come to a pretty pass. We've always been able to hold our heads up, and now, because of your looseness, this happens on me doorstep. Well, here's an ultimatum. You give her up, or you get out. One or t'other. And before you do either, you'll get a bucket and clout and wipe that filth off.'

'I'll be damned if I will!' Larry's hands went to tighten up his belt, but not finding one, he hitched savagely at his trousers.

'What's up?' Jinny's cry pierced the men's voices. 'What's out there anyway?' She looked towards the front door.

'Summat that should never have been . . . our name's like mud in the town. Are you going to do it?' Frank turned to his son again.

'No.' Larry walked firmly towards the stairs, and Frank cried, 'Good. Good enough. Then get out!'

'I'll do that an' all.'

Larry mounted the stairs, and Jinny, her hands gripping her blouse, looked in desperation from her son's retreating figure to her husband. Never had she seen Frank like this. Frank was easy-going, peace-loving. He thought the world of Larry. Like herself, she felt that deep inside he housed a pride and feeling for his elder son that he did not have for any of the others. So much so that for years now he had openly acceded to him. When there was a question to debate, whether about pit or politics, he would sit and nod at Larry's cool reasoning, commenting from time to time, 'Aye. Aye; you're right theer, lad.' And now he had ordered him out.

Automatically patting her hair into place, and taking off her top apron, which she always did when

187

going out the front way, she went down the path to the gate. Looking over it, she saw at first only a number of whitewash marks on the flags. Her sight was not too good, and she scorned glasses, except for reading, and so she had to step on to the street and peer towards the pavement. And from this point of vantage, the marks took shape and formed lines of writing, writing done in letters inches high. Slowly she read the crude printing:

Pam had a little Larry without any dough,
So Pam dropped Larry in the cold, cold snow;
But her rich Daddy's kisses were not so hot as his,
So to the Barn came Pam again – Fizz, fizz, fizz.
                    Sucker.

Being unable to believe the evidence of her eyes, Jinny stared at the pavement, and she had to read the words again, and yet a third time, before she could take them in. Then shame, belittling and humiliating, covered her. All she had worked for in her life, which could be summed up in one word – respectability – was gone, trampled in the dirt of the whitewash on the pavement. There seemed no use any more in fighting or struggling to put a face on things. Even the façade of her brusque manner, that had helped so much in warding off the neighbours' bold approach, she could see now as useless. Slowly, almost humbly, she went up the path and round to the back door, and filling a bucket with water, and taking up a cloth and brush, she went to the gate again, and under the covered scrutiny of eyes behind curtains and over garden railings, she scrubbed away the words.

For the tenth time in half an hour Larry went to the opening of the barn and looked out across the rain-drenched grass. It had poured steadily from seven o'clock that morning, and now a cold wind was added to it, making the June day reminiscent of December. From its beginning it had been a hell of a day, and it wasn't over. How, he was now wondering, would Pam react to his decision? She had promised that as soon as her mother was strong enough she would make the break; but would she? Would her love for him be strong enough to break the ties that reached from across the Atlantic? It wasn't her mother he was afraid of now, but the man – he could feel his power in the silence that surrounded him – for his name had not been mentioned between them since the night they had come together again. At first, she had said, 'We must talk about it . . . about him', but she never had, and they had lived and loved hungrily, in the precious time that she stole from her mother's or father's watchful eye. They would laugh and joke, then become painfully silent, and the silence in turn would be broken by a passion of feeling, of taking greedily until, drunk with grasping, they sent each other reeling to their respective homes, she by her car, and he by bus or on foot. This divided departure always irked him, to see her drive away in a car placed a world between them. He could tell himself that any fool could have a car nowadays – half the fellows in the pit had cars now; he could have one tomorrow if he wanted one – but the thought brought no comfort. He was, there was no doubt, in the position to buy himself a second-hand car, but would he ever be in the position to provide her with a car like the one she had now?

Straining his ears, he was listening now for the sound of the car on the road, and thinking he heard it, he moved from out of the shelter of the barn, but the wind, lashing the rain at him, drowned all sound but that of itself, and he returned to the barn again.

It was their arranged plan that if she could not keep an appointment, he should wait at the barn between six and seven of an evening; that is, if his shift permitted. Today, they were to have met at two o'clock, but she hadn't turned up. He was on the third shift, and, in the ordinary way, he should have gone down at three-thirty. But there would be no more shifts for him, fore, back, or night. No, by God. He might live to regret a lot of things he would do from henceforth in his life, but leaving the pit, never.

The thought of his release made him buoyant for the moment, and he had a desire to dash out into the pelting rain and walk and walk, even run. He was free, free from the earth. No more would that winter be one continuous night; no more would the sweat stand on him, not from the heat or dripping water, but from fear – fear of the roof dropping in; fear of being trapped; fear of an explosion. Of all his fears, his fear of an explosion was the greatest, and the one he would have denied most, for had it not made the coward in him deny himself promotion? Years ago, he'd had the idea of becoming somebody in the pit: an overman, a deputy; who knew – assistant manager. He knew, as he put it to himself, that where brains were concerned he could have bought and sold the deputies that were over him. Most of them knew their immediate job, and that was all. It had been his determination to go into the thing thoroughly that had caused him not to go in for it at all. And the truth of 'Where ignorance is bliss . . .' came to him when he had done so much reading that he saw in the smallest spark from a coal-cutter, or the veriest suspicion of one from chock releases, the cause of an explosion; or when the cutter picks struck iron or copper in the seams, then his new knowledge would say . . . pyrites. And only a spark would be needed from that to ignite fire damp and air, and that particular section, he knew, would have had it.

A deputy might know all this, but if he wanted to hold down his job he didn't visualise it happening every time he entered the pit.

No more listening to talk of Aneurin Bevan and was he or was he not the reason why the Labour Party hadn't got in. The talk of some of his mates made him sick; the less they had in their heads the more they had to say. And it was the same with members of Parliament. Some hadn't the sense to realise that their past efforts had already borne fruit, that they were no longer appealing to a mob of ignoramuses. He had been sickened when listening to some of his own party, listening to their infantile reasoning and cheap slating. The pitmen were the top dogs now, they had said. Top dogs! Top dogs of what? Who wanted to be top dog in the bowels of the earth? And 'princely' had been another term used when comparing the miner's life of today with that of fifty years ago. They could have their princely lives . . . Princes of darkness, princes who had still to crawl on their bellies, princes who walked like permanent hunch-backs most of their days; princes who breathed, chewed, and swallowed death in bespangled dust. Princely! Why didn't they try the princely life? If, in the future, he should have to live from hand to mouth, his existence would, he felt, be more princely than it was now even with his swollen pay packet.

'Pam.' The name sprang from his thoughts and he was out and across the open space to where she was struggling towards him. His arm about her, he half carried her to shelter, and there, in the comparative dryness of the barn, she gasped and leant against him.

He held her closely, saying, 'I thought you weren't coming. Did you get my note? That's silly' – he gave a short laugh – 'you wouldn't be here if you hadn't. What a night to bring you out. I'm sorry I had to send it. Look, take off your mack and I'll shake it.'

He went to undo the top button, but his hands moved from it to her rain-drenched face, and holding it between his palms he murmured, 'Why are you so beautiful? . . . It drives me mad.' Then pulling her close again, he murmured thickly, 'My love. Darling!

192

Darling!' With each word he jerked her nearer and nearer to him, but when no answering endearment or responding pressure of her body came to him, he paused and raised her face, saying, 'What is it?'

Her eyes, looking deep into his, were troubled, and when she made to disengage herself from him, he did nothing to stop her. She was looking down at her clasped hands when she said, 'Ron's here.'

The muscles of his face tightened swiftly. His expression lost its look of adoration, and the protectiveness left his manner.

'Did you know he was coming?'

'No,' she said dully; then added emphatically, 'No, of course I didn't. He walked in this morning out of the blue. I thought he was still in California . . . that's where he wrote from last. He . . . he wanted me to go out.'

'Why has he come then?'

'I think it's my father. He must have sent for him.'

Her head was bowed, and her thick glistening lashes hid her expression from him, but gripping her by the shoulders he jolted her head up and stared into her face; then, after a moment, he said bitterly, 'You're glad he's come. You're glad he's back.'

'Don't be a fool.' She pulled herself from his hands. Then her expression softened, and she whispered, 'Larry, how could I be?' Then, more gently still, 'How could I be? How could I?'

Her tone drew the tenseness from his limbs, and gripping her hands and holding them to his chest, he said rapidly, 'I know, I know. I'm a frightened fool.

But listen. I've left the pit . . . and home. I got my marching orders from there.' Her widening eyes asked why, and he said, 'It doesn't matter, but I'm going. And you're coming . . . now, tonight. Just think, London tomorrow, Italy by the weekend.'

'But Larry . . .'

'Now, no buts, it's all arranged. I'm packed up, actually packed up.' The excitement was making him quiver.

'I can't come tonight, Larry.'

'Why not? You said . . .'

'Yes, I know. I know.' She moved her head restlessly.

'You're coming tonight.' Again he was holding her. 'You're not going back to him . . . not tonight or any other night.

'Do you mean to say . . . ?' He strained back from her the better to see her face. 'Do you mean to say you would stay with him tonight after . . . ? You couldn't. Pam, you couldn't.'

'Who said I was going to? Not that; but I've got to return home, I just can't run away. I've got to tell him and my mother.'

'But you'll come?'

'Not tonight, Larry.'

'You're stalling. Pam, if I thought you'd go back on me again I'd . . .' There was a terrible threat in his unspoken words.

'I won't. Darling, darling, I won't.' She flung herself on him, pulling his arms about her, her cheek tight pressed to his, trying to soften his anger and

194

allay his fears. 'I love you. Don't you know I love you? Haven't I proved it? If you only knew what it's been like at home, these past weeks. My father has been on every minute, and when my mother came out of hospital and got to know I thought she would die. How can you doubt me? But I can't just leave tonight; I've got to have time.'

'Time for what? I tell you, Pam, I just can't let you stay the night with him there. I'd go mad with the thought of you and him.'

'But I promise you, Larry, I promise you.'

'Promises are no good. I just couldn't stand it. Not again.'

He went to pull himself away, but she held him, and he muttered, 'I could put up with anything – all the tongue wagging in the world, but I tell you I can't bear to think of you and him . . .'

She lifted her face from his shoulder in order to be better able to convince him by the truth in her eyes. But her gaze became fixed on the opening of the doorway and on a figure moving through the rain towards it.

In the moment when in one swift jerk she freed herself from his arms, murmuring, 'Oh, God!' Larry too became aware through her wide-straining eyes of the man approaching, and when the heavily coated figure filled the doorway there was no doubt at all in his mind who it was. In a searing flash he took in the details of the man whom he hated as passionately as he loved his wife. He was as tall as himself, but broad with it, twice as broad; and he saw that it wasn't fat. The face was square and healthy-looking, and altogether he was the antithesis of his idea of her husband. Although he looked middle-aged, there was a virility about him, a youthfulness that belied his years. Here was no over-fed American, with a belly on him and thickening jowls; nor was the light of lustful ownership in his eyes.

This new picture did not soften Larry's hate or lessen his fears; in fact his jealousy took to itself a new aspect – he felt resentful towards her for not having prepared him; he felt that she had done him a double wrong in marrying someone as presentable as the man who was staring at him.

'We . . . ll.' The word was slow, drawn out, and soft, and his own voice when it barked back, 'Well!' sounded loud and uncouth in comparison.

The man took off his soft hat and dashed the rain from it. Then, looking at Pam, with only a touch of reproach in his voice, he said, 'This could have been avoided, you know . . . if you had done as I asked this afternoon. I gave you the chance to tell me.' He could have been censuring her for some slight misdemeanour.

Biting on her lip, in a childish manner of distress, Pam shook her head twice before saying, 'I couldn't, Ron. I didn't want to hurt you.'

'Hurt me!' The man made a sound in his throat. 'I don't think that would have troubled you very much. However' – he sighed, and once again dashed the water from his hat – 'now that I'm here we'll have this out. You'll have to make your choice.'

'She's made it.' Larry's voice was deep and guttural.

The two men confronted each other, and in the older man's eyes there seemed reflected now some of that hate that was pouring from Larry's.

'She's got to tell me herself. She happens to be my wife.'

'She should never have been your wife, and you know it. She was mine. You got her with your money and your showy car, that's how you got her.'

The man's nostrils widened, and it was some seconds before he answered, 'If I thought that was all that made her my wife I wouldn't be here now, and if you think she can be bought so lightly, why do you want her? I may tell you, sir' – his voice rested on the title – 'that I didn't know of your existence until her father wrote last week and informed me of the whole affair.'

Larry's eyes flickered towards Pam, but her head was turned from him. 'Well, you know now,' he said.

The man turned away and said softly, 'Pam.'

Slowly, she turned towards him, and Larry, watching her face, which to him was so beautiful that to look upon it brought a sort of pain, saw it now showing distress. Her eyes were full of sadness, her cheeks without colour, and her lips trembling.

'I'm sorry, Ron.'

They were the words she had spoken to him the day she had come back to him, and she was saying them in the same way now . . . She can't do it! The cry was loud in his head. She can't do it! She's mine.

'I believe you,' said the man; 'but why didn't you tell me before? I would have understood. At least, I would have tried. It would have made it easier for you and prevented all this.'

'I . . . couldn't hurt you.'

'But you have hurt me.'

'I know.'

The fact that they were talking as if he wasn't there made Larry rear. He wanted to lash out at the man, see him grovelling in the mud, but in spite of himself he was forced to stand aside and listen. 'You know what it will mean if you make this decision, don't you?'

Pam said nothing, but continued to look at her husband with a troubled stare.

'I could make you happy. I know I could. You may not think so now, but I could. You haven't given us half a chance.'

It was too much. 'Look here.' Larry almost sprang forward, and the man, without looking at him, said, 'Will you be quiet for a moment? I am talking to my wife. Your turn will come, and by what I can gather you have lost no opportunity lately. Pam' – complete master of the situation and speaking with evidently controlled quietness, he brought her distracted attention to himself again – 'look at me. I can give you so much that you need . . . not only in material things – and you are not unappreciative of those, are you?' He paused a moment before continuing, 'But socially and intellectually, and the last, although you may not be fully aware of it yet, is a need that you will miss if you are deprived of the opportunity to develop it.'

The man's slow polished tone added weight to the inferred slight. But Larry's hot retort was checked by Pam's voice, full of regret, as she said, 'I know, Ron, I know. And I don't want to do this, not to you, but I can't help it. I should never have married you. I'm to blame for it all. I do care for you, really I do, but not in the way I care for . . . Larry. I don't want to do this to you; you have been so good . . . Oh, I'm so sorry, Ron.'

The last words ended on a broken cry, and the man stood quite still for another moment or two, then dashing his hat once again, he said, 'There's little more to be said then.'

Relief and joy should have been racing through Larry, but her decision had left him strangely numb. She was coming to him, yet in some odd way he felt she was sorry she had to, as if she were being forced against her will.

'You understand that I will take the car?'

There was no reply from Pam to this.

'And about the jewellery.'

Larry watched her tongue flick over her lips as she said, 'You gave them to me.'

'I gave them to my wife. My mother had worn them, and her mother, and her mother . . . they belong to the family. The fob' – he made a small gesture towards the breast pocket of her suit, above which showed a gold pin, and then to her right hand, where, on the middle finger, was set a ring similar in

199

appearance to costume jewellery, in so much as it was ornate, but bearing, instead of the usual bright-coloured stone, three half hoops of glittering diamonds – 'they could never be replaced, not with money. And the others, Pam.'

She was silent while she twisted the ring on her finger.

'I am starting for London tonight. I would like to take them with me. You brought them all over?' There was a question, and a touch of censure, here. 'Perhaps you would let me have the key to the box, and that of the car?'

Her lids were drooped and her head lowered as she pulled off the ring and unloosened the fob and handed them to him. And when she fumbled in her bag for the key, her whole body slumped.

There was a shame about her that Larry could not bear to witness. He silenced the voice which was telling him that she knew she was going to leave him, but nevertheless had brought his jewellery, and stepping to her side, his lip curling back until his mouth looked ugly, he said, 'And you say you didn't buy her! Well, you've got your money back . . . and now we're all square!'

The blow was so swift and so unexpected that it caught Larry completely off his guard and sent him reeling and dizzy against the black timbers of the barn. It had been delivered straight between the eyes. For a full moment he did not know where he was, but when his vision cleared he saw the man before him and Pam clinging to him, beseeching him to go.

200

Like an enraged animal he sprang towards her, crying at her, 'Out of the way!'

'No, no! You mustn't. Ron, Ron, go. Please – oh, please!'

He gripped her arm, trying to tear her from the man, but swiftly she turned and clung to him now, holding him with a strength that was phenomenal. 'You mustn't! You mustn't! Let him go. Please, do this for me, do this for me.'

'Get out of the way!' It was the man's voice speaking to Pam, cuttingly cold now. 'Do not deprive him of this satisfaction. He'll need to remember something with satisfaction before life has finished with him. His hell will start when it is borne through his thick skull that he is depriving you of a way of life to which your education has fitted you. If he were a man he wouldn't be doing it, but he is a boy . . . immature.'

He seemed bent now on getting Larry from her struggling hold, and his taunting became even more pointed. 'Yes, you can go black in the face. What does it matter what your years are, or how long you've worked? I've had dealings with your kind. You're like children: deprive you of something and you scream and yell and hit out.'

'Ron, Ron, stop it. For God's sake, go.'

With a great effort, Larry tried to fling her from him. Inside, he was screaming and yelling and hitting out; he was battering the self-assurance and the cultured poise which he both hated and envied out of the man. He knew he had hated this man before he'd set eyes on him, but he had never imagined that the sound, more than the sight of him, would fill him with a rage that almost amounted to madness.

Pam, still clutching at him like a frantic octopus, was sobbing wildly. Short of swinging about and hurling her against the wall he could not rid himself of her. The man looked at her and listened to her cries for a moment longer, then, with a final flick of his wet hat, he settled it carefully as if its angle was of importance, turned slowly on his heel, and went out.

The rain must have stopped, for apart from a gentle sizzling there was no sound now but Pam's sobbing. And still clinging to Larry, she continued to cry until, from the distance, she heard the sound of the car starting. Then, and then only, did she relax her hold, and almost in a state of collapse she gave way to greater sobbing still.

Although his arms were about her and he knew she was his, he had no feeling of victory. Instead, he felt humiliated and beaten. He put up his hand and touched his swelling nose. The pain was shooting through his head like a knife.

She moved her head against him. And he forced himself to ask, 'You're not sorry?'

Her head moved again, and he growled, 'You'll get a car and jewellery.'

She murmured something, but he could not catch her words, and when he lifted her chin and looked on her tear-stained face, he said bitterly, 'I believe you are sorry.'

'No' – she gave a series of short gasps – 'no, I'm not. But he was good, and I hated to hurt him, that's all.'

As she gasped again, he said, 'Don't say that!' The words seemed squeezed through his teeth. 'I can't bear it. You didn't feel like that about me.'

'I did . . . I did.'

'Oh, God Almighty!' He pushed her from him. 'Do you want us both?'

Silently she stood before him, the tears running down her face. She couldn't truthfully give an answer to that question, for it would have been Yes.

9

THE PROPOSAL

Before leaving the house Jessie made it her business to wait until she saw some woman dressed for 'out' leave her gate and come down the street. She watched from the side of the curtains, and when she saw Mrs Gourlay resplendent in her new summer coat and hat sailing towards the house she opened the front door, and making a to-do about the latch she closed it just as Mrs Gourlay came abreast of her.

'It's a nice evening after the rain.'

Mrs Gourlay nodded. 'Yes, it is, Jessie. By, it was a day yesterday. Talk about June. Pity anybody on their holidays. Still it's few who'll be on holiday with the rail strike and that. Strikes, strikes, nothing but strikes . . . dockers, railwaymen, sailors. Did you ever! Well, let them get on with it, as long as our men keep in . . . we've had enough strikes to last our lifetime.'

Jessie did not say the mines wouldn't keep working very long if there was no way of sending off the coal – her personal worries far overshadowed those of the nation at the present moment. So all she said was, 'Yes, you're right.'

After traversing a short way in silence, Mrs

Gourlay, glancing sideways at Jessie, said, 'Off for a walk some place, Jessie?'

'Well, not for a walk exactly. I'm just going to Mrs Boucher's.'

'Mrs Boucher's?' Mrs Gourlay's eyebrows moved slightly upwards, and her head inclined to one side with polite enquiry.

'She's drawing a club the night.'

'Oh, is she? And you're having a draw?'

'Yes, a few to get some things.'

'Is it a money draw or the store?'

'Money.'

'Well' – Mrs Gourlay moved her bright leather handbag from one arm to the other – 'I'd be careful about dealing with Emma Boucher if I was you, Jessie. Of course, it's not my business, but once you get into her clutches you're there for life. If you wanted a club or two, why didn't you try Mrs Hanley's? She'd have been only too happy to oblige. You know where you are with her. A shilling a pound for the draw, and the store dividend, that's all she asks, not a backhander when you get your ticket. Why, Mrs Tollet had to pay Emma Boucher five shillings down for a five-pound money club, and when she got her draw and only gave her half a crown back, she had something to say. And she was in hot water a few years back, you know, for money-lending. Tuppence a week for the loan of a bob she was charging. Jessie' – Mrs Gourlay shook her head slowly – 'you want to look out with her. Are you short?'

'Well . . . yes. I've been buying things, you see.'

Again Mrs Gourlay's head went to one side, and Jessie could almost hear her turning over in her mind this new construction on how of late she had come by her money.

Mrs Gourlay's manner became more motherly, and at the market place she left Jessie with a final warning: 'Mind, Jessie, don't say I didn't put you wise.'

Jessie had few prejudices, but clubs was one of them . . . likely because she had been clothed by them all her life. But out of desperation the idea came to her that if it was known she was drawing big clubs, her new affluence would be put down to their benevolence. Mrs Boucher was a well-known figure in the town and had lived all her life by her clubs and money-lending. The latter had installed her in a new house at the far end of the town, and it was the distance from her own immediate quarter which suggested to Jessie the likelihood of her little plan working. That it would eventually make her out to be a liar she didn't mind.

The events of the past few days had in a way been more upsetting than the effects of Larry's rejection, which had hurt only herself; but now Willie and the minister were involved. Willie, she knew, was bewildered. She had no proof that she could show him of her mother's hoard; not even the sovereigns, for these, together with what money she had left, she had placed in the bank. She had done this on the advice of Miss Barrington – the only person in whom

206

she had confided. Although at times she still stood in awe of her she had always proved a sympathetic and good employer. But what, after all, was the good of Miss Barrington's trust – she lived in another world. It was her own world she had to convince, and if Willie couldn't believe her it was going to be difficult to convince others. And then there was the minister. She hadn't seen him since Saturday night. She had been unable to face him on Sunday, so had stayed away from the service; and twice during the past week, when a knock had come on the front door during the evening she hadn't gone to open it but instead had bolted the back door and gone upstairs. But sooner or later, she knew, she would have to face him.

For the past two years, life had been, to say the least, painful, worrying and nerve-racking. It was still painful, but it had also become difficult, for she was facing an undreamed-of issue, the defence of her morality. As much as she wanted people to be in no doubt as to her moral integrity, she wanted, nevertheless, first and foremost, all suspicion wiped away from the unsuspecting minister. She knew her own kind too well to try to convince them by talk alone – with them, seeing was believing. So Mrs Boucher had come to her mind in the nature of a brainwave.

In Mrs Boucher's front room she sat with nine other women, and in the course of time drew out five lots from the hat. Only one of the women present was from her own neighbourhood, a Mrs Patty, but one was enough. Jessie, after handing Mrs Boucher five shillings and ignoring the shrewd questioning in the older woman's eyes, waited deliberately for Mrs Patty, determined on the way home to give her something in the way of information to carry back to the street. But the parrying remarks about the weather and the numerous strikes had hardly begun when her whole evening's effort was wiped away by a voice which came from behind them saying, 'Hello there, Jessie. This is a coincidence. I was just on my way to see you.'

Jessie stood still as the minister moved to her side. She looked at him for a moment, and pressed back the urge to cry at him, 'Oh, go away. For God's sake, go away.'

Mrs Patty, too, stopped, her eyes brightly darting from one to the other.

'Isn't it a glorious evening! And they say you don't get good weather in the north. Oh yes, I know all about last night.' He flapped his hands at them both. 'But let me tell you, you don't get evenings like this in the south . . . slow, warm twilights.'

Of one accord, they moved on, the minister walking between them. 'You're Mrs Patty, aren't you?' he said. 'Janet's mother. She's a fine child, and quick.'

Mrs Patty was gratified and went into a detailed account of Janet's virtues which filled the time until they reached the street. Jessie did not once open her mouth, but her thoughts were racing. She'd have to tell him; that was the only thing to do. If he went on blindly like this, like as not he would be reported to

– well, whoever they reported Baptist ministers to. It was a shame . . . Oh, why were people so bad-minded? He was the nicest man she had ever met – yes, Larry Broadhurst included. Larry Broadhurst could never be nice in the way this man was nice. There was a natural gayness about him, and a quick sympathetic tenderness. And it came to her that it was strange he should be a Baptist minister, or a minister at all for that matter.

It would also happen that after the heavy downpour of rain almost everyone seemed to have turned out to do their front gardens, and three times the minister called out a greeting to a weeder. Then, just as they reached the Macintyres' house, the door opened and Willie came out.

'Oh, hello there.' The minister half stopped.

'Hello,' said Willie, who, however, did not hesitate in his walk but continued at an even pace up the street.

After saying a faint farewell to Mrs Patty, Jessie entered her cottage and stood aside to allow him in. He preceded her into the kitchen, and there he turned to meet her. And his face was no longer jovial. Quietly and to the point he asked her, 'What is it, Jessie?'

She did not answer but moved to the table and adjusted the lace centre-piece, first one way and then the other.

After watching her for a moment, he went on, 'There's something wrong. When you didn't come to either service on Sunday I came round on Monday evening. I had the feeling you were not out, but you didn't answer. Wouldn't it be better to tell me?'

It should be easy now he had given her an opening, but she found that she could not look at him. She turned away from the table and took off her hat and coat, and with his gaze intently on her, he said, 'I haven't known you very long, Jessie, as regards time, but I have the feeling that there hasn't been a time when I haven't known you. I shouldn't be saying this now, and I wouldn't have, only I'm uneasy inside – I have the unhappy faculty of sensing trouble. On Sunday evening after the service I enquired after you from Mrs King. It was from then.' He came and stood near her. 'Tell me everything, whatever it is.'

She turned now and faced him. 'I'm not coming to chapel any more, Mr Ramsey, and it would be better if you didn't call here any more.'

He stared at her for a long moment before saying, 'Tell me the rest, Jessie. Go on, all of it.'

She swallowed hard, then brought out in a shame-faced whisper, 'They're saying . . .'

'Yes?'

She turned the chair round and sat down. Her hands were clammy with sweat. 'I'll have to start from the beginning . . . about my mother.'

'Go on then.' He pulled up a chair and sat opposite to her, and haltingly, with bent head, she told him how she came to have the money and what she had done with it. And when no word of censure came from him, she looked up to find him smiling, a quiet amused smile.

'I guessed so much from what Dobson told me.'

'But he didn't know.'

'Yes he did. He knew she had money put by, but he couldn't do anything about it.'

'You think I did wrong in withholding it?'

'No. No, I don't. If anyone worked for that money you did. But go on.'

Jessie went on. She told him of her spending, of Willie, and very haltingly of Mrs Macintyre's visit. When she again looked at him his expression bore no amusement, yet it was not as troubled as she had expected.

'That's the world over,' he said, 'and there's little you can do about it. Will you marry me, Jessie?'

She blinked twice. Then, like some gormless creature, her mouth fell open.

'It may sound sudden, I know, and although you won't believe it it's got nothing to do with what you've just told me. I would have asked you sooner or later. I knew on Sunday when I looked for you and you weren't there. I missed the smile in your eyes, and the feeling of security that you give me. You see, I'm always doubting myself. You might find this hard to believe, but I am. All this hail-fellow-well-met is a façade. The long and short of it is I should never have been a minister, but my father was one, and well . . . Anyway, from the first day I met you in this kitchen when you faced up to Dobson you have been a source of strength to me, and then on Sunday I knew . . . I knew I loved you, Jessie.'

'No.' Jessie shot up from her chair. 'It's . . . it's . . .

you can't. I'm older than you. It's because I'm older.'

He did not move, but smiled up at her. 'How old are you?'

'I'm thirty-one.'

He laughed softly. 'I'm twenty-nine.'

She swallowed and stroked her neck. Her mind was whirling. She had just received the biggest shock of her life . . . a minister had asked her to marry him. He said he loved her. But he was like a boy to her – he didn't look twenty-nine. He could never look twenty-nine, while she, she knew, looked and felt far older than her years. It was fantastic, and anyway she had only known him a few weeks. Her . . . a minister's wife! His wife! Half fearfully, she looked down on him. His face was . . . good. It was, she thought, a lovely face, fair and open. But he was a genleman with education; why should he want her? There had been nothing in her to hold Larry, so what could such a man as this see in her?

As if he were reading her thoughts he said, 'You don't know it, and you'd never believe it because you're so full of humility, but you're beautiful. There's something shining through you.'

She turned from him, again helpless to answer. No-one had ever said such a thing to her. It made her hot. Her, beautiful. He was a strange man . . . boy. Yes, that's how she thought of him, as a boy. Yet, he wasn't a boy, he was more of a man than – she did not name the name – and he said he was in love with her and she could be married. Her mind leaped across the street. That would give Larry Broadhurst something to think about, her marrying the minister. And not only him, it would stop the tongues wagging in the wrong way. But what was she thinking? She couldn't do it. Her and this man. He was a stranger; she didn't know him or anything about him, only that he knew a lot about books and was kind. But even with his kindness and being younger than her, she stood in awe of him. She had to force her words out, and she stammered as she began, 'It's ve . . . ry kind of you, Mr Ramsey, but . . . but, I . . .'

'My name's Alan, and it's not kind of me. If there's any kindness that's going to be done, it's you who are going to do it. But don't say anything now, think it over. I know there is someone else in the running.' He smiled broadly. 'Willie . . . but all's fair, you know.'

She gazed at him. Anyone listening to him would imagine that men were falling over themselves for her favours. That was the niceness of him – he had the power to make you feel wanted. But she couldn't take him, she wasn't fitted for him and his life. Larry, no matter how clever he might have become, would still have been no mystery to her; her love and adoration was based on knowledge of him. She could even see herself as Willie's wife, but this man's – never.

He stood up and came towards her, and, unclasping her agitated hands, said, 'You don't dislike me, Jessie?'

'No. Oh no.'

'Do you love Willie?'

'No, no.' The truth was easy there.

'Well then, I can wait. For a time at any rate. I am not staying here, Jessie. They are too set in their ways. It's sad when you come to think that an old die-hard hypocrite like Dobson, and that's all he was, could hold them, make them believe, while moderation smacks to them of the devil. When I heard of you stripping the walls of those tracts, my heart leapt to you. Jessie, don't look so scared. Am I so awful?'

'Oh, Mr Ramsey.'

'Alan.'

The colour that was flooding Jessie's face had in this moment brought beauty to it, and his eyes were making her desperate with embarrassment, when relief came in the form of a series of sharp knocks on the front door.

'Excuse me a minute, there's someone at the door.' Hastily she withdrew her hands and went through the front room, and before the door had swung fully open, Lottie's voice had begun.

'Oh, Jessie, I had to come the front way. I tried your back door twice earlier on, and I came over last night and couldn't make you hear. Can I come in?'

Jessie knew that there would be a number of eyes on the doorway speculating as to whether Lottie would be admitted or not. 'Yes, yes, come in, Aunt Lot.'

'Oh, Jessie, we're in a state. Jinny's in a state, and I've been sick. And last night Larry went off. There was a row. He's gone off for good with Pam. And her Dad's been up, and Jinny's nearly mad, and Frank – I've never seen Frank like he is.'

The latch in her hand, Jessie stared at the brown paint on the back of the door. The gossamer thread of hope that had persistently lingered was broken. Slowly she turned and went towards the kitchen, with Lottie behind her, gabbling on, 'And Jinny won't look at me, she won't speak. I'm going to have a baby, Jessie.'

'Ssh!'

Lottie, standing in the doorway, looked at the minister. He had heard what she had said. Well, ministers weren't men, they were like nuns and things. You could say things in front of ministers you couldn't say in front of men, so she repeated to him, 'I'm going to have a baby and Jinny, me sister's, mad at me.'

'Do you want a baby?'

'Oh yes, I love bairns. Lena won't let me near Betty, and the poor little thing's funny like Mary Tollet in Cranwell Avenue. But I can mind bairns. I've always minded bairns.'

'Aunt Lot!' Jessie's voice sounded a little like Jinny's, and Lottie said, 'Oh, all right, Jessie.' Then she added, 'There's been no tea or anything. The house is all upset, and I daren't go to the cupboard 'cause Jinny might go for me.'

Alan Ramsey glanced at Jessie, and there was a gently humorous light in his eye as he said, 'A cup of tea is always a good stand-by in times of trouble. Could I make one?'

'No, no,' she said, 'I'll do it.' And as she went into the scullery a wave of sickness assailed her. He was gone – it was over. Well, she'd known it would happen, hadn't she?

A touch of the anger she had felt that night she had confronted him in the street returned. He would get what he deserved, as so would she. They would pay each other out. There was only one thing she wished. She wished he could know that the minister wanted to marry her. Not a pitman or a workman of any kind, but a minister, young, attractive, and a gentleman. Yes, a gentleman. She put a match to the gas which had been turned on for some seconds and it lit with a loud plop. A gentleman with a college education, and she couldn't see him checking her pronunciation when she opened her mouth, as Larry had done after he had come out of the army. He was an upstart. Behind her love for him she had always known it. That's why he had gone after Pam Turnbull in the first place. He wanted to rise, he wanted to write and be thought somebody, and the bitter truth of it was, if he did write and become somebody the wrong he had done to her and the American man would be forgotten, even condoned.

The way of the world drained her anger from her. She made the tea, and when she returned to the kitchen Alan Ramsey came immediately to her and took the tray, while Lottie, laughing now, said, 'Your minister's funny, Jessie; he's been making me laugh. He said he knew a woman once who hung her baby out to dry on a line. He didn't, did he, Jessie?'

Jessie looked at the minister, and his eyes were

waiting for her. He smiled and in his smile she could see love for herself and pity and tenderness for Aunt Lot, and she thought, I'd be a fool if I didn't take him.

10

AND THE THINGS THEY FEAR

During the past few days Willie's world had been knocked upside down – his mother had been proved right, Jessie was carrying on with the minister fellow. What he should do, he knew, was to go in and ask her point blank what she was up to. But he found he couldn't. He had always thought Jessie as straight as a die, but he had seen them himself going into the house together on Wednesday, and he had stayed over an hour – he had timed him himself. Letting Aunt Lot in, his mother had said, was just a cover – the fellow had never been off the doorstep that week. And if you could pick anything out of Aunt Lot's prattle, they were thick all right. It was fantastic and bewildering. The man hadn't been in the town but a few weeks, and if rumour was true he wouldn't be here many more. And yet, Willie thought, with the faculty he had for seeing two sides of every question, who could blame Jessie if she did take the chap? He was a good catch, and she wanted something after the dirty deal she'd had. But why had she let him himself cotton on to her? She should have told him straight out in the first place. He had, he supposed, as usual been slow. But he hadn't wanted to rush her after her mother died. Still, she had known fine well he was courting her – hadn't he done all the business of the funeral for her? Yes, she knew all right. She hadn't really played fair; as his mother said, she had made a fool of him. He hadn't minded standing aside where Larry was concerned, but he didn't feel the same way about this other bloke.

And then there was Larry. To leave the pit and go off like that without as much as a goodbye, after all the time they had been marrers. Why, they had been like brothers; closer than brothers, for Larry could hurt him where no-one else could. The pain of Larry's departure was like a knife inside him, and the unusual emotion of hate was in him for Pam Turnbull. Women! The trouble they caused. But Pam Turnbull wasn't even a woman, not as he thought of women, she was just a piece, fancy-tongued, and fancy-dressed.

'Hello there, Willie.'

'Oh, hello, John.'

The man, his bait tin tucked under his arm, joined his step to Willie's, and together they walked down the main road to the pit gate.

'Won't be doin' this much bloody longer if those Johnnies don't get them trains movin'. Seen the paper this mornin'?'

'No,' said Willie.

'Negotiating now. That's what happens when unions split. They've got to negotiate each other afore they can negotiate the bosses. What's the good of a bloody union if it doesn't speak for you all? Divided you fall, united you stand.'

'Aye, that's about it,' said Willie.

'And the dockers had a do at Liverpool last night, didn't they? Wanted to lynch one of their blokes.'

'Aye?'

'Aye. The country's in a bloody state, and they can't blame the Labour Government noo, can they? Aye, and if you believe all you read, wor coal mines are aboot worked oot. Some bloke writin' in the paper this mornin' about bringin' industry to West Durham, 'cause wor pits are nearly worked oot. Aa'd like to write that bloke to come doon the Phoenix or the Venus. What d'ye say, Willie . . . eh?'

'Aye, you're right.'

The man cast a sidelong glance at Willie and said in an altered tone, 'Aw, lad, I wouldn't take on aboot Larry Broadhurst like that. Larry was always too big for his boots to my mind; but he's done a dirty trick noo, and that American chap is not goin' to think any more of the English 'cause of it. But as I said to the wife in joke like, Larry's payin' the Americans back in their own coin. But she said the Americans' wartime activities was ower. I thought that was a good 'un, I did . . . war-time activities. Still, he shouldn't uv done it. The fellow's a nice bloke; real toff, they say. Old Turnbull and his missus are nearly up the lum; and I saw Frank yesterday. My, he looked bad . . . properly down and beaten, he looked. That family's had a run of bad luck and no mistake. And noo they say Aunt Lot's goin' to have a bairn.'

'What!' Willie stopped in his tracks.

'Hadn't you heard then?'

'No.'

'Well, that's how it is. Me missus was at the doctor's when Jinny took her. Jinny didn't let on – she wouldn't – but Lottie told me missus last night. Bright and airy she was. It's the Bog's End fiddler. I hear he did a bunk.'

'My God!' Willie rubbed his mouth with his hand, and his face expressed his shocked horror. 'Aunt Lot. Why, man, it's awful.'

'Aye, it's awful. It's bad enough when they're really sensible, but Aunt Lot, what'll she do with a bairn? And if it's like her . . . Well, here we are.'

They turned in at the gate, and were immediately caught up in a stream of men, one of whom said, 'Hello there, John. Hello, Willie.'

'Hello, Stanley,' they both answered.

'Aa wonder if we'll get goin' this mornin',' said Stan.

Willie looked at the man with the hollow cheeks and blue-marked skin.

'There was a fall near the gap in number seven last night – Jimmy Tollet's just been telling me. They were testing for fire damp.'

'Find any?' asked Willie.

'Not that Aa know of, and they don't go shoutin' about it if they do. We'll know when we get down, if they won't let us along.'

'The whole bloody rabbit warren is full of gas,' said John. 'Ted Fuller said the gas took his light

221

yesterda'. He reported it and the dep put up a new canvas sheet.'

'Bloody lot of good that'll do. Stone dust's the only answer, and more of it. It's got to be mixed with every ounce of coal dust in the pit or else one of these days we'll all bloody well pop through the top.' Stan laughed with macabre mirth. 'Last week I would have come straight up into wor back garden, and Aa've just set me peas, but noo that we've moved back to the West four junction Aa'll likely come up in the Wear somewhere near Durham Cathedral. Aa can see meself crawling up the bank and gannin' straight to the church and givin' a word of thanks for me survival.'

'Shut up!' Willie's tone was unusually sharp and Stan, laughing louder, said, 'Why man, what's up wi' ye . . . got cauld feet?'

Willie did not answer but swung away and joined the press in the lamp house, and John remarked soberly, 'Willie's aal for a laugh, but not aboot that. He hasn't forgotten when he was shut in. The young uns don't throw it off like we did, Stan, and you've go to throw it off if you mean to go on.'

Willie, walking with the other nineteen men of his section along the main road towards the loading station, felt a sadness settling on him, which had nothing to do with Stan's joking. Down here his mind was taken up completely with the loss of Larry. Sometimes they had traversed the two miles to the face and Larry had not opened his mouth, but he had been there, part of the ordered plan of life. Lately, he might have been a bit short at times, but what did that matter? He had understood . . . there'd been a lot on his mind . . . a whole lot. If only he had said he was going. But to go off like that without so much as a 'so long' – it wasn't playing the game. He should have told him. Surely he must have known that he wouldn't condemn him for anything he did.

'Hold your hand there a minute.' The order came from their deputy as they approached him at the loading station. He was standing to the side of the widened road, along which ran a mass of cables. He was in the middle of a telephone conversation, and he nodded a number of times, saying only, 'Aye, all right,' before hanging up the phone and turning again to the men.

'You can't go inbye yet . . . bit of a hold up.'

'Owt wrong?' The query came quietly from a number of quarters.

'Nothing serious.'

'Why are they keepin' them? They should be up by now, it's long after four.'

'They'll be along shortly. There's been a slight fall at the tail-gate end of number six.'

'My bloody hide-out,' came a voice. Then with a short laugh: 'I bet Geordie Burns has been rattling the foundations with his ruddy shuttle car.'

'More likely young Broadhurst fired a shot in the face roof to release a chock, or put one under Bill Turner's Joy loader.'

On a ripple of laughter came a censuring voice,

saying, 'Broadhurst'll release those roof chocks once too often. It's illegal . . . it should never be done.'

'Oh, illegal, my God! If we did nowt illegal there'd never be any coal got out. They're shoutin' enough about production now.'

The voices trailed off and the men stood grouped together. Now and again a man's eyes would slowly move and take in his surroundings as if he were only now becoming aware of them; which was more than likely, for in their scurryings to and from the coal-face the roads became just roads, and here the conveyor belt, coming from number eight face and pouring the coal into the chutes, was not a piece of ingenuity that had saved the torturing grind of the ponies and the agonising sweat of men, it was now just a piece of accepted pit mechanism.

The lights from their caps shone on to the others' faces, showing them up with womanish whiteness against the dirty grey depth in which they stood.

There was the sound of steps approaching from the shaft end of the road and the group turned as one and watched men up to twice their number turn off a side road near the stables and go into their own district. Then, without comment, they turned away again, and their eyes seemed now to focus on a door of about four feet high set in a recess.

After a time the unity of their waiting began to split, and an oldish man sat down on a heap of stones and opened his bait tin, bringing his head down to shine the lamp on to its contents. The whole action caused a ripple to pass over the men, and they moved about and laughed, throwing quips at the unperturbed figure.

'What's it the day? Jam and breed again?'

'Why, no, man. His missus has put him up chicken sandwiches and caviere.'

'No! Go on!'

'Aye; hasn't she, Sam?'

Sam said no word. He spoke little but he ate a lot, and slowly now he opened two slices of bread and there, to the amazed and amused eyes of the beholders, lay the thick creamy breast of a chicken with the deep-brown crisp skin still intact.

A roar went up against the quippers, and a voice cried, 'Divn't let on, any of you, mind, aboot this. Let it be known that we bring chicken doon here and they'll dock wor wages, they will, begod!'

Sam's eyes twinkled, and as he bit deeply into the sandwich the phone bell rang. The deputy went to the wall and, picking up the receiver, listened. After a number of nods, he said, 'OK, Philip'; then turned to the men, saying, 'It's OK, you can get going.'

In twos, they now moved towards the low door. Willie and John were once more together, and were the last to pass through. They did this bent double, and when they entered the mother-gate their backs, although straighter, were still bent.

When the blast hit Willie it came like a kick in his middle, and knocked him into a sitting position. He was aware of men tumbling about in front of him as the sound of the explosion vibrated around the walls. He had been sitting on the ground for what seemed minutes but what his alerted mind told him was no longer than a second or two. The air was thick with the mixture of grit and coal dust, and the space towards the air doors became choked with gasping men. Staggering drunkenly, they stumbled back into the roadway from which they had moved only a few minutes earlier. The deputy came out last, banging the door firmly behind him, and leant against a prop and drew in great gulps of the clean, circulating air; then pulling himself up, he gasped, 'You all here?'

He moved his lamp and counted, then going to the phone he tried to make contact with the affected area, but there was no response to his repeated hellos.

The men were breathing more easily now, and their eyes were on him and their ears listening. They heard him get in touch with Johnson, the shift foreman, before he turned and said, 'Get going to the shaft . . . except one or two of you. I want someone to come to the tail-gate with me. Johnson's in the Bottle district, he won't be able to get here right away. They're notifying up top.'

There was a shuffling movement of all the men forward, and the deputy, who may have been thinking of wives and families, looked at Willie, saying, 'You, Willie, you were at the back end and seem all right.'

'Aye, Dep, I'm all right.'

'I am an' all, man.'

'And me. I'm all right, man. I'll only have to come back anyway.'

'Well, you'll come back with the rescue squad,'

said the deputy to the man in question, 'but for the present, all get going. I won't be but a few minutes after you. If any of them's been near the tail-gate and the return airway's all right, I can signal along. Look, give Sam a hand there, he's a bit shaken.' He pointed to where Sam was sitting, once again on the heap of stones, his head drooping towards his knees. 'Get him moving. You could stay at this point, Bob, and you, Stan, and I'll phone you back if need be. Come on, Willie.'

Willie moved to the deputy's side, and from the expression on his face there was no indication of what he was thinking as together they moved into the darkness.

They had gone some way when Willie asked, 'What's the chances?'

'Hard to say, yet it wasn't much. If it had been we wouldn't be here now.'

'God,' said Willie, 'I hope you're right. Frank Broadhurst and Jack's in there.'

The deputy said nothing to this for a moment; then he said caustically, 'Well, it'll be news for their Larry . . . I hear he's left.'

Willie made no reply, and the deputy went on, 'Dirty way of doing things, if you ask me. No notice, no nowt.'

Even in such circumstances as these, a protest of defence was hot on Willie's lips when the sound of a dull thud in the distance came to them. They both halted, and their eyes darting about them, seemed to feel at the air.

'Current's changed,' said Willie.

Swiftly now, they turned and ran. But having traversed but a few yards, they pulled up. The air current had once again changed and was back to normal. They stared at each other in the two beams of light, and the deputy said softly, 'A fall could do that . . . change the air. That's likely what it was. Are you going on?'

'Aye, by all means.'

Turning, they moved inbye once again, and as swiftly as the rough road permitted they made their way towards the tail-gate, and it was when they were within actual sight of it that a sound as if the heavens were being split by thunder rang round them. In a split second they had gone down before the blast and were enveloped in a sheet of flame.

Fighting now like madmen, they tore at their burning clothing. The deputy's helmet together with his lamp rang against the stones behind the props, and Willie, in tearing off his coat and shirt, dislodged his own lamp. Frantically, he made an effort to save it, while fighting the flames around him. But, in so doing, precipitated it into a far crevice of the piled rocks.

The flames out, and now in total darkness, Willie gasped, 'Are you there, Dep?'

The answer was a muffled groan, and Willie, moving towards the sound, touched the deputy where he lay on the bottom.

'You all right?'

'It's . . . me face . . . God!'

'We've got to get moving.'

'Oh, God Almighty!'

'Look, grab hold of me belt . . . come on.'

With one hand the deputy groped at Willie's waist, and when Willie felt the tug at his belt he moved round on his knees, grabbed at the rail of the tub track, and using it for a guide, he started the laborious journey back to the loading station.

There was nothing but darkness, frightening darkness full of malevolent life; it was thick and heavy and had a power of pressure. Willie felt he was swallowing the blackness as he gulped the dust-filled air. The pace was excruciatingly slow, and they both kept their mouths as near the steel rails as was possible. Not more than a few minutes had passed in this way when the deputy gasped, 'I'm gonna . . . leave loose, Willie. I canna get along like this. You . . . carry on . . . I'll take me time.'

'Like hell,' said Willie. 'You come on in front, and I'll follow.'

So saying, he crawled behind the deputy, and the slow-moving journey began again. Then, without any warning, the deputy's crawling stopped abruptly, and Willie asked, 'You all right, Dep?'

There was no answer, and with a rising feeling of panic Willie's hands moved over the prostrate man. He could feel his heart beating, so he guessed he had passed out with the pain, and thought it must have been an outsize pain to make Charlie Cock pass out, for he was as tough as they came.

He had no means of reviving him, so all there was

229

for it, his dizzy mind told him, was to get them both to hell out of here as quickly as possible. So, easing the deputy to one side, he put one arm about his naked body and with the other hand gripping the rail he dragged them inch by inch along in the everlasting blackness.

Taking a rest for a moment, Willie's mind began to reason. It must be ten minutes since the explosion. This road connected directly with the loading station. By now there should be lights dancing towards them, that's if Bob and Stan hadn't caught it an' all. He should be seeing the lights any minute now . . . Well, he'd keep moving. It would be a shorter distance to walk, he encouraged himself.

After a few more minutes, which seemed like an hour, he stopped again . . . abruptly. He knew now why there were no lights, no sound, nothing, only eternal quiet and darkness; and on the thought his teeth bit on the steel rail of the track. Then lifting his head, his grip tightened around the dep and he moved forward again. He would carry on, he told himself, until he came to the fall.

11

THE TEST

'Darling, don't be so impatient. We have all our lives in which to trot about the continent – what does a day or two matter? Didn't you realise you'd need a passport?'

'Yes, I realised that all right.'

'Well, did you expect them to give you priority? Come on, let's do a show. Something funny . . . that Victorian thing. One of the characters on the stills looked the image of that fellow who gave us a lift from York. Do you know, darling' – she snuggled closer into his arms on the couch – 'it was more fun begging lifts than coming primly by train. I enjoyed every minute of it. What do you say we do it from Calais? There's no strike on there, it should be easy.'

Her face was below his, and he looked searchingly into her eyes. Either she didn't really mind roughing it or she was putting on a good act. He hated to think it was an act, but his common-sense told him it was. Yet hadn't she plumped for this third-rate place? A bed-sitter with breakfast. It bore the smell of countless predecessors – its furniture was shabby and dirty – and the fact that he was being charged six guineas a week in advance was already beginning to have its effect. How long would his three hundred last at this rate, plus the eating out? For himself it wouldn't matter, but he was developing a nightmarish dread of the time when she would be forced to compare what she had given up with what he was offering her.

He wanted to get away. He wanted to get away from London and from England and as quickly as possible. There was an uneasiness about him whenever they went out – the fellow was in London. It was a thousand-to-one chance that they would meet, yet such long shots very often came off. But why was he worrying? She loved him, she worshipped him. Hadn't last night proved it? Of one thing he was certain: no man had ever been loved as she loved him. There was a mad ecstasy in her loving that was the antithesis of her apparently cool, poised self. It had been a mad night, a night that had been impossible to foretaste in dreams.

'Oh, darling, your arms are like iron. No, no' – she pushed his face aside – 'we're going out. What time is it? Let me get up. Oh do, please.'

The last was in the form of a command, and his hold slackened. And he despised himself as he watched her swing her feet from the couch and stand up – some tones of her voice had the power to put him in his place. But what was his place? Springing up, he caught her to him and kissed her with such fierceness that they both overbalanced and fell once again on to the couch. Here they lay looking at each other and laughing until she said, 'My lord and master, now that you have proved your maleness may I get up?'

He let her go, perturbed again in his mind that she could read him so easily, and perturbed also at her manner, which was new to him, bright and brittle.

'What time is it?'

He looked at his watch. 'Quarter past six.'

'It isn't that, surely – it's fast.'

'It gains a bit, but only a minute or so. It was three when we came in, you know.'

'Put that wireless on if the thing works. I bet it doesn't, it looks so ancient. I'm going to have a wash. Do you think I dare ask the old dear for a bath tonight?'

'Why not?' Larry went to the old-fashioned set which was standing on top of a battered sideboard and fiddled with the knobs, and Pam, pouring some water from a jug into a bowl, said, 'You know, darling, you can get lodgings for next to nothing in some parts of Italy, but not the Florence section. You're not really struck on Florence, are you?' Without waiting for his answer she went on. 'The Duckans – they're friends of Arlett, you know, my French friend – they lived for two years in an old villa. They rented half from a family who had a little farm. It didn't cost the two of them more than three pounds a week, and they fed beautifully. Oh what a noise!'

'It goes, anyway,' said Larry, shouting above the voice of the announcer. 'It's the news. Good Lord, this watch is fast.' He turned from the wireless, adding, 'Strikes, strikes, strikes. We've all gone mad. But why worry. Where is the place you say?'

'Twenty-seven miles from Rome. Oh Lord' – the soap skidded from her hands and shot over the linoleum and under the sideboard. Laughing, they both went down on their knees to retrieve it, and their shoulders touching, they turned, and slowly put their lips together and softly and gently kissed. It was a quiet moment, and they stared into each other's eyes while the voice above them rambled on. Then the voice paused, and resumed the news on an altered tone in which there was that touch of personal regret used by some of the announcers to differentiate the sad from the gay.

'It has just been announced that an explosion occurred at four-thirty today in the Venus coalmine, Fellburn, County Durham. The explosion has trapped twenty-eight men working at the face. It is feared there is little hope of finding the men alive. Also a deputy and another man from the in-going shift, who went to investigate, are missing. They are believed to have been caught by a fall following the second explosion which blocked both the inroads and outroads of this section. The under-manager and the agent, who happened to be in another section of the mine at the time of the explosion, led a rescue team to clear the fall, behind which they believed the two men to be. Tapping has been heard from time to time.

'This mine employs up to three thousand men. All those working in the mine at the time of the disaster have been withdrawn. The trained rescue squads of the mine have been reinforced by the permanent rescue corps from Houghton-le-Spring.'

Rising slowly from his knees, Larry stared at the box from which the impersonal voice had set a seal on his life and actions. Pam, gazing up at him from the floor, suddenly jumped to her feet, crying, 'Larry, don't take it like that. Look at me . . . Larry.'

As if he were just recovering from a stunning blow, he blinked and brought his dazed eyes to her face. 'Pam . . . my God!'

'Listen, Larry. Come and sit down.'

'No . . . wait a minute.' He shrugged her hands off. 'I've got to think . . . Pam, two hours ago – four o'clock – me Da and our Jack would be up by then.'

'Of course they would. Come and sit down. Don't take it so badly, dear. Poor souls. Oh, pits! They're dreadful places. It's the women I think of at a time like this.'

'But what did that announcer say? He said the deputy and another man went to investigate, men from the in-going shift. It could have been they weren't up.'

'Don't be silly; you said they'd finish at four.'

'They should do, but there's no hard-and-fast rules. If something went wrong they'd want to put it right before the next shift took over.'

'But it could have happened on any other face, or whatever it is, there's so many of them. Look, my love, don't worry. What can you do now? Come and sit down.'

235

Gently she led him to the couch, and when seated, she gathered his rough hands into her smooth tapered ones. She was no longer bright and brittle, but tender. 'You've left the pit, darling, and there'll always be accidents in pits. You couldn't do anything if you were there.'

'I'm a trained rescue worker.' His voice was dull and flat.

'But there are dozens of trained rescue workers.'

He swallowed, wetted his lips, then rubbed the moisture off with the back of his hand. This instinctive, earthy action was one he never indulged in when in her presence.

'Larry, listen to me.' Her voice, though still tender, was firm. 'You've got to face up to this thing right now. It's just as well it's happened. The pit and all it entails is behind you. You have always wanted a new way of life – well, you are starting on it. There'll be more accidents in the Venus pit, and in all the other pits. Look at the one in Easington in 'fifty-one. Then that one in Horden about two years ago. There'll always be accidents.'

'Pam, I've got to find out.'

'Find out what, dear?'

'If my father and our Jack are all right.'

'But you said yourself . . .'

'I've got to know.'

Pam's face had paled, and she asked quietly, 'And what will happen if they are in it?'

He did not look at her but rose from the couch, and taking up his hat went to the door. But before he could open it, she was upon him, her arms twining his neck. 'Larry, Larry . . . don't go. They won't be in it. Oh, Larry, darling. Darling.'

He held her gently. 'Pam, I've got to phone and find out. But don't worry.' He lifted her face to his. 'It can't touch us. Nothing can touch us. At the worst it can only delay our going, that's all.'

Slowly he took her arms from his neck, and in a fixed, almost fascinated stare, she watched him go out. Then moving to the window, she looked down into the street and waited for his appearance. When he stepped on to the pavement and crossed the road, her eyes went with him. On the far side, and at the end of the long street, was a telephone kiosk. She watched him go in, and then gripping the coarse, musty curtains in both hands, she closed her eyes.

After a long while, she looked up the street again. Larry was still in the box, and when, after what seemed to her half an hour at least, he moved into the street again, she could not watch his coming but turned from the window and sat down. Even when the door opened she dared not look at him.

He came in quickly, his breathing short and loud as if he had run from the box. It told her all she wanted to know, and when he stood before her she kept her eyes fixed on his feet.

'We've got to go back, Pam – they're both in it. Me father and our Jack, at the face. And Willie's one of the two men behind the fall.'

'No . . . no, we can't. I won't go back.' She was looking at him now, her face as white as his. 'I

237

couldn't, I couldn't. Where would I stay? I'd have to go home . . . I tell you I couldn't bear it. I don't know now how I managed to come away on Wednesday, they were so upset. If I go back now, they'll wear me down.'

'You needn't go back home, you could find lodgings in Chester-le-Street or Durham.'

'Yes, and what then? I know what will happen . . . I'll be there for life.' Her voice had risen. 'If anything has happened to your father and brother do you think your mother will let you go? No. You'll be tied there, and me with you.' She did not move from him, but she swung her body from side to side as if struggling for release. 'I couldn't bear it. I hate Fellburn and all it stands for. I tell you, Larry, I couldn't do it.'

His eyes seemed to have sunk into the back of his head, their expression lost in the blackness. There was no vestige of colour in his face, and his lips were now a hard straight line. He looked at her in silence for some moments, then said, 'You'll wait for me here then?'

Now she did move. She turned from him and went to the window, and with her back to him, she said, 'You expect me to stay in a place like this on my own? Doing it together, it's different, but alone I couldn't put up with it. This!' She waved her hand back to take in the room.

'I'll leave the money with you; you can go to some place decent.'

She moved impatiently. 'How long do you think it would last in London? Oh, Larry.' She swung round to him. 'What can you do if you go back? Nothing that isn't already being done. I'm sorry about your people, oh I am, but you can't better it now. Larry' – she moved to him, speaking softly again – 'send a wire and get your mother to come to the phone somewhere, but don't go.'

He did not answer, but stared at her fixedly as she went on, 'No-one will think any the worse of you.'

'No?' he said quietly. 'Nobody but myself. I've got to go back now. Even if my father and Jack weren't in it, I think I would have had to go back. I've worked in that mine since I was fifteen; I know it, every cranny of it, and officially I've never left the pit, I didn't give my notice in.'

'But you hated the pit, every minute you were down. You said you did.'

'I know, and I still do. I can't explain it, but I'd never be able to look a pitman in the face again if I didn't go back.'

'I'm only a secondary consideration then?'

He moved his mouth as if he were chewing, and the words came out painfully, 'You're my life – you know you are – I can't see me living without you, but in a case like this . . .'

'In a case like this, the first test, I'm put in my place. No, don't touch me.' She stepped back from him. 'They were right, they said it wouldn't work. Once a pitman always a pitman, and me fighting to make them believe you were a frustrated literary genius.'

'Do you realise that my father and brother are probably dead?'

'Then if they are, what can you do? You made a decision, you should stick by it. That decision involved me.'

'You forget there's still my mother. How will she feel now there's only Aunt Lot and Lena there?'

'How do you think my mother felt? It nearly killed her when she knew I was seeing you again, and on Wednesday night she collapsed. I didn't tell you, but she did, and I felt like a criminal, a murderer. She has worked for me for years, and what do I do? Throw it all up for you and bring disgrace on her. But did I hesitate? No. You wanted me, I must come to you. Now I want you.'

'If you want me you'll come back with me.'

'And be a laughing-stock? No, I couldn't. I won't. Nor am I going to live in slums on my own. If you leave me now . . .' She paused and her voice sank, and she repeated, 'If you leave me now I'll go back to Ron. I can, you know. He loves me, he would have me back . . . it depends upon me.'

A combination of anger, fear, and pain filled his eyes with mist and blotted her from his sight, and he pulled at his collar to ease the feeling of choking in his throat. In this moment his hate equalled his love. 'Don't go too far, Pam,' he said.

'Don't go too far,' she repeated. 'I mean what I say – if you leave me now, I'll go back to him. I won't be made a fool of.'

The mist cleared and he saw her, the side of her he had shut his eyes to, the side that had prompted her to bring all the fellow's jewellery from America, knowing that she might leave him. He thought of the man's words. 'You are depriving her of a way of life.' He could see in this moment that she wouldn't have been without that way of life for long; with her push and tenacity she would have driven or carried him to a height from where he could provide her with what she wanted. He would have been crude clay in her hands because she would have led him with the other side of her, which he knew to be all love and tenderness, and this present side he might never have known. But now it was confronting him and it had the power to enrage him. Yet he controlled his rage and once again pleaded, 'Pam, you wouldn't do it . . . you couldn't. Look, I promise you on God's honour, if you come back it will only be for a couple of weeks. Your mother needn't know you're back; you can, as I said, get lodgings in some place near. You could go to Newcastle or Sunderland.'

'No.'

It was final and he knew it. She was no longer a beautiful girl, soft, yielding, maddening. She was facing him as a woman, a sophisticated woman, who because she knew what she wanted could rule her heart.

He watched her turn swiftly and go to the bed and pull one of her cases from beneath it. Having unlocked it, with quick, deft movements she began putting oddments into it, such as a brush, a comb, slippers, and lastly her nightdress, a thing so fine that she was able to cover it with both hands as she rammed it into a corner. Following this last action, she turned to him. 'Well?'

She had turned the last screw and she expected it to break him. When it didn't, she cried, 'You're a fool – a fool!'

He made no answer, and she cried again, 'Don't you realise what I'm going to do? I'm going back to him.'

Still he said nothing. His body seemed numb, and a curious numbness too had come upon his mind. Everything she had done and said in the past few minutes he seemed to recognise as if he knew it had been bound to happen and had rehearsed it in his own mind. And it wasn't finished yet. He must wait until it was finished. He could not, at this stage, walk out on her; he must let her do the walking out. He must give her that satisfaction. But no matter which one went first, this was the end. He knew he was looking on her for the last time in his life; he knew that never again would he be called upon to feel the pain that had the power to freeze his body into numbness and clamp down his emotions, rage included.

Even when finally she came near to him, so close that the faint perfume she always wore wafted gently into his nostrils, and looking into his eyes said, 'You can't let me do this,' he remained silent. The link could never be mended now, even if he had said 'All right, have it your own way.' The mend would only be a temporary job, for, as much as he loved her, he would have fought against her now, defying her to lead him whither she willed. Life would have been a fight between them, his conscience acting as a one-sided arbitrator.

She left the room door open with her cases standing before it while she went downstairs to call a taxi. This she set as a final of final tests. When she returned and the cases were still there, she moved slowly towards him; and now she was the old Pam again, her eyes bright with tears, her voice breaking as she said, 'You can't do this to me, Larry. You can't let me do it. Larry, darling, it's not too late.'

Her face was close to him, and in spite of the tears raining down it, he had the odd feeling that if he were to relent now she would hate him, not for his lack of strength, but for depriving her of the chance to retrieve that which deep down her soul craved.

His lips were stiff with numbness as he said, 'You know where to find him!'

Her eyes swimming with her tears darkened; her head went up and she stared defiantly at him for a moment, then, turning quickly away and picking up the two heavy cases and a number of oddments, she went laboriously down the stairs.

Nothing in him moved to check her when he heard the car draw up to the door. He looked at his watch. It said twenty minutes to seven. He shook it gently, thinking it must have stopped – life couldn't change in twenty-five minutes. But as he stood staring at the watch he knew it could change in seconds . . . an explosion in itself is but a matter of seconds. His life had been changed when the explosion hit the mine

. . . no, not changed, brought back to its beginning.

The numbness began to lift and he had the desire to throw himself down somewhere and cry – cry as he had done secretly when a lad, cry like a girl, a woman . . . like Jessie Honeysett must have done.

On this thought an involuntary reaction in him caused him, too, to turn suddenly and cram his things into a case and make ready to go.

12

THE PIT

It was quarter past nine on Saturday morning when Larry reached Fellburn. He had been unable to get a seat on the long-distance buses, but had done the journey almost as quickly in three lifts. The first, on one of the hundreds of lorries packing the roads, had taken him as far as Doncaster; from there he had got a lift in a private car to Durham; and from Durham it was but a short bus ride to Fellburn.

The bus stopped right opposite the Turnbulls' shop, and it so happened that Mr Turnbull was arranging a display of goods to the side of the open door. He glanced up as the bus stopped; then, straightening his back, he looked at Larry across the distance. For a moment their eyes met, and Larry saw that all there was to know Mr Turnbull already knew, for behind the hatred in his eyes there was triumph. With burning bitterness he thought, she hasn't been long in passing on the good news. Or was it the man himself who had phoned them?

All night he had refused to think of the man, fearing he might snap under the strain of his jealousy. At one point during the long ride, when the lorry was crossing a bridge, he had looked at the driver, who, although his eyes were open, seemed asleep, and he had thought, a push, and a twist of that wheel, and we've had it. But before the thought could take shape in any way the driver had turned to him and said airily, 'Cheer up, chum. It can't be as bad as that. Wife left you or summat?' Yes, his wife had left him, for she had been his wife as she would never be her husband's wife. And as he walked down the street a stiffness came into his muscles that had no connection with the tiredness assailing his body. The street was strangely quiet. On his side there was no bustle of women, no early gardener getting in a bit of digging between shifts, and on the other side there was no-one in front of the cottages doing windows or steps. This lack of audience to his return did not affect him one way or the other. The town was lying under a disaster, and his affair would be swamped beneath it. For this much he could at least thank God.

Three nights ago, when he had passed through the front gate, it was, he had told himself, for the last time, and he had felt not the slightest regret – she had outweighed home and all it stood for – yet here he was back. If she had outweighed it three nights ago, why was she not outweighing it now? Her question came to him: if they are dead, what can you do?

He opened the back door and stepped slowly into the scullery and stared at the strange back bending over the sink. A woman turned and exclaimed 'Good God!'; then, wiping her hands quickly on her apron, she added, 'It's you, Larry. Oh, you give me a shock, I thought it was . . .' She stopped. The movement of her hands became slower, and she went on with naked frankness, 'Well, you've come back, that's something in your favour anyway.'

His face tightened still further, and he asked gruffly, 'Where's my mother?' But before the woman could answer there was a scuffling movement on the stairs, and the next moment he was enveloped in Lottie's frantic embrace. 'Oh, Larry, Larry! Oh, you've come back, Larry. Oh Larry! Oh Larry!'

'Be quiet,' said the woman; 'you'll raise the house, Lottie . . . I'll make you a cup of tea, Larry. Have you had any breakfast?'

Larry diffidently patted Lottie's back, and muttered, 'I want nothing, just a cup of tea.'

'Oh, Larry, I said you'd come back. I told Jinny you'd come back. Poor Jinny.'

Larry pressed Lottie's straining body from him, and looked down into her tear-ravished face. 'Is me mother in, or . . . ?' He did not say, 'at the gates?' And the woman put in now, 'Give ower, Lottie, and leave Larry be for a minute. Yes, she's in. She's bad, Larry. You'd better prepare yourself for a shock.' She did not pause to break the news but went on, 'She had a stroke last night. She's sensible enough, but there's one side gone. The doctor says she should go to hospital for the time being, but she won't. She wrote on a piece of paper asking him to leave her here. We've got her in the front room, it's easier there. We brought your bed down, not knowing you'd be back.'

Slowly he pushed off Lottie's clinging hands and

went along the passage, as the woman admonished Lottie, 'Now you stay where you are.'

The front-room door was open and he could see the foot of his bed. Two women were standing, one on each side of it, their backs bent. 'Up,' said one, and together they heaved.

He was in the middle of the room before they were aware of him, and he saw that, like the woman in the scullery, they were not close neighbours such as Mrs King, or Mrs Adams, or Willie's mother. One was a Mrs Preston, and the other was Mrs Patty, both from the top end of the street. When they straightened up, he saw his mother, and she him, and they looked at each other.

One of the women, after making wordless sounds of surprise, said, 'Well, there you are, Jinny, we'll leave you for a bit. We'll be back.' She patted the sheet straight, touched Jinny's hair where a wisp had fallen about her ear, then, picking up a bowl from the floor, she went out, followed by her partner who carefully and soundlessly closed the door after her.

Unable to withdraw his eyes from his mother's, Larry moved to the bedside. His heart and conscience smote him with such force that for a space her plight held him. In the short time since he had last seen her, she seemed to have shrunk to half her size. The whole of the left side of her face was affected – the corner of her mouth stretched upwards to meet the dragging skin from her eye. Her left hand lay still on top of the bedspread, while the fingers of the right hand moved swiftly about it in a plucking motion, as if to prove its power of life.

Slowly he lowered himself on to the bed, and taking the moving hand between his own, he held it firmly. The right side of her face crumpled, the tears rolled down her cheeks, and her body began to shake. In one swift movement he hitched himself up the bed and put his arms about her. And like that they stayed, saying no word, only clinging together.

Again and again, stereotyped sentences formed in his mind, made up of words that would fit the occasion, such as 'There, there. Don't worry, you'll get better. No matter what's happened, you'll be all right. I'll see to that'; but he could say none of them, for he needed no confirmation to know that she would never get better, not to be herself again.

When he laid her back she turned her eyes towards the piece of paper and a pencil lying on the side of the table, and taking the paper up and placing it on a book, he held it for her, and in a small drunken scrawl she wrote one word, 'smallholding'.

The word expressed everything she was feeling. Never more would she hear talk of Frank's lifelong desire, never more would she see through his eyes the military rows of vegetables and fruit bushes. The pit had got him as over the years he had secretly feared it would.

Larry could not bear any longer to look at her agonised face, so without a word having been spoken between them, he went out, and, evading Lottie, whose crying of relief followed him upstairs, he went into his room.

In the doorway he paused for a while and looked about him. The room, like his life, was in complete upheaval, bedding lying on the floor, nothing in its place. It looked as if his mother had been in the midst of clearing the room of everything that would remind her of him when the disaster had occurred. His books were in a heap on the floor together with some old clothes. He went deliberately and picked from among the clothes the old suit he had worn in his going and coming from the pit, and swiftly now he changed into it, and although, being hung in a private locker kept apart for clean clothes, it had never come in contact with coal dust, it nevertheless carried the smell of the pit on it, and its odour cried to him, she was right, what can you do? You can't untrap the dead. But you can trap yourself.

Swiftly, as if to escape the thought, he ran down the stairs, and at the foot stood Lottie. She had the child in her arms and it was crying, not loudly, yet in a strong monotonous way. The sight of it reminded him of Lena, and he realised he hadn't seen her. She would be at the gates. A spark of pity for her assailed him, for with her temperament and saddled with a handicapped child she would take life hard.

'Betty's been whining all night. I've given her a bottle, haven't I, Mrs Fowley?'

'Yes, you've been good, Lottie,' said the woman. 'Now take it into the kitchen and keep it quiet; you don't want to disturb Jinny, do you?'

'No. All right. Oh, Larry.' Her swollen eyes looked their joy at Larry, and for a moment she seemed on the point of laughing with her pleasure, but the darkness that lay on the house had the power to still her natural reaction.

Mrs Fowley pushed her gently away with one hand while with the other she restrained Larry's departure. And when Lottie was out of hearing she closed the scullery door, and turning to him said, 'You'd better know right away about Lena. She's done a bunk. She told Mrs Patty she couldn't stick it, not after she heard there was no hope. That was late on last night, and our George saw her get on the first bus this morning. She had two cases with her, that's why he thought it was funny, and mentioned it. Mrs Patty didn't half go for her last night. She said it had to come to all of us sooner or later, and she had that helpless bairn to think of. And then there was your mother. Well . . .' Mrs Fowley paused, and her eyes rolled around in their sockets as if she were indulging in an eye exercise. Then she sighed and went on, 'You should have heard her . . . Lena. She said Jinny was your look-out and you'd have to come back, seeing as the girls were on t'other side of the world. As for the bairn, it could be put in a home somewhere, she said. She didn't feel it was hers anyway. She said it was like it was because of your grandfather or somebody. But none of us thought she'd go off, we thought it was the shock making her go on like that. Well, there it is, lad. I'm sorry.'

He made no comment but turned from her and

went out. It seemed as if the tentacles of an octopus were winding about him.

In the warm morning sunshine he shivered. His mother, Lottie, and the bairn, all helpless in one way or another, would depend now for their existence on him and through him the pit. The prospect was more horrifying at this moment than the ordeal he was about to face, and he cried out within him, I can't do it . . . tied for life, I just can't do it. I'll see them fixed in some way, but I can't stay on for ever. My God! no.

The crowd at the gate was thick and, in the main, was comprised of women. They stood crowded together, yet separated into small groups. The groups could be easily distinguished, as each seemed to converge round its own central figure. There was very little sound, no crying, no loud voice shouting against the owners as would have been the case twenty years ago. Policemen were keeping a path clear to the gate and as Larry, his eyes lowered, went up it a hand gripped at his arm and he was pulled to a halt, and he looked down into the agonised face of Mrs Macintyre.

'Larry.' Her voice was like a croak. 'Larry.'

He patted her hand but could say no word of comfort; as with his own mother, he could only feel for her.

'He was knocking in the night; he was still knocking.'

He moved swiftly away, his conscience crying loud in his ears now, 'She's blaming you, and she's right.

If you hadn't gone when you did, it's a thousand to one you'd be with him now.' For a moment the weight of the whole disaster seemed to fall on his shoulders. He had quarrelled with his father, and left him in bitterness, when, up to a month ago, he had never had a cross word with him. He had died in the bitterness. And Jack, too, was dead, and thirty-five others. It was as if, in his scurrying to a new life, he had pulled the roof supports with him, and the result was this.

'Hello there, Larry.' As he pressed through the guarded gate into the press of the yard a back overman, the captain of a rescue party, spoke to him. 'Late, aren't you?'

He looked hard and spoke tersely, and Larry said with a sheepishness he loathed himself for, 'I took a couple of days off. I was away when I heard.'

It was obvious to him that Bill Catley knew nothing of his private affairs, and it caused him a certain amount of wonder that when he had not been on call for the squad some fellow had not provided the answer for his absence.

Bill Catley was one of the older men of the pit and knew what strikes and tight belts meant, and he said reprovingly, 'You can't wonder about them going on about absenteeism, you young'uns'll never larn. Aye well, I suppose you weren't to know.' And in the same tone he went on, 'I'm sorry about your father, lad. He was a good man was Frank, none better; steady and reliable. There'll soon be none of them

253

left . . . Look, they've divided the squads up now. Report to Stanley Blake.'

'Is there any news at all?' asked Larry.

'Nowt that's good, I'm afraid, lad. We've established a fresh-air base in the return drift, and trying to get to the Duckbill district that way; but it's a hell of a job. We found the separation doors at the foot of the intake gone west. The air was putrid. The canaries nearly had it. They're sealing off sections now to try and get the ventilators going.'

'What about the mother-gate?'

'Hopeless. The second explosion brought God knows how much of the roof down.'

'And the fall in the main road? Willie . . . Willie Macintyre?'

The overman shook his head. 'They're not through that yet. Once they are, and the roof's held, then . . . well . . .'

He left the sentence unfinished, and Larry moved away to the dressing-rooms. Once inside, it was evident that his affairs were known here. It was also evident that at some time he had been under discussion, for there was a quick movement of eyes, and the greetings that were sent to him were slow and tentative.

'Hello, there . . . got back?'

'Hello there, Larry.'

'Wot-cher.'

Under normal circumstances there would have been no greetings – you don't greet a member of the family with stilted politeness if you see him morn, noon, and night; a nod of the head or the immediate delving into some topic would more likely be the normal procedure. Yet in the half-glances and the greetings there was a quality that Larry felt but would not put a name to. He could not think that it was relief, that they were relieved to a man that although he had, to their way of thinking, done a dirty bit of business, he had, nevertheless, when put to the test, and the test at rock-bottom was the pull of the pit, turned up trumps.

Larry gave no greeting except the curt lift of his head, and after pushing towards his locker and changing into his things he turned to a man and said, 'Who we under?'

'Ralph Telham. They've split up. There's squads from all over the place here. We're on report now.' The man put his head down and spoke into his own locker more than to Larry. 'I'm sorry about your dad and Jack, Larry. And Willie. But still, he could be all right, there's still a chance.'

'Who was he with?'

'The dep.'

'Just the two of them?'

'Aye. They were knocking till just a while ago, which makes them think they're in a pocket. They surmise there must have been another fall further along, and they're getting some air from the old workings near the seven quarter seam. They would have tried to get in that way, but it would have taken longer.'

The man waited while Larry changed, and together

255

they went out into the crowded yard and towards the first-aid post. The familiar scene was no longer familiar. All about him were strange men. Here and there he recognised a 'big pot'; an area surveyor, an agent, a pit manager, and three men he knew to be local doctors. There were parsons and priests, and standing talking to two men covered with grime was a Member of Parliament.

As he made to go into the first-aid post the whirring of the shaftwheel ceased and his, with every other head in the top end of the yard, moved upwards. The cage had come up; it could mean news. Almost instantly, like wind over grass, a message would sweep across the cage landing, down the steel steps, and into the yard.

It did. They could see them . . . they would be through any minute now. Nothing more. There was no: The deputy had said this, or Willie had said that; there was no shout: They're alive and kicking.

He turned into the first-aid post and made his way towards the overman Bill Catley, whom he had encountered in the yard, and stood before him, where he was surrounded with equipment. And without any to-do he was handed a helmet and breathing apparatus, and instructed, 'You weren't here when they were told. We're to go to the fresh-air base in the main section and get our orders and be checked over from there. They've just gone up. Come on.'

Following him, Larry went through the yard and up the steps and on to the platform, and joined the men with whom he had practised time and again for just such a moment as this. But never during his training had he imagined going to the rescue, the hopeless rescue, of the three men closest to his life. Between a gap in the heads of the men and the space between two trucks he saw, away over the town in the far distance, a strip of yellow green . . . the fells. In the middle of the strip was a minute black dot. It could have been the barn. As the cage rattled to the surface the dot seemed to melt before his eyes, and his mind could not hold it, even had he wished it to.

Crushed on his hunkers in the cage, pressed knee to knee and with the arid smell of clothes soaked in sweat and dust about him, and dropping with the usual sickening swiftness into the earth, he cried in protest against all the facets of his life. 'God! God! God!'

They stood a short time later like strange beings from a dark and unknown planet, waiting for the word to move on. Their faces bulged with the breathing apparatus, but the nose-clip, the mouthpiece, the bag, the liquid-air pack did not appear as appendages to their bodies but part of themselves, and one with the congested depth. All about them was movement, apparently chaotic, but in fact so organised that no man made an unnecessary step . . .

Inside Larry's chest was a feeling comparable with nothing that he had felt in his life before. The torments of his love bore no resemblance to the anguish with him now. In his own eyes he was as dust – in the local idiom, he was a nowt – and he knew in this moment that as long as he might live he would never regain a full conceit of himself. All the kindness, all the devotion, yes and the love, that Willie Macintyre had openly bestowed on him was alive now and filling the narrow road which was a shambles of heaped stones, mangled rails, and props, and bowing before that love was the knowledge that in his heart he had scorned the simplicity of this friend and had looked down on him for it. And now he was unable to take his eyes from where he lay at the side of the track.

Willie did not look dead; through the grime on his face he looked asleep, and for a moment Larry questioned whether that could not be the case. He wanted to cry to the doctor who had just risen from his knees, 'It could be shock. Why don't you try artificial respiration or something?' But he said nothing, only continued to stare down at the burnt body of his friend. Willie was dead, quite dead, and three days ago he had left him too without a word of farewell. He had left him without even a thought.

The doctor signalled to the stretcher bearers, and gently Willie was lifted from the blanket on to the stretcher and a sheet was placed over him, and for the last time he rode the main road.

Larry did not watch the departure, but stared ahead into the opening they had made through the fall, and when, at a signal from the captain, they began to move off in pairs he took his place in the short procession. Slowly and carefully, like men walking on the sea bed, they went. For a distance of four hundred yards the road appeared normal, then abruptly they came to the reason why Willie had stopped knocking. There had been a fall almost at the beginning of the old working leading to the seven quarter seam, from which enough clean air had seeped into the pocket to keep a man alive.

Now they came to the obstruction that had formed the other wall of the pocket. There was no telling to what depth it went. After the captain had climbed some of the strewn boulders and examined those near the roof, he signalled two men up beside him, and carefully removing some top stones, passed them to the men, who in turn passed them to their mates. Then stopping, he signalled again, indicating that the fall was slight.

Working with seeming lazy slowness, they shored up a hole big enough to afford the passage of one man at a time. Larry was the sixth man through, and as he entered the last stretch of the road which led to the tail-gate a suffocating sickness assailed him, and for a moment he knew panic. His mouth-piece and nose-clip were in place, and the air was flowing smoothly from the air pack into his breathing bag. The sickness was not that caused by carbon-monoxide, but by fear, fear of what he would see once they reached the face. Men would be strewn about, and among them would be his father and Jack. But swiftly the fear of his own reactions was wiped away as the man in front of him, the Welshman who had chipped Willie on that fateful Saturday when Pam Turnbull had come back into his life, suddenly sank on to his knees and muttering only one word,

'Sweating', rolled over on to his side. The distress signal passed swiftly on to the captain, who, turning, made motions that the man should be taken back.

With the aid of another man Larry hoisted him up, and together they dragged him to the hole, and going one at a time through it, they moved slowly back towards the base. But long before they reached it, Larry knew that the weight he was carrying was a dead weight.

When once again Larry went up the road he knew no fear, but as a few hours previous when in the lorry he had been tempted to end it, so now the temptation was even stronger. All he had to do was to open his mouth and it would be over in a matter of seconds. He had always known this in theory, but Taffy had proved it in actuality. Taffy had felt little, there had been no time. Perhaps a tight pain in the chest, a feeling of sweating, and then . . . nothing . . . blessed nothing. The desire for escape from life filled his mind and took the place of the dread of what he would see at the face. It took away the dread of life lived without Pam, and the dread of life lived with his mother and Aunt Lot, and Jack's grotesque child, and . . . the pit . . . the pit with its present nightmare always looming in the background.

There was a tap on his arm, and he followed the direction of the pointing finger through the zig-zag of lights. There was a signal coming from the end of the tail-gate. The way was blocked, they were returning. As if being granted an unwanted reprieve, he slowly turned round and went back to the station.

It was thirty-two hours later before they entered the actual face. Fresh-air bases had had to be gradually moved nearer to it to enable the rescue team to work from each end simultaneously and to allow them to be relieved at short intervals. Although the captain had offered to relieve Larry of the task that lay before him, he had curtly refused. It was now six o'clock on the Sunday evening, and but for two short rests he had been on hand all the time. This was his third trip to the face, and now they were moving in.

During his years in the pit he had experienced three mine disasters, and they had all been the result of roof falls and each in its own way had been gruesome enough. The memory of them had stayed vividly with him for months afterwards. But this was different. This hell, this shambles born of poisoned air and flames, this madman's world of twisted rails and tubs hanging like baskets from crevices. The word horror was inadequate – burnt, twisted, grotesque creatures, sprawling at angles that weirdly suggested motion. The orders were to move each man out as they came to him. But when he bent over the first body, he could not touch it. It was the captain who gently turned it over. It was not his father; he knew it wouldn't be Jack, for they would find him near the duckbill loader.

Crawling over the debris of twisted cables and roof chocks, he came across a box. It was locked and he did not touch it. He knew it held detonators, and everything that could be left was left for the investigators to check up on. The result of all enquiries usually revealed carelessness, and this one would likely be no exception. Detonators that should be taken up at the end of the shift were left in odd corners. It was illegal, but nobody reminded anyone else of the illegality; so it went on, as did the firing of tight roof chocks. Well, there were plenty of loose roof chocks now. They were strewn right and left.

The captain picked up a tattered book. It was the deputy's report book, and near it lay a bait tin quite intact.

The seventh man they came to was Frank. Larry recognised him even before he was identified. It was the recognition of blood to blood, and his heart cried out with the simplicity of a child, 'Oh, Dad, I'm sorry. I'm sorry. I would never have left you like that. You know I wouldn't. You understand? For God's sake, say·you understand!'

But there was no swift release to the pain of regret as slowly and painfully he eased his father along the coal face and, with each pull on Frank's body, an agony of mind that he likened to being crucified filled him. And when, in the tail-gate, Frank was laid on a stretcher he took one end; the ambulance member did not deter him. And when at the foot of the actual shaft, standing amid the ready helpers, he still gripped the stretcher, he knew he was doing it now not only because he did not want to be separated from his father but because, as long as he held the stretcher, he would be forced to stand. He knew that once released from it he too would drop.

And it was as he had forecast. When obliged, in turning, to place the stretcher on the ground, he sank down and was relieved for the moment of any more pain by an obliterating blackness, and together Frank and he were taken up into the daylight. The cage carried them slowly this time, even gently, as it had never done before.

The town was still, the shops were closed, and no traffic moved on the main road. The day had started quietly and the quietness had grown with each hour. When people stirred they did so softly; when they spoke, their words, broad as they might be, did not rise with the sing-song intonation and fill the air, but hovered close about them as if loath to jar this day of sorrows. The funeral route was black with people; and as the long line of hearses moved slowly to the cemetery, women cried, men cried, and small children were unusually silent.

Larry was the only representative of his family. The one uncle and three cousins he had were scattered over the country. The uncle was confined to his bed, and the cousins for varying reasons could not attend. Cables bearing frantic messages had come from Australia, but no-one expected anyone from there. Neighbours and friends flanked him, but seemingly he was alone. Of his father and Jack, he did not think 'I am walking with them for the last time' because for days now they had been strangely nearer to him than ever they had been when alive. Some part of each of them had burrowed into his being; he felt he was no longer one but three men. But he would recognise the responsibilities of two only, his own, and his father's. His mother was his responsibility; so was Aunt Lot, but Jack's child . . . Here his particular self was constantly proving the point against Jack's pleading. The child was Lena's; she should be found and made to take it. Yet within himself he knew that Lena had gone for good, and that what was finally to become of the child would rest with him. And at the moment these three people represented his world, and their combined pressure lay on his shoulders like a roof fall.

The cemetery lay on a rising fell on the outskirts of the town, and from any part of it could be seen the shafts of the two pits. As the heart-breaking service went on, and names were called and the coffins lowered, and flowers sprinkled and muffled sobs and moans filled the air, heads would be lifted to the pit wheels, and like monster eyes in which was reflected nothing but indifference the wheels stared back and seemed to say, 'You asked for it. Who started me anyway? You want coal and more coal. You must pay for it.'

Frank and Jack were laid side by side, and as Larry stepped blindly back from the grave, he too seemed forced to raise his eyes over the mass of heads. The wheels looked at him. First the Venus then the Phoenix, and at the sight of them he yelled in his head, 'Damn you! Blast you!'

A woman near him quietly fainted, sliding down between two relatives as if she had just decided to sit, while another, unable to control her sobs, verged on hysteria. A man, whose son had just been lowered, gave a cry like a wounded animal and, turning from the grave, his hand shielding his face, he pushed his way aggressively through the crowd.

At last it was over, the dead were left in the bower of flowers. And it was of the flowers that Larry was thinking as he walked out of the gates. Never in his life did he want to see or smell another flower. Always would he be reminded of that grave when he saw a bunch of flowers. The smell of them was strong in his nostrils now and filling his head with a sick ache. He felt their scent would remain round him for ever.

'The missus is making you some tea, lad.' It was Bill Preston who spoke to him from the opposite seat in the car.

'With Jinny being bad,' he said, 'we won't come in.' He included the others with a lift of his head. 'We'll show her wor respects later on. She'll have enough on her plate the day, and the women are the best hands at dealing with that kind of thing.'

Larry nodded. There was no need to express his thanks to these four men; some day the opportunity would arise and he would repay them for their and their wives' kindness. Perhaps under exactly the same circumstances as this present one.

They alighted from the car at his gate and each went his own way. Larry entered the house by the back door, and having closed it, he stood for a moment leaning against it. Lottie's voice came to him from the kitchen. It was tear-filled and broken. She was saying to the whimpering child, 'There now. There now. I'll get you a bottle. Ssh, now! There now.'

He moved from the door as Mrs Preston came into the kitchen. 'You back, Larry?' she said. 'I've been thinking: Wouldn't you go to our house and have your tea?'

'Thanks all the same,' he said.

'All right, Larry. I know how you feel about it. Jinny's in a bit of a state, but don't let it worry you too much. She'll get over it. We all do. To a certain extent anyway. We've got to, else we couldn't go on.' She nodded sadly, confirming the truth of this, for she had lost her eldest son eight years ago.

Larry went into the passage, then stepped back again into the scullery and said with some awkwardness, 'I'm not ungrateful for all you've done, Mrs Preston, no matter how I might appear.'

'Oh, go on' – she waved him away. 'I'm only too glad to do it. If Mrs King hadn't been hit an' all, I would have never got the chance to do anything. This street's had it and no mistake this time. Five gone. I'll do all I can for your mother, Larry, so don't worry.'

'Thank you.'

Before going in to his mother he looked into the kitchen. The table was set for tea, and the room was tidy. That was all that could be said for it. The sparkle and sheen of Jinny's daily rubbing was no longer visible. A week had covered her lifetime's effort –

there was dust on everything. Mrs Preston was quite a hand at tending the sick but she could sit in a muddle and remain happy. As for Lottie, surroundings did not affect her. She too could have remained happy in a pigsty, provided she liked the pig.

Lottie, catching sight of him, turned from the child. 'Oh, Larry, you're back.' Her crying broke out afresh and he motioned her to be quiet, saying gently, 'Don't, Aunt Lot. Now, now. Now try not to.'

She came to him and clung on to his hand, saying, 'Oh, Larry, I've been crying and crying. I couldn't eat nothing. And Betty cried, she did, Larry, right out loud. 'Twas as if she knew, 'cause she's never cried out properly like that. She's gettin' to know me now. Will Lena come back, do you think? I hope she doesn't. Mrs Preston says she will, if it's only to get her share out of what they've collected. Thousands and thousands they've . . .'

'Be quiet, Aunt Lot!'

'Oh, all right, Larry, don't be vexed with me . . . I was only saying. And I feel so bad, Larry. But don't worry. I'll look after you and Jinny, and the house an' all. You'll see, I'll make you a pot pie like Jinny.'

She too was looking to the future . . . the funeral was over. Firmly he loosened her hold and said, still gently, 'All right, Aunt Lot. I know you will.' Then leaving her still talking he went into the front room.

The blinds were drawn and in the gloom Jinny looked an old woman of eighty. She was propped up and had fallen a little to one side, but her eyes searched his face and drew him to her. He sat down slowly on the bed and, leaning towards her, laid his head on her shoulder, and when her good hand passed over his hair the tears rose to his throat and almost suffocated him.

13

THE ANSWER

Jessie, carefully placing the six long-stemmed rose-buds up to their neck in water, remarked to the young woman by her side, 'It's important that you see that the crocks are full, Clara. The water must come right up to the flower, if not they'll die tomorrow.'

'It would worry me, I want to get out. We've been closed for twenty minutes now, and it nearly six o'clock on a Friday night an' all.'

'Worry you or not,' said Jessie sharply, 'this is what's got to be done, and the sooner you learn the better.'

'I don't intend to learn. And what's to learn anyway? Stuck out in the back here, emptying smelly jars.'

'They're only smelly when you don't change the water. You'll be having Miss Barrington after you, I'm warning you.' She turned to the girl. 'Why don't you try?'

'Try what?' said Clara pertly. 'Get used to this solitary confinement? No fear. I'm leaving the night, she can do what she likes. Me mother says I can. She says I was daft to come here, anyway, when I can start at four-seventeen in the factory. And it's the

269

Durham gala the morrow and she's keepin' open when the town'll be nearly empty. Stingy old scare-crow.'

Jessie turned to the girl, her intention being to plead the cause of the flowers and to point out that likely within a few weeks she'd be allowed to serve in the shop; but, looking into Clara's mascaraed eyes, she saw the futility of it. She knew why Clara had answered the advert for a young lady assistant. She had seen herself waiting on men, men who would come to buy flowers, but who she expected would see a greater charm in her painted beauty.

Very few men actually came into Miss Barrington's shop; most of the custom came by phone from the residents of The Hill. That generally only women came to the shop was a blow to Clara. Her dreams of suddenly being swept off her feet by a fellow who could afford to buy three dozen roses had soon faded. No, Clara was fed up and she was leaving. 'And,' she repeated for the second time, 'I'm leaving the night.'

Without being told, Miss Barrington knew that her young assistant was about to leave, and without notice, and she was worried, but not about Clara. She'd had four Claras in six months. You could always get Claras, but the Jessies were hard to find at any time, and more so these days. Miss Barrington was asking herself now what she would do if Jessie should leave – Jessie knew the business as well as herself. She must, she told herself, take action im-mediately and do what she'd had in the back of her mind for some time, make her a partner. She'd had no intention of taking any step in this direction for some years yet, but now she feared she might have left it too late. If all she heard about this parson was true, he was a determined young man. Moreover, he seemed to know a good thing when he saw it, not like the other fool of a fellow who threw her up. If the parson had been staying in the town there would still have been a problem, for parsons want their wives as part-time workers. But the rumour said he was leaving and urging Jessie to go with him. Of course, it might all be quite a lot of exaggeration, but there was no gainsaying the fact that Jessie had become a new creature these past few months. In fact, since her mother died. And the change, Miss Barrington suspected, was not only outwardly. Jessie had an assurance now that she had not even shown signs of in all the years she had known her.

Miss Barrington put her head round the office door and called softly, 'Jessie.'

Jessie came into the darkened shop. 'Yes, Miss Barrington?'

'Come in a minute. Has that girl finished?'

'Not quite.'

'She's no good, hopeless in fact. Not the type at all. She'll be telling me she's leaving tonight. I shouldn't be at all surprised.'

Jessie said nothing, but wondered, and not for the first time, at the sagacity of her employer. She certainly knew a great deal about girls, for it was only to herself that Clara had blown her head off these past weeks. To Miss Barrington she had been politeness itself.

'Sit down a minute. Close that door.'

Jessie, a little mystified, closed the door, which was rarely or never shut, and sat down on an old-fashioned high desk stool.

Miss Barrington did not believe in beating about the bush and, in her usual way, she came straight to the point: 'How would you like to come into partnership with me, Jessie?'

Miss Barrington was looking down on her order book, and Jessie stared at her smooth, rounded profile. The proposal had shot through her with the force of an electric shock, causing her heart to race, her eyes to screw up, and her lips to fall apart.

All day she had been praying inwardly to be shown the way, to be shown the right thing to do. She had prayed that before tomorrow she would know that the feeling she had for Alan, which she never likened to love, was foundation enough on which to say she would become his wife. He himself had no doubts but that she in time would love him as he did her. And she felt that once away from Fellburn and its painful associations this could even be possible. During these past three weeks she had been drawn closer to him than to anyone in her life before. Never had she been able to talk to Larry Broadhurst, even, as she had done to him. Something had quickened in her when she saw his compassion for the people during the disaster, and the tireless way in which he had worked. He had been mentioned in the paper, and his congregation, instead of censuring him, were speaking of him now as 'our Mr Ramsey'. He had even been asked to reconsider his decision to leave, and two of the members who had been most bitter against him had spoken to her last Sunday.

'Beautiful day, Miss Honeysett,' they had said. And these words, she knew, spelt reprieve from scandal. Yet, in spite of their changed attitude to both herself and him, he was still determined to leave. Tomorrow she was to tell him if she would go with him . . . and here was her answer.

A vague dream, a dream that floated in the back-water of unconsciousness, a dream that she had allowed no breath of air to sustain, for in her mind she had recognised the impossibility and the futility of such as her ever having a flower shop on her own, had been given life. Even when, some months ago at Madame Fonyer's she had been jerked into a small conceit of herself, it had not embraced the idea of a partnership with Miss Barrington. If her dreams had taken shape at all, it would have assumed a little one-window shop in a side-street, which would have been in no way comparable with being a partner in Barrington's, with its double windows, its exclusive clientele, and enviable position in the High Street.

'Well, Jessie?' Miss Barrington continued to look at her book. She entered some figures and waited.

'But, Miss Barrington, I have no money. Just what's left. About a hundred and twenty pounds. It wouldn't be . . .'

Now Miss Barrington turned and looked at her.

'I'm not asking you to put money in, you'd be a working partner. You've always worked hard for me, Jessie, very hard. I haven't been blind all these years. What's more, you love the flowers. You've got to love them to make a business like this really go. I'm not getting younger. When I die everything I have goes to my nephew in Canada, and he doesn't need it, and he certainly wouldn't want the shop. And I'd like to think that when that time comes you would take it over. Well, how about it, Jessie? It would all be done legally, no promises, no hearsay or she-say.'

'Oh, Miss Barrington.'

'You will then?'

'Yes, oh yes. I don't know what to say. I never dreamed. Believe me, I never dreamed of such a thing. Yet it is a sort of answer. I was thinking about going away, Miss Barrington.'

'You were, Jessie?' Miss Barrington simulated surprise.

'Yes, but I couldn't now. This is the answer I prayed for.'

Miss Barrington smiled gently. There was something so simple, so honest, so kind about this big woman. She was a rare quality in these days of brashness. She leaned forward and actually patted Jessie's hand. 'I know you never aspired to the shop, Jessie. If you had, I doubt whether I would be making you this offer now. In a way, I was going to say, you are too self-effacing; but no, it's a rare quality and pays in the end.'

'Oh, Miss Barrington, I don't know what to say.'

'Well, that's a good thing, too. There's too much talking these days. Talking without thinking. People don't think any more, so they jabber. Which reminds me. Send in that potential film star, then give her those Esther Reads to deliver to the Pratts on her way home.'

Jessie stood up. 'I'll take them, Miss Barrington; I think she's . . . she's thinking of leaving.'

'Oh, so she is, is she? Well then, neither of us will be surprised. I'd have been more so if she hadn't been. Send her in and let's get it over. Candidly, I'll be glad to see the back of her; that painted face of hers jars on the colours. And go when you're finished, I'll be here for some time yet.'

'All right, Miss Barrington. And . . . and . . . oh, thank you so much.'

Jessie moved into the shop on unsteady feet, and after telling Clara that Miss Barrington wanted her, she stood in the middle of the cool, stone-shelved room and looked bemusedly about her. She was to be a partner, a partner in this shop; from now on everything she did would be partly for herself; and one day the shop would be hers. Not for a long, long time, she hoped, but one day.

It was the greatest thing that had ever happened to her, and she had the desire to drop on her knees and give thanks, or to tell someone the news, someone who would care. But who would care? Only Alan; and when she told him, it would be his answer. The thought brought with it a deep sadness. Perhaps if she asked him, he would stay on. No, no, she didn't wish that he should stay on, nor did she wish that she should go. The fact that the swift events of the past few minutes had tied her to the town was filling her with relief, and she shook her head as if brushing something away that could not be removed by hand. Quickly now she turned to the bench, and taking the Esther Reads from a tall vase she laid them on a sheet of green paper, through which the gold-printed words 'Barrington: Florists' shone. Her hands stopped their work and her mind came back to the present. How soon would it be before it read 'Barrington and Honeysett: Florists'. A joy swelled her throat, bringing with it the rare feeling of gaiety. It was as she had realised in Madame Fonyer's that Saturday afternoon, there were other lives to live. Yet before she had finished wrapping the flowers a sense of guilt had dimmed the joy and her mind was swung back to the immediate past. And she thought of Willie and of the house across the street where so many lives had stopped at once. Five weeks ago today . . .

Jessie arrived home at half-past seven, and on entering the cottage the neat brightness of its new dressings took on a brighter hue still. She wouldn't have to leave it now; the little world that had been born out of her deep protest against the cramping and narrow existence would still be hers to enjoy. She hadn't realised just how much she had come to love the home she had made out of her one-time prison, until this moment.

She had with her a large bunch of flowers: roses,

sweet peas, and three carnations. The latter were forced and their life was ending, but they still held a radiant elegance in their scarlet fluted petals. Even before removing her hat and coat she went into the little scullery, and filling a vase with water, placed the three blooms in it, and having stood them on the corner of the book-case she stood back to admire them, thinking, 'It's as Miss Barrington says, you've got to love flowers.'

She joined her hands together under her chin, closed her eyes tightly, and swung around. It was the action of a young girl, and one that Jessie had never been stimulated to indulge in. She brought herself to a stop and leaned her head against the mantelpiece. 'Eeh! I'm silly, quite daft . . . like a lass. But who would have thought this would happen to me . . . partner in the shop . . . a share in it. I'll be working for myself. It's fantastic. It's really too good to be true.' She straightened up. 'What have I done to deserve it?' Her humility brought her to her knees, and leaning upon the couch, she buried her face in her hands and, without words, she prayed, giving thanks from her heart for this wonderful gift, for the kindness of Miss Barrington, and lastly, with her face pressed tightly into her hands, for the answer to her prayers, that she need not leave her home, that she need not leave this street, and that the pain that the presence of Larry Broadhurst created was still acutely with her.

Soberly now she stood up. The young girl had fled, the woman was back, quiet and restrained. She took

277

off her things, then went about the house opening the windows to let in the cool evening air. As she was pulling down the front window, she saw Lottie come out of the gate opposite. Lottie must have seen her but she gave no sign; instead she went up the street as if she were going into the town. And this unusual conduct from the effervescent Lottie caused Jessie to wonder, for it wasn't the first time Lottie had done something similar in the past two weeks. And Lottie wouldn't do anything like that unless she'd been told, and told repeatedly.

She went into the scullery and put the kettle on, and she was setting the tray when the latch of the back door was gently rattled. On the door being unbolted, Lottie, the picture of furtiveness, sidled into the yard.

'Are you in, Jessie?' she whispered.

Jessie smiled kindly. 'Well, what do you think, Aunt Lot?'

'I mean, are you by yourself, Jessie?'

'Yes; come in.'

'I won't stay a minute, but I just wanted . . .'

'Come in.' Jessie marshalled her up the yard – the inside walls of the cottages might have straining ears, but the back-yards were easy amplifiers of sound, and you could be almost sure, intentionally or otherwise, someone would be listening in.

In the kitchen, she said, 'I've just made a cup of tea, would you like one, Aunt Lot?'

'Oh, yes, Jessie. Eeh, I always come when you're making tea. Oh' – she pointed to the flowers – 'aren't

278

they lovely! I love flowers. Carnations. Our house used to be like this' – she moved her arm around the room – 'all bright, especially at the weekend. Jinny always bought herself some flowers; Larry used to give her the money. She spoke the day, Jessie, more than she's done afore. She was upset, and she said some words right off.'

'What does the doctor say?' asked Jessie from the scullery.

'Oh, he says she's doin' nicely, but he says Betty's got to be sent away. Larry and him were talkin'. But I see to Betty. I do. I can see to her. I feed her and wash her face and hands. And Jinny doesn't want her to be sent away. She got all worked up. She likes her on the bed – she lies and looks at her. But since Mrs Preston fell down and hurt her leg and Mrs Adams and Mrs Patty can only take turns at coming in, the doctor says something must be done.'

'Have you had no news of Lena?'

'No. Larry went to the police 'cause there's money for her because of Jack, and he says she's got to take Betty. But Mrs Adams says she won't care a damn about the money, she'll have likely gone to Charlie Burton. He was a dealer that went round, and Lena used to go about with him afore she met Jack. Mrs Adams says she'd be lying low somewhere, and there's one thing sure, she won't come back and look after Jinny and the house. Larry's gone up to Durham to see if a woman will come and be housekeeper. He tried in the town but they're all in the new factory. Jinny cried and tried to get up. The doctor says she'll never get up if she worries. Can I have one of these biscuits, Jessie?'

'Yes, of course. Help yourself.' Jessie came into the kitchen, put down the teapot, and closed the kitchen window – Aunt Lot was talking as if she were at the other end of the street. As she poured out the tea, she said, 'Have some bread and butter. And that's strawberry jam. It's home-made, from Dalton's.'

'Ooh! Dalton's. Dalton's sell nice stuff. I put Larry's bait up with jam and he brought it back.'

Lottie stopped eating, and the brightness left her face and sudden tears came into her eyes, turning their faded blue to an opaque jellyness. 'I do try, Jessie, I do me best. And I'm not so sick now; but I feel tired and I don't want to get up. But I do because I want to look after Larry. And the other day he went for me. Jinny was in a stew 'cause she couldn't make me understand, and the bairn was crying, and she rarely cries, you know, Jessie. And oh, Jinny was upset, and Larry had to hold her, Jinny, I mean, and she kept crying and saying, a menagerie, a menagerie. What's a menagerie, Jessie?'

'I'll give you some more tea,' said Jessie, taking the cup from her hands.

Lottie did not press for an explanation but went on, 'It was then that I said "If Jessie . . ." '

Her hand went swiftly to her face and covered her mouth, and her eyes looked over it, rounding themselves into circles.

Jessie's face became set, and there was pain in her voice as she asked, 'Tell me what you said, Aunt Lot.'

'Eeh, no. It's as Larry said, if I come over I can't help meself. He said if I came over here again he'd send me away when the bairn was born because I couldn't keep me mouth shut. I tried. I did, didn't I? I didn't say anything.'

The words came clipped and hard as Jessie said, 'Go on, tell me why he said that. He won't know; and he won't know you've been if you don't tell him.'

'Oh no, I won't tell him . . . that's if . . . if it doesn't slip out. All I said to him was, Jessie, should I come over for you when Mrs Preston took bad, 'cause you would clean up in a jiffy for us and make his bait and things, and he went for me. Eeh, he did go for me. Larry's never gone for me like that, never. He yelled at me, Jessie, and pushed me out of the kitchen. It was nothing to say, was it, Jessie? 'Tisn't as if . . . well, I told him you were going to marry the minister.'

'Who told you that?'

'Mrs Preston; her Harry's Ada goes to his church. You know Ada?'

Jessie rose from the couch and taking the teapot went into the scullery to refill it. There was a deep sickness in her, and the bitterness that had been wiped away on the day Larry came back returned. She could see him, almost hear him raging in case she could come into his house, for it was his now. The desertion for the second time by Pam Turnbull had not, as one would have expected, shown herself up in favourable comparison, but had evoked a feeling that seemingly could be expressed by nothing but his rage. For a moment the temptation assailed her to take the opportunity that Alan Ramsey offered and marry him. She was never more aware than at this moment that never again would a man of Alan's standard ask her for his wife. Other women could have the same chances repeated even again and again, but this opportunity would be the one and only in her life, and she had an overpowering desire to show Larry Broadhurst that she was wanted, and by somebody of a class above himself. She had a swift mental picture of her wedding. It could be by special licence, next week or the week after: it would be from this house, and she would make a splash. By, that would be paying him back in his own coin, for he would have to witness it, at least some part of it, for he was tied to the house with even stronger chains than had ever tied herself. His mother, Lottie, the child, and another one coming. Why, with those tentacles binding him it must for him be almost like being buried alive.

Jessie bowed her head over the stove. Her anger was being wiped away on a wave of pity, and she murmured down to the grid, 'I would rather that he had gone off with her than he be saddled like this.'

'I'd better go now.' Lottie was at the scullery door. 'It's been lovely, Jessie. If I keep me mouth shut he won't know nothing and I can come again . . . well, I've always come over, haven't I?'

'Yes. Yes, of course.'

'And there's no harm in it, is there?'

'No, no. Only you'd better try and not say

anything. Don't mention my name at all, Aunt Lot, that's the safest way.'

'All right, Jessie.'

'I'll let you out. And you'd better go back round the bottom corner, it won't look then as if you've been here.'

'All right, Jessie. Bye-bye. Oh—' she paused. 'You know what the morrow is . . . Durham gala day. Eeh, we used to all go, didn't we? Eeh, we had some times. That's why Jinny was so upset the day. Bye-bye, Jessie.'

'Goodbye, Aunt Lot.'

Lottie was gone, walking quietly down the lane as if Larry might hear her step, and Jessie, back in the house again, sat down on the couch. The thrill of her new position was gone. The fact that she could yet accept an offer of marriage was as nothing, because inside herself she was Jessie Honeysett, the scorned and unwanted woman with, she knew, nothing about her. He had raged at mention of her going into his house. He was going to give her no loop-hole through which to retrieve the past out of the chaos of the present. Even in extremity he would have none of her. She gripped her hands tightly between her knees and slowly rocked herself.

14

THE MENAGERIE

Jinny lay staring ahead of her, her eyes gazing through the open door and across the passage into the kitchen. At her laboured request her bed had been moved from the wall and placed with its head to the fireplace. It was from here she could see more of what was going on . . . or what was not going on. The worry in her mind now, superseding even the pain of her loss, was the fact that there wasn't enough going on in the house. Neighbours popped in, but they popped out again, and it hurt her more and more as the days went by to see her son, his face set in a fixed blankness, trying to cope with the routine of the house after having returned from the pit.

Lottie's efforts drove her almost into a frenzy. She wanted to scream at her; and she became frightened at the racing of her heart when she tried to make her understand. Sometimes her thinking would be clear, and at these times she would have an urge to get up. She even attempted to. She would get one leg over the side of the bed, but do what she might the other wouldn't follow, and her efforts would make her exhausted and bring her to tears. Then her mind at times during the long days and longer nights would revert to her youth, with nostalgic longing, and she would keep repeating to herself, 'If only we could know . . . if only we could know,' and this trend would invariably recall her grandmother and the particular story of the menagerie, and she would mutter, 'She didn't tell me that story for nothing . . . she must have known . . . she had second sight; she must have known my house would become like a menagerie.' This would be followed by a cry from her heart, 'Oh Frank! Frank, come back!'

Voices came to her now with startling suddenness from the scullery. It was Larry, going for Lottie again. He was trying to clean the place ready for the woman coming – a woman was coming to take charge of her house. She would open all the drawers and take out the good stuff and use it for every day; and help herself – they all helped themselves, and her good china and dinner ware would be broken and chipped.

This thought spurred her to fresh effort, and she had moved her body to the side of the bed and was struggling to rise when Larry came into the room.

'What you trying to do? There's plenty of time for that.' He lifted her up straight again, then said, 'Come on; drink this.'

His voice was kind but stiff, and as she took the cup of milk from him with her good hand and lay sipping it, she thought, I've made him into an old man; he'll never be young again. And as Jessie had, so she said to herself, I'd rather have seen him gone with the other one. I would, I would. He's tied for life, and he knows he is – it's written all over him –

and even if in time he forgot her and wanted any woman, who'd take him with this saddle on his back? Three helpless creatures and another coming! Oh, my God! What was to become of them? If he'd only married Jessie things would have been different, Jessie would have looked after them. But he had come to hate Jessie. She had seen it in his eyes and heard it in his voice when he went for Lot this morning when she gave herself away about being over the road. What if he carried out his threat and sent Lot away? Oh no, no. She could get angry with Lot, but she couldn't bear the thought of her being sent away, even if it was just to be boarded somewhere. She had looked after Lot all these years. And she wasn't daft or barmy, just silly, just silly. And yet not so silly . . . she had a big heart, had Lot. What had she done last night anyway? – only gone over to Jessie's. And she'd always gone to Jessie's.

And in the kitchen this was just what Lottie was repeating between her bursts of weeping: 'I've always gone to Jessie's, Larry.'

She was whimpering to herself now, as she sipped at her cocoa, and Larry turned on her, his voice low and rasping. 'Shut up, will you, Aunt Lot? I won't tell you again. I've warned you mind, what will happen. Go on into the room.'

Lottie, still sniffing, obediently rose and went out, and Larry, dropping on to the stool she had vacated, rested his head in his hands.

From whichever way he looked at it life was like a nightmare. He could see no end to the chaos. It did not really matter a great deal what he did, there was no longer a path along which he could direct his efforts. He went to work; he came back to the house – he did not even think of it as a home now – he saw to his own meals, for he had forbidden Lottie to make any more attempts at cooking, and he had also kindly but firmly refused to accept any more meals for himself from the neighbours, saying that he could manage. But he did not refuse them for his mother.

His threats to send Lottie away were merely idle threats, for even if he could find a home for her, he knew his mother would resist any such move to a point that could easily cause her end. But about Lena's child – he did not think of it as Jack's – he had no such scruples. His mother would just have to put up with whatever could be done in that quarter. The child had cried a lot of late, which the doctor said was a good sign – a good sign of what? He was getting rid of it as soon as possible. No woman could be expected to put with it an' all, for she'd have her hands full with his mother and Aunt Lot. And it caused him to wonder if the woman would come in any case now on Monday to look round; it wasn't a very hopeful sign that she wouldn't put off going to the Gala in order to call today.

The Gala! All the years he had been at the pit he had never missed the Gala, although of late years he had harboured thoughts that certainly were not in unison with the mining community. While he had listened to speeches on the Labour Party's policy he had thought, What is it all but a lot of hooey?

Whatever they do for us they do a darn sight more for themselves. Public-spirited, me foot. The ones that are out of the pit are climbing on their knowledge. I don't blame them for that, it's all this talk about living to serve that makes me sick.

But today he did not think along these lines, for in his imagination he was walking behind the Lodge banner, staring at the fluttering black crêpe that told of the men who had followed the band last year but who would follow it no more. He could see Jack, in particular, walking proudly, looking up at the hotel balcony on which the Labour speakers would be standing, accompanied this year by the visiting Russian delegates. Jack had liked such spectacles; he had liked the noise, the shouting, the drinking and the laughing; and today when the hundred thousand miners and their families swelled Durham to suffocation there would be all that.

For himself he had liked to go to the service in the Cathedral. Jack had always chided him, saying, 'Why, man, you're a bit of a hypocrite; you never put your nose inside the church door but on Gala day.' And it was true, he didn't, yet the Cathedral had always held an attraction for him. Although he hated the pit, he was proud in an odd kind of way that, as a miner, the Cathedral was his. And he had, over the years, made himself acquainted with its history, and when standing in a tightly packed throng the music and emotion would lift him out of his cynical self, and he would feel the impression of the centuries in the breath-taking, over-powering splendour of the stone pillars. And although likely he would be stuck right behind one, he knew from where each echo came. That one would be from the Chapel of the Nine Altars, where sat the Founder of Durham's University, William Van Humbert, cast in his academic white marble; or he would see in his mind's eye the galleried chapel with the altar of Our Lady of Pity and St Peter, crucified head downwards. Last year Pam had stood close pressed to him, and after the service was over he had walked her to the Miners' Memorial, for she admitted that although she had been in the Cathedral she had never looked at it.

> 'He breaketh open a shaft from where men
>   sojourn.
> They are forgotten by the feet that passeth by.'

Already they would be forgotten in the hectic jollification in Durham today, for those nearest and dearest to the dead would not be there, while for the rest, Life must be lived. The latter either would already have got over their particular sorrow or it was yet to come.

His memory having touched on Pam, a licence forbidden it except in the dead of the night, do what he might now he could not press her away into temporary oblivion. He felt her near him – it was as if his arms had just released her – and the gnawing ache and emptiness rushed upon him again and brought him to his feet. He began to move about the scullery continuing the job he had been on with, that of trying to bring some semblance of tidiness into the muddle of crockery, pans, and food; but suddenly the ache became umbearable and he tore out and up the stairs to his room. Yet once inside, he could not immediately indulge his personal feelings, for the unmade bed, the dust and untidiness, shouted at him and he stood looking about him like a bewildered stranger. He put his hands on his head and muttered words unintelligible even to himself; then dropping on to the side of the bed he said quietly, as if he were reasoning with another person, 'This can't go on. You'll go off your head. If that woman doesn't come you'll have to get somebody.' Then, from the depths of his tortured self, the voice that was for ever crying 'Pam! Pam!' came tearing up through his being to the surface, and with her name on his lips he turned and buried his head in the pillow, and with his hands gripping their fill of feathers he writhed until with a gasp he drew in a great breath, then lay still.

When after some time he rose from the bed, he went and stood near the window. He could look out today without any fear of being seen, for the street was deserted. He stared at the cottages opposite, and his eyes went to Willie's door. Of the losses he had sustained in the past weeks that of Willie was not the least. Willie's death had left a soreness behind that was not present in the miss of his father or of Jack, for Willie had loved him. The word sounded unmanly and strange, yet he knew it to be true. And the feeling Willie's loss had left on him was also akin to betrayal, for had he not gone off on that particular day he would undoubtedly have been with him and the deputy. Mrs Macintyre had passed him in the street the other day without as much as a nod; a cut which was like a slap in the face. She, too, thought he should be where Willie was now. It would have been no use telling her he wished to God he was; that he envied the dead their peace, their release from responsibility. No more had they to strive to get through a day, then strive with equal intensity to seek oblivion at night. Why, he asked of the empty street, should he have been picked out to shoulder the dead weight he now carried? Hadn't he the right of a man to make his own life? What had he done that everything should have gone wrong for him?

As if in answer, there came into his line of vision the figure of Jessie. She was not dressed in her best, for she was returning from the shop, yet her clothes were not the drab garments he associated with her. His immediate reaction at the sight of her was to step back into the shadow, but he checked it, for the curtains were drawn almost together; he could not be seen, or his reactions noticed. If, prior to his return home, he had stopped to dissect his feelings about Jessie, he would have said they consisted mainly of pity mingled with remorse for having hurt her; but now the sight of her evoked neither pity nor remorse, what he felt was resentment, keen resentment against her. He did not remember the years of her devotion, but he remembered her look when she confronted him under the lamp and laid the blame for Aunt Lot's behaviour at his door. It could have been yesterday that it happened, so fresh in his mind was her scorn of him. As he watched her go indoors he thought, Well, she's got her own back all right. She must be crowing and thinking differently about her mother's tracts now: 'As ye sow so also shall ye reap.' I've proved that one for her. Yet she herself had played fast and loose with Willie, if all tales were true. Faint snatches of conversation overheard came back to him. Jessie Honeysett was going strong with the minister, and Ma Macintyre had gone for her. The minister, they had said, was a catch in a lifetime for the likes of Jessie. And he was a fine fellow an' all.

He remembered the minister. They had knelt side by side, but for different reasons, more than once during those dreadful days, but he had not thought of him then in connection with Jessie. Now he thought maliciously, He'll look like her son, not her man.

A cry from downstairs brought him to the door, and when he reached the landing Lottie was at the foot of the stairs crying, 'Larry! Larry! It's Betty. She's something stuck in her throat – it's choking her.'

He stilled the retort 'That's the best thing that could happen' and going down the stairs none too hastily he went into the kitchen, and there he saw the child really choking. She was blue in the face and gasping for breath. From the front room came his mother's agitated cries: 'Tip! Tip her . . . up . . . upside down.'

He had never yet touched the child – to him it was a repulsive thing, something not quite human. It was as much as he could do to make himself look at it now. Its face was swelling, and in another few minutes it would undoubtedly be gone. He looked coldly down on to the struggling child and repeated to himself, 'This is the best thing that could happen,' and stepping in front of Lottie, with his arm outstretched, he stopped her from picking it up, and said with strange quietness, 'Get a glass of water.'

Even by the time she came back it would be too late.

The child's gasping and choking were horrible, and he could not bear to look at it for one moment longer. And he was turning from the sight of it when his mother's voice came at him. It came with the force of a blow in his back, seeming to come from just behind him, and the words were almost coherent: 'Pick the child up – do you hear me?'

He swung swiftly round and looked across the passage to see her standing on her feet, clinging on to the foot of her bed. The wild look in her eyes bored into him across the distance, frightening him, as big as he was, and as swiftly again he turned to the pram and whipping the child up he held it by its feet, as he had seen her do with Gracie when a baby, given to convulsions. The surprise at seeing his mother on her feet was forgotten for a moment, for the child, after holding its breath for what seemed an age to him, made a great hawking sound, reminiscent of an old man, and out of its mouth spurted a hard crust of bread, the remains of Lottie's pacifier.

Lottie, rushing back up the passage, gave another

cry, but it was the sight of Jinny on her feet again that caused it. The glass tipped and fell to the floor and she let it lie there – Jinny took precedence and the needs of the child were forgotten for the moment. She rushed into the room to her sister, crying, 'Oh, Jinny! Oh, Jinny! You're up. Eeh, it's a miracle.'

'Help me back.' Jinny's speech was thick, and as she clung on to the bed with Lottie clutching at her in clumsy assistance, she said, 'Bring the child. Go on . . . bring it.'

Before Jinny was half settled in the bed Lottie excitedly rushed to do her bidding. She came into the kitchen, laughing and crying the words at the same time: 'Everything will be all right now.' Then she stopped, pushing the tears of her mixed emotions up her cheeks with the back of her hand. Larry was nursing the bairn . . . he had it in his arms. 'Eeh, Larry,' she said quietly, 'that's the first time I've seen you nurse her.'

'Be quiet, and pick that glass up, and get a cloth for that water.'

'Yes, Larry . . . Jinny wants her. It's wonderful, she was standing . . . All right, I'm going.' She dashed out of the room, exclaiming as she went, 'Eeh, it's wonderful.'

Larry moved awkwardly towards the pram. The child was breathing evenly now, and as he looked down on it, it turned its head slowly and pushed its face into his shirt until he could feel the soft warmth of it coming through to his skin, then the small fist opened and shut as it clutched at the air, and he noticed that the nails were dirty, and not only the nails but the skin between the fingers held dirt too.

Jinny's voice came again from the bedroom. 'Bring her in here,' it said.

Larry hesitated a moment before deliberately putting the child into the pram again; then going out of the room without once raising his eyes to the bed across the passage, he went into the scullery and said to Lottie, 'Go and tell my mother you'll bring her in directly; she's going to have a bath.'

Lottie went out exclaiming excitedly, and Larry, going to the roller towel on the back of the door, rubbed his face vigorously with it, and in rubbing the sweat away he tried to erase the memory of the past few minutes.

The preservation of life is strong in all pitmen, for they are consistently trying to prolong it in themselves and often fighting a battle to preserve it for others; yet he had come near to taking a life in that he had made no effort to save it. But for his mother's voice the child would now be dead. He did not think, as he had done a few moments earlier, it would have been better so. His mind had shut down temporarily on the trial the child's existence was to the household and to himself in particular; he only knew that there was a strong feeling of relief in him that his conscience had escaped carrying this further burden.

The woman came on Monday. She came while Larry was at work, and it lay to Lottie to show her round. The woman looked long and hard at Jinny. She

295

looked long and hard at the child. She took a cup of tea that Lottie made for her and she laughed with her; then she left, leaving a message for Larry. The message was: 'Tell him it would be too much for me. It's me back; I couldn't see to her.'

15

RANCOUR OF REMORSE

The summer had passed. It had been a wonderful summer, everyone felt there had not been one like it for years, but there were those who said they would be glad to see it snow, and they thanked goodness that the nights were cold now which entailed . . . a big fire.

Whereas a hard winter is often said to kill the germs of illnesses, the rarer event of a hot summer is thought to multiply them. Bill Catley, looking down on Larry where he sat in the first-aid post, said, 'It's been the heat, man; it's been too much . . . underneath and on top an' all. You can't stand a double dose all the time. Why, I felt pretty much the same meself last week. How do you feel now?'

'Not so bad.'

'You go back home and turn in.'

'No, I'll be all right.'

'All right be damned! You look like a corpse. And it isn't the first time you've been like this lately. You go and see the doctor afore he comes and sees you. That's the damned funny thing about it: a third of wor blokes what fill the surgeries are swinging the lead, as brazen as brass they are about it an' all. Why, man, I'd be ashamed. They didn't stoop to owt like that in my young days . . . if we were bad we had to work it off, for it was work or starve then. But now . . . why, man, they divvn't knaw they're born. And I told them at the Lodge the other night they'd be sorry. It's the swing of the pendulum, I said. It's been swinging t'other side for a long time but it's bound to follow the law of gravity and swing back. And who'll be acting as its earth pull? I said. Why, the very ones who are filling the doctors' surgeries now for certificates. There I go, ranting on; but there's some of them gets me goat. Get yersel up, Larry, and gang hyem and take a few days off; I can vouch for you all right. An' don't you be a bloomin' fool. You think over what I was saying to you yesterday. With your headpiece you'd do much more good up top knocking sense into some of the hot-heads. I mentioned you to Davy Powell last night and he said to look him up. He could give you a push, could Davy.'

Larry got to his feet, wiping the sweat from his face as he did so. 'It's good of you, Bill, but I'm not the man you want for that job. There's dozens already in the Union breaking their necks to climb. Count me out; I've enough troubles.'

'You're a fool, Larry.'

'Aye, I might be, but you can only fight for something if you think it's worth fighting for.'

'Why, man, don't say that . . . we're all in this together, no matter what the hotheads say.'

Larry, slowly buttoning up his coat, said quietly, 'I'm in it because I must, that's all. If I could make as much at any other job within twenty miles I'd leave the pit tomorrow.'

On his way to the door he nodded to the first-aid attendant, saying, 'Thanks, Barney.' Then, turning to where Bill stood watching him, he said, 'Thanks all the same, Bill, and I'll try and get in tomorrow.'

'That's all right, Larry. You take it easy.' The old man watched him leave, and then turning to Barney, he said confidentially, 'He's two different kinds of a fool, and if he doesn't come up top soon he'll go up top.' He patted his forehead. 'You mark my words.'

A drizzle was falling as Larry walked along the main road, and he took off his cap to let the rain cool his head. Bill had said take it easy. That's what he wanted to do, take it easy; say To hell with everything – with work and worry and feeling, especially feeling. What was going to be the end of it all? Marry Clara? He let out a harsh laugh that startled a passer-by who turned a head in his direction.

Clara was the third housekeeper he had had in four months, and Clara was bent on marrying him; indeed she hardly bothered to cover up her aims. Every day he heard of the offers she had received to look after Mr So-and-So who lived alone. She had been a widow for eighteen months, and her desire once more to become a wife would have been laughable had it not also been frightening. Even though he would not admit to himself that he was scared of Clara, nevertheless he was. Once or twice lately he had had the strong urge to go and get drunk, really blind, but what he might do or say under the influence both of the drink and of Clara had deterred him.

He was feeling now that some of the present strain would ease if he could go in and say 'Pack and get out!' But should he do so it would mean starting all over again to find someone else. If it had meant just housekeeping for himself he knew he wouldn't have had much bother, but the three inhabitants of the house seemed to frighten off any but those who were badly pushed for a home, or those who saw in him, as Clara had done, a future husband. But afraid of her or not, there was one thing he was determined to have out with her as soon as he felt fit enough, and that was the bills. It was costing just twice as much to run the house now as it had done in his mother's managing days. Clara was a good enough cook, and he couldn't complain about the food but the amount of stuff she ordered was colossal. When, a fortnight ago, he had tentatively approached the subject she had said, 'Well, I can't do on less; Lot eats like a horse. She must be carrying a regiment.' But what did it matter? All he wanted at the present moment was to get his head down.

He went into the Galloping Fawn, and calling for a double whisky he drank it in one go; then made his way home, telling himself he would sweat this out.

He was never afterwards sure what made him stop at the scullery window. A broad slit of light was showing where the curtains had not been pulled together, and through it he caught a glimpse of two figures. They could have been Clara and Lottie, but something about the second figure's height and width showed him it wasn't Aunt Lot. The woman was short and fat and not unlike his mother. It was this resemblance that made him pause. Then it was the keen activity in the scullery that drew his attention. A large attaché-case stood on the narrow scullery table and into it Clara was packing food. He saw her put in numerous tins and bags, then he watched her stand on a chair and bring from the back of a high shelf on which a conglomeration of articles was usually stored a bottle of sauce and another of pickles. So that was it! No wonder the bills were high.

For a moment he checked a swift move towards the door. If he exposed the little game she would go, and then where would he be? Rid of her, he told himself. But when he went to push open the door he found to his amazement that it was locked; so taking his knuckles he rapped twice on it. Following this, however, not a whisper or a sound came to him, and not till after he had knocked twice again did he hear Clara's voice, and now it came from the direction of the kitchen: 'Wait a minute, can't you! What's all your hurry?'

Clara's surprise on opening the door was quite genuine. 'Larry! You . . . what's the matter?'

He did not answer her, but pushing her to one side went straight through the scullery and into the kitchen. The woman was sitting there with the case by her side. But Clara, forcing her way past him, said brightly, 'This is me sister from Gateshead – you

haven't met – she just dropped in. You're not looking
too good . . . you shouldn't have gone. I told you
Well' – she indicated a chair – 'sit yourself down; I'
get you something.'

Her tone implied two things: she was evidentl
nervous, but she was mistress of the house.

Larry looked from her to the woman who wa
smiling inanely at him, then with a swift movemen
he bent to lift the case from her side up on to th
table, but its weight checked his swing and in a flash
the woman's hands were over his.

'Here, what you doing? Leave me case alone.'

Clara, too, now had her hands on the case. 'Put i
down!' she said. 'That's a nice way to treat my visitor
Well, I must say! What's up with you? Look, leav
go.'

'You leave go.' With a sweep of his arm he knocke
them both aside, and lifting the case on to the tabl
he opened it.

'Those are my groceries,' said the woman in
dignantly.

'Yours!' He turned on her. 'Yours? What I've pai
for, and have been doing for weeks.'

'I can have you up for that. You be careful wha
you're saying.' Clara was now playing the part of th
wronged woman; her prim neatness was bristling.

'Get your things and get out!'

'What?'

'You heard what I said.'

'I won't. I want notice.'

'You've had all the notice you're getting.'

302

'Oh, have I? That's where you're mistaken.'

Larry rounded on her, his eyes narrowed and his voice deep in his throat. 'If you're not gone within fifteen minutes I'll call the police.'

The little woman became agitated. 'I wouldn't stay where he was, Clara, if I was you. Get your things and come on. Go on, do.' She pushed at her sister and Clara, after looking at Larry for a moment, flung round crying, 'You won't hear the last of this. I'll make you pay dearly for this, just you wait and see.'

Turning to the case once again, he tipped the whole of the contents on to the table, and the woman, snatching at a brown paper bag, cried, 'That's mine, that's me wool.'

He looked at the food. There was, he made a rough guess, about three pounds' worth; butter, boiled ham, gammon, sugar, tea, even a tin of lambs' tongues. And this, he had not the slightest doubt, had been going every week.

In less than the time he had given her Clara was downstairs again. She was red in the face and looked furious. There were no tears about her. 'I want me pay,' she demanded.

'I paid you in advance, and you got it on Saturday. I pay you no more.'

'You . . . !' She came out with a string of invective that left him blinking, for he had never heard her swear before.

'Get going!' he said.

She got going, and as she passed the front-room door she glared towards Jinny, where she was sitting

303

in a chair before the fire, holding tightly on to Lottie; and she cried back at Larry, 'I wish you luck with your handful. You'll never get anybody to do what I did, never.'

The door banged and they were gone, and after a moment during which he stood passing his hand alternately through his hair and across his mouth he went slowly into the front room, and Lottie, released from Jinny's grip, came rushing to him.

'They locked the scullery door an' all, and I couldn't get in. She always did that when she came . . . her sister. Oh, Larry, are you bad?'

He went to his mother and said, 'I'll find somebody. She's been helping herself all along.'

'Sit down, lad, sit . . . sit down,' said Jinny. She felt tired with holding on to Lottie in an endeavour to stop her from interfering. She had known that if Clara was given enough rope she would hang herself, but she hadn't thought it would come about so soon. And she felt a great relief now that Clara was out of the house, for she knew what women were, women who had lost their men and were still young enough to crave for another. Clara had made no bones about her intentions, and a man in Larry's state of mind, Jinny had thought, would be capable of any folly.

'You're not well, lad,' she said.

'A bit off colour, that's all.'

'Go and . . . see the doctor.'

'No, I'll go to bed and sweat it out.'

'You won't sweat out . . . out what you've got. Go to the doctor.'

'All right,' he said. 'And don't worry, I'll find somebody, somewhere.'

'I'm not worrying,' she said, 'not . . . not about that. But go to the doctor. And look—' She pulled herself slowly to her feet and, taking three shaky steps, said, 'That's better, isn't it?'

'Yes, fine. Yes' – he tried to show some enthusiasm – 'but don't overdo it, and you'll be out and about in no time.'

'Yes, yes, I will.'

'Will I make you some tea, Larry?' asked Lottie.

'No. The quicker I go the quicker I'll get back. Do you think you could put those things away off the table and put them in their right places?'

'Oh yes, Larry, course I can.'

She went out airily, and he followed, saying over his shoulder to Jinny, 'I won't be long.'

Jinny waited till she heard his step going along the side of the house and the front gate click, then she called sharply, 'Lottie! Lottie!'

Lottie came running in from the kitchen, 'Yes, Jinny? Oh, isn't it nice to have the house ours again? Oh! I didn't like her, I didn't. Oh, the things she made me . . .'

'Sit down.'

'Yes, Jinny.'

'Now listen, and pay . . . pay heed to what I'm saying. I want you to go over to Jessie's and say . . . say . . . Jinny says will . . . will you come over a minute?'

'To Jessie's? But, Jinny, Jessie won't come across here.'

'Be quiet . . . and . . . do . . . do what I tell you . . . and don't say Larry's bad and he's gone to the doctor's or . . . or anything. Just say what I tell you.'

There was hardly any hesitation now in Jinny's speech, she was sounding almost like the old Jinny, and Lottie replied the same as she had always done, 'Yes, Jinny.'

She went into the scullery, and taking an old raincoat from the back of the door she put it over her head and went out. The rain was coming down heavily and she stood crouched in Jessie's doorway as she knocked rapidly on the door.

Jessie, opening the door and seeing who it was, exclaimed, 'Why, Aunt Lot! You're drenched. Why are you out on a night like this?'

'Jinny sent me, Jessie. Eeh, the drops'll wet all your floor . . . your nice carpet.'

'That's all right. Come on into the kitchen.'

In the kitchen, she took the coat from Lottie's shoulders, saying, 'Jinny sent you? What for, Aunt Lot?'

There was no eager enquiry in her tone – Lottie had likely been upsetting the housekeeper and Jinny had sent her out of the way.

'She said for you to come over, Jessie.'

Jessie was on her way to the scullery with the coat, and she turned very slowly about and repeated, 'Jinny said that?'

'Yes.'

'You're mistaken, Aunt Lot.'

'I'm not, Jessie, that's what she said.'

'But she knows I couldn't.'

'Larry's not in.'

'That doesn't matter – he'd soon find out I had been. I couldn't, Aunt Lot.'

'But Jinny's set on it, Jessie – I can always tell when she's set on a thing. And it isn't about me, Jessie – she doesn't want you to take care of me or anything, 'cause we've been fine lately. She's even talked to me about the bairn coming. She's going to make some things. She's been lovely to me. Just now and again when she got mad she'd go for me, but I didn't mind, Jessie. I didn't mind. She didn't like Clara, and she stuck up for me when Clara went for me for not doing things. She told her she was being paid for it. Four pounds Larry gave her a week, and then she was pinching all the stuff.'

'Has Mrs Barrett left?'

'Yes, Larry sent her flying.'

Jessie turned from Lottie, and said softly, 'Where is he now, what shift is he on?'

'Night shift, Jessie.'

'What does Jinny want to see me about?'

'I don't know, Jessie.'

'Are you sure?'

'Yes, honest. Honest, Jessie. That's all she said to me, honest, Jessie.'

Jessie moved the coat about in her hand, and she muttered, 'I can't go. No, I can't.'

'Oh, Jessie, it won't take you a minute, and

nobody'll see you. It's pouring cats and dogs and nobody'll be out.'

Jessie stood pondering. If this invitation had come six weeks ago she would have taken it, for up till then she had been unable to quench the faint embers of hope that periodically glowed in her, but after having come face to face with him she had no longer fanned the ember but had faced the situation squarely. He hated the sight of her. She had been going along the main road to catch the Newcastle bus at Pelham's Corner when he had come out of Brown's, the chemists. Only by turning completely about could he have avoided her, and as he came on his eyes had looked at her with a dark, bitter light in them. It was as if he loathed her. She had stood by the bus stop trembling, and had told herself that it was final, that she didn't need any more proof. Yet in the night she had asked herself why . . . why should he hate her? The boot should be on the other foot. Did he hate her because she no longer dressed like a tramp? And she had retracted for a moment, thinking, I would dress like ten tramps . . . if . . . But no. She had not allowed herself to finish, but had stated firmly, 'I'll never be less than I am now, never! I won't go back . . . for him, nor no-one else.'

'Are you coming, Jessie?'

'No, Aunt Lot.'

'Aw, Jessie.'

'Tell Jinny that I can't. She'll understand.' And she placed the coat about Lottie's head again and gently led her to the front door.

308

When Jinny received the message she bit on her knuckles for a moment; then said, 'Give me . . . the pencil.'

Lottie handed her a pencil and pad from the mantelpiece, saying, 'She says it's no use, Jinny, she can't come. She's frightened of seeing Larry, I think, but I told her he wasn't in; I said he was on night shift.' Lottie preened herself at her cleverness and rested her arms on top of the mound of her stomach while she watched Jinny slowly writing on the pad.

Jinny's mind was back to normal, even if her body wasn't, and for weeks now there had been nagging at her the thought that there must be something she could do to make her son's life bearable, and the only answer that had come to her mind was for her to . . . get on her feet again and take the burden of the house off him, for it was the burden of the house as much as his private misery, she felt, that was getting him down. And then when Lottie brought her the news that the minister had left the town and Jessie had not gone with him she immediately began to scheme. If Larry and Jessie could be brought together; if they could but speak, just speak, things would right themselves, for if Jessie had refused the minister there was only one answer, she still loved Larry. Emily King had said it was because she had been offered a partnership in the shop that she had refused the minister, a partnership such as that was too good a chance to miss, and she was wise to keep in with old Miss Barrington for she was rolling in money; but Jinny could not think that Jessie had given up the chance of becoming the minister's wife but for one reason. At this point Larry had engaged Clara, and of the three housekeepers Clara had been the most dangerous. But now she was gone, and thanks be to God for it.

'There' – she folded the note – 'slip across . . . with that. And . . . and don't come back without her . . . Go on.'

Once again Lottie left the house, and Jinny, her hands locked in her lap, sat and waited. She looked about the room. Jessie would get a shock when she saw the place. It wasn't dirty, but it was far from clean, as she meant clean. There was no sheen, and not a flower anywhere. But that hadn't been Clara's fault. Larry couldn't stand the sight of flowers – even her big geranium had upset him, actually made him retch. Larry was bad, not in his body but in his mind. He had never been the same since the accident. They said that the men never got over what they saw, on top of which he was carrying the knowledge that he had quarrelled with his father the last time that he saw him alive. This would have been enough without Pam Turnbull. She was back in America now, Emily King said, and going to have a baby. Jinny shut her mind down on this; she would not question who the child's father would be.

A wail from the kitchen made her turn towards the room door. Betty had woken. Well, she'd have to cry till Lottie came in. But here they were now, coming in the back way. She moved excitedly in her chair. Why couldn't Lottie use the front door? She had gone out that way. The excitement rose in her, bringing a smile to her face. It would be good to see Jessie again at close quarters. She had always liked Jessie, even, she thought at times, more than her own daughters, for they had never been very mindful of her.

When Larry filled the room doorway Jinny gaped in surprise. This would put it all wrong. Jessie was to be sitting quietly talking to her when Larry should walk in, and when they had spoken to each other everything would be all right. He wouldn't even go for her for sending for Jessie. Not that he ever went for her. He might go for Lot, but with her he was always gentle.

'Where's Aunt Lot? The child's raising the house.'

Jinny turned to the fire. 'She won't be a minute, she's just gone out on an errand. You're back quick. Was the surgery empty?'

'No. Packed out. I couldn't stand and wait, I'll go in the morning. The things are still on the table; I asked her to put them away. Oh, what's the use!' He turned into the kitchen and going to the pram picked up the child.

It was strange, but the flat, pushed-in face was no longer repulsive to him. He often held her now, and he felt that she knew him, for she always became quiet when he looked at her. At such times he seemed to sense a faint glimmer of intelligence coming into its eyes, but that it would only ever remain a glimmer he knew only too well. There was nothing about the child that made him think 'That's our Jack', yet it was as if when he lifted her, he was once again 'minding Jack'. The kinship that had been between Jack and himself was there between the child and him, and he had in the past weeks come to understand how his mother could not bear that the child should be taken away.

'There, there,' he said; 'you'll be changed. Be quiet now. There, there.'

The child's low whimpering ceased, and he took a napkin from a pile on the top of the sewing machine and, sitting down, began to change her. He had just dropped the dirty napkin on to the floor when he heard Lottie coming in by the front way. He heard the door close and Lottie's voice saying, 'She's in the front room.' He turned his head a little to see who was with Lottie because all the usual visitors to the house certainly knew where his mother was; at the same time he tried to hide his efforts, for he didn't like to be caught doing a job like this. And then the child seemed to spring from his knee, and it was only by the quick clutch of his hand that he caught her. He was on his feet, the child half-naked hanging over one arm while in the other he held the napkin. His entire face looked on fire as he gazed at Jessie.

It was close on three years since she had been in this house, and the Jessie Honeysett looking at him now was in no way connected with the docile, adoring woman whom he had courted since she was a girl and he a boy. Although her face was flushed she appeared to him composed, even uppish. He could see her thinking again along the lines of her mother's tracts – 'and the mighty have been brought low'. This must be a crowning satisfaction to her, to see him having to change a bairn, he who had turned her down for someone smart, intelligent, and beautiful, someone who had twice thrown him aside. Hadn't she already got enough of her own back without having to see him do this?

'What do you want here?' His voice whipped her with its anger, and she did not immediately answer. Then, glancing at Lottie, she said quietly, 'I came to see your mother.'

'You should wait until you're asked.'

'I was asked.'

Jessie's face was drained as white as a piece of linen now, and she turned to the room door where Jinny was standing holding on to the framework with both hands; and Jinny's eyes were beseeching her with some message she could not read.

'I sent . . . for Jessie. It was me . . . I sent twice. I wanted to see . . . her.'

Larry's infuriated gaze passed on to his mother. He seemed on the point of saying something; then, turning from them all, he went to the pram and almost threw the child into it.

After one look at Jinny, Jessie went along the passage again and out of the door, and as it closed behind her Jinny slowly shuffled into the kitchen, and there, looking at her son, she said, 'You'll live . . . to regret . . . the night. The only one . . . in the world who's . . . been any good to you . . . or could be still . . . and you spit on her. When . . . when . . . you should go down on your knees for all the wrong you

313

did her . . . There was still a chance . . . up to now
. . . you could have had her back. She let the minister
go . . . there was a chance . . . but not now. I could
see it in her face . . . she has a . . . a pride in her now.
You're my own son but . . . but you're a fool.'

He remained standing with his back to her, and
when he heard her shuffling into the room and the
unusual procedure of the door closing behind her, he
went and sat down by the table and, putting his hands
on it, he locked them like two steel bands together.
There was a rhythmic opening and shutting in his
head – he felt tormented, burnt out, ill; he felt . . .
Just how did he feel? He stared at his clenched fists.
Why had he acted like that? Why did he always
become enraged now at the sight or thought of her?
It wasn't right; he knew it wasn't right. That feeling
should have been kept for the other one, but it seemed
as if he couldn't think of Pam clearly at all now in
any way. At times he had great difficulty in even
recalling what she looked like, and yet she remained
as a heavy dull ache that he felt would never leave
him. And although the ache became activated by
bitterness at times, it was not Pam's conduct that
caused this feeling of humiliation that was constantly
with him now, but Jessie's. Jessie scorned him; she
was glad he was being paid out. Of late, he'd found
himself recalling how he had talked when he was
courting her. He had been the big fellow who was
going to 'break eggs with a stick', the chap who was
going to use his brains. And what had he done? He
was a pitman still, and likely to remain one all his

living days. He knew why he hated her, because she sat snugly in her little cottage and watched the tables being turned on him. She was going up, effortlessly up, while he . . .

Lottie came into the room and now she, too, closed the door and stood looking towards him, her hands as usual resting on her stomach. Lottie's pregnancy should have made her a grotesque sight. Her arms, legs, neck, and face all remained long bony structures, while her stomach and hips were of such roundness as to make her a caricature of a Dickens character. Yet her condition had brought to her a comeliness and had seemed to steady somewhat her mercurial mind. Her flashes of penetrating simplicity were more frequent, and at this moment some inner guidance told her that her Larry needed help, and that she was not to be afraid of his temper or outbursts as she sometimes was, but she was to talk to him like the day Jinny let her tell him that Pam Turnbull was back. She went to him and put her hand on his shoulder.

'Larry.'

He made no answer, but moved his arm as if to shove her off.

'Larry, don't take on. I had a job to get her to come, but Jinny wanted to see her, and she won't think worse of you seeing you change Betty.'

He moved his head from side to side but did not turn on her demanding that she should be quiet, and so she went on, 'Jessie's smart and looks nice now . . . lovely, and her name's been painted on the flower-shop next to Miss Barrington's, but she still wears a green overall in the shop and she's not stuck up about it or anything. She's always the same, is Jessie; she's always lovely to me and I know she's the same inside.'

'Aunt Lot.'

His voice sounded tired, but there was no reprimand in it, and she said, 'I know. I know, Larry, you're bad and that's why you went for Jessie, and she's upset. But she's done nothing, only been kind.'

'All right, Aunt Lot; all right.' His head moved in a rocking motion downwards towards the table.

'Jessie still loves you, Larry; that's why she wouldn't marry the minister.'

His head stopped moving; it was as if he were listening.

'She nearly cried the night I let on you stopped me coming across, but she didn't. But I knew she would have a good cry after I went, like I do in bed at nights after Jinny's been on at me. And now Jessie won't ever come back over here, not again she won't. It's as Jinny said, she's the same Jessie but she's different. You know what I mean.' She waited, looking down on his beloved head. Then softly she brought out, 'But you, Larry . . . you could go over on the quiet, and you could tell her you didn't mean it.'

There . . . she had said it, and he hadn't turned on her. She waited for him to bounce up knocking the chair over as he did so, but instead his head fell quite suddenly on to his arms, and to her complete amazement, Larry, her Larry, began to cry, a crying that you could hear, not the quiet kind that he had done over the accident, but a noise that filled the room and spurted from his mouth and eyes with such intensity that for the moment she was afraid. She watched him bite on his arm, and her face twisted up and her own tears flowed. 'Larry, Larry, don't.' Her arms went around him and she pulled his head to her, and he hid his face on her breast. And she held him tightly to her, trying to stifle the terrible sound, and she talked as she would have done to Betty: 'There now, there now, it's all right,' only this time she added, 'When you go over you'll feel better, I know you will. I know you will, Larry.'

A faint trace of light was coming into the sky. He watched it through the frame of curtains. It was the longest night he had experienced in his life. He had woken out of a feverish doze about half-past one and, being unable to sleep again, had got up and sat by the window . . . and thought. And his self-inflicted dissection had been anything but pleasant. Now he was waiting for a light to appear across the road. It would come on about half-past six, and when it did he knew what he must do.

During the war, when waiting for orders to attack, he had known this empty sick feeling, and the crossing of the road to Jessie's cottage would be an attack that would need courage, more courage than he possessed.

When the light came on in the upstairs room he rose and, going very quietly downstairs, made himself a cup of tea. He did not put on a collar and tie, but as when he had slipped across the street years ago so he went to go now, his shirt neck open, his coat thrown over it. Once outside the back door, he stood uncertain, and looked up at the sky and shivered. Then, pulling the collar of his coat over the bare skin of his chest, he slowly went down the path, out of the gate, and across the road.

After a long, fear-filled moment of hesitation he raised his hand and knocked once on the door.

And when there came no immediate answer he experienced a temporary feeling of relief and thought, 'Thank God, I couldn't face it anyway.' And shivering, he went to turn quietly away when the door opened, and Jessie stood there. She was wearing a thick, warm-looking, rose-coloured dressing-gown and her hair was tousled from the bed. She did not utter a sound, nor when he attempted to speak did any words come. His mouth was as dry as sand and his tongue seemed swollen. He could not remember saying 'Can I come in?' but slowly, as if in answer to a request, she stood back, pulling the door with her, and he, with head bowed, stepped into her house once more.

16

NO COMPROMISE

His heart, thumping against his ribs, demanded air, and he drew in a long slow breath and raised his head. He was in the kitchen, a room, he would have said, he knew as well as the kitchen of his own home; but even the shape of it seemed altered; it was as transformed with light and colour as was the woman before him. Somewhere in his mind he recognised that he had been building on finding the old Jessie, that once he was within the walls that had held her for so long she would reappear. But these walls were different walls, this house was a different house.

He looked at her with as much humility as he could gather, and said, 'I'm sorry, Jessie.'

She did not answer but returned his look, and her whole attitude baffled him. He had been a fool to come. It was as he'd thought, she was crowing . . . But Aunt Lot had said . . . Damn Aunt Lot! Suddenly he felt dizzy, and the room for a moment turned up end in a black sweep.

'Sit down.' She pulled a chair towards him, and he groped at it and sat down and put his hand to his head.

'I've got a cold coming on . . . I had to come over.

The way I spoke to you' – he kept his hand over his eyes – 'I'm sorry.'

'That's all right.'

The words sounded calmly indifferent. What more did she want him to say? What did she want him to do? Through a haze he looked up at her. She had not fallen on his neck with an 'Oh, Larry! Oh, Larry!'; this woman . . . this Jessie was not the old Jessie Honeysett, and the road back to her was going to be difficult, and in this moment all the resolve of the night vanished – he didn't want any more difficult roads, what he wanted were arms to hold him, hands to soothe him, and a voice to foster his self-pity, someone to mourn with him for his lost life, someone to tell him of the great things he could have achieved had he had the chance to travel, for how could a man write unless he travelled; he wanted someone to look after the house and those in it, to take the burden off his mind and shoulders . . . oh yes, he wanted someone to look after the house. And then he wanted someone to love him, love him just for himself like the old Jessie had done . . . God, he was going to pass out. No, by God, he wasn't, not here he wasn't, not in front of her . . . he must get over home.

'Here . . . drink this.'

He took the cup from her hand. He hadn't been aware that she had left the kitchen. It wasn't ordinary tea he was drinking, but was laced with something . . . brandy. Jessie with brandy in the house! That proved there was nothing left of the old Jessie. It was a wonder her mother didn't haunt her.

'Jessie.'

'Yes?'

'Do you hate me?'

He was looking down into the cup, and the answer when it came was not a definite no, holding forth promise, but a no that was calm, without emotion, and it caused him to think, Hell! I'm not doing it, I'm not going on my bended knees. What does she want anyway? I've come over, haven't I?

He thrust his hand out to put the cup on the table preparatory to rising, and was amazed to see it fall on to the floor and break into pieces. The table had seemed near enough.

Words of apology came into his mouth, but he couldn't speak them. His mind began to chant one word, Pam . . . Pam. Over and over it went . . . Pam . . . Pam. Getting louder . . . Pam . . . Pam, until it became a scream, and he put up his hands to stop it. But the chant engulfed him; it took on form and swirled about him in tongues of flame and fire . . . Pam . . . Pam . . . Pam . . . until in one great sweep of flame it bore him to the floor.

The bed was near the window – there was more light there should he wish to read or write. It had been Jessie's idea, and the curtains were not pulled so close as usual; he had only to turn his head and he could see across the street, past Mrs King's door one way and beyond Willie's the other. He still thought of the door of number ten as Willie's. He glanced at the clock. It said five minutes past one. In another few

minutes she'd be here. He was feeling a bit hungry
. . . It was odd to feel hungry; he hadn't bothered
whether he ate or drank during the last five weeks.
Had he been lying here only five weeks? It seemed
like five years, so much had happened within his
mind, so much torment, so much loneliness, so much
longing. And these feelings had been worse than any
such he had experienced when he was well. He knew
that they had been the aftermath of delirium, when
he had fought to hold Pam in his arms and pin her
beside him in the bed, when in nightmares of sweating
he screamed for her and woke to find Jessie, her
hands on him holding him down. It was then he
would cry out to her in his aloneness, 'Don't leave
me, Jessie! . . . Don't leave me, will you? . . . You
won't leave me?'

He could never clearly remember her answer, only
that what she had said made him feel safe. Sometimes
he would wake to find Mrs King or Mrs Patty by his
side . . . but they weren't Jessie. He found himself
watching the door for her coming; and then the street
as he had done years ago; and he didn't question
why.

Last week the doctor had said, 'In another week
you'll be on your feet; and then a couple of weeks'
convalescence at one of the homes and you'll be
yourself again.' It was strange and frightening when
he realised he did not want this week to pass. He did
not want to leave this bed, he wanted to lie here for
ever in this new calmness. He knew, without being
told, he had just escaped a serious mental breakdown;

he seemed to have worked it out in the severe bout of influenza. He had now a feeling of being drained; any effort, mental or physical, tired him. Jessie had said to him yesterday, 'Why don't you write?' . . . Write! He had felt hurt, slighted in some way – he wasn't well enough to write. And anyway, what was there to write about? . . . 'Write?' he had said. 'What can I write about?'

He had asked the question like a child, and he had kept his eyes fixed on her back as she moved around the room.

'Write a novel about Aunt Lot and everything.' Her voice was very level.

'About Aunt Lot? Who'd want to read it?'

'You never know.'

'What could there be of interest in it?' He had merely asked this question to hold her attention, to keep her in the room talking; he was not interested in what would be the substance of her answer. But when she had said, 'It's a way of life', he had thought, yes, there's something in that. And then she had gone on, her back still to him, 'If you were to write it all down, you'd get it out of your system, you'd feel better . . . Write everything.' She had paused. 'Everything about me, yourself, Aunt Lot, Willie . . . and Pam.' She had brought in the name as if it was of no more consequence than the others, then had gone on, 'Start with Aunt Lot. I feel that life revolves around Aunt Lot . . . And then the explosion.'

He had stared at her and said, 'Jessie. You don't

mind any more?' And she had answered, 'No, I don't mind any more.'

But what had she really meant by this? He didn't know now whether she still loved him or not. There was a strange elusiveness about her that constantly troubled him; it seemed to him as if she were waiting for something. But what was she waiting for? For him to say he wanted her? Well, couldn't she see he wanted her? He couldn't see life without her. The house . . . everything had altered because of her – she only went to the shop in the mornings now, while the rest of the time she cleaned and cooked and put things in order. He knew that he couldn't go back beyond five weeks ago when the burden of his mother, Aunt Lot, and the child lay on him, not to mention the house.

There she was, coming down the street now, looking younger than ever he remembered her. And his eyes came with her to her door, and when it closed on her he moved restlessly.

Lottie came into the room. She was panting slightly and laughing.

'You know, Larry, what I'm laughing at?'

'No.' He lay deep in his pillows looking at her lazily.

'He's kicking. He's been at it all morning. And Jinny says he's gonna be a footballer, and I should go and see about having him signed up.' She bent her long length forward and giggled and pressed her hands to her stomach; then added, 'Jessie's in. I've done all she said. The shepherd pie's lovely and brown on top, and the lemon sole's for you . . . Oh, the pie smells lovely. I put it in dead on eleven. She cooks lovely, does Jessie . . . You better, Larry? You've got some colour.'

He smiled at her and said, 'I feel a bit hungry.'

'Oh, do you, Larry; I'll tell Jinny. She'll be pleased to hear that.'

She went out, and he turned his head and lay looking out of the window. And as he did so a man came down the street and stopped at the door opposite. He was tall and slim and vital-looking, and the sight of him brought Larry up in the bed. It was the minister fellow.

When the door opened he saw Jessie's face, and she was smiling as she never smiled at him, and her hands were out, both of them, in welcome.

When the door shut them from his gaze he lay back. The indolent feeling had gone; his body was taut and his face tight. What could he be after? And the way she had looked at him, with her hands out . . . What if . . . ? No, no, not Jessie now. Jessie wouldn't do that . . . let him down. Not like Pam; Jessie was made of different stuff. He flung round in the bed. So was he. A few years ago he'd have knocked the man down who would have suggested that he would play the dirty on Jessie Honeysett.

It was fifteen minutes before Jessie's door again opened. He watched her come hurrying across the road, and when he heard her voice downstairs he waited with open impatience for her appearance. He was feeling all worked up, but that no doubt was

325

weakness, the result of the illness – the doctor had said he mustn't worry about anything, just to let things slide. Well, he wasn't going to worry, he wouldn't mention the fellow. Yet – the sweat broke out on his forehead – what if she went off with him? What would become of them all? The sweat rolled down his face, and when Aunt Lot came into the room with his tray he sat up and demanded, 'Where's Jessie?'

'She hasn't time to come up yet a bit, Larry. She's got a visitor, she's goin' over home for a bit. But she said she won't be long. Enjoy your dinner. I told Jessie you were hungry.'

Left alone with the tray he stared at it. The sight of the fish made him sick. Or had he been feeling sick before he saw it? He pushed the tray on to the table and lay looking at his hands clutching at the eider-down – they hadn't the strength to grip. They were white and boneless-looking; that fellow looked young and full of life . . . The thought brought a still greater feeling of weakness to his body. But Jessie wouldn't do that on him . . . she couldn't . . . That's exactly what she must have said about him when he was going mad over Pam Turnbull. Had he ever gone mad over Pam Turnbull? Yes . . . yes. Why start that hypocrisy; was there not a scar in his heart that would never be erased? But the wound pained no longer. At least not in the daytime; only sometimes in the night when there was no antidote to loneliness and he would see her standing cool and aloof looking at him. Jessie, too, was cool and aloof.

He brought himself up sharply in the bed. That was it. That was why she had given him no encouragement – there was the other fellow all the time. She had looked after him, as she would after anyone who threw himself on her mercy. And he had literally thrown himself on her mercy that morning he had passed out at her feet. And in showering her mercy on him she had thought to heap coals of fire on his head . . . He could see all her actions now smacking of the minister's influence.

When he heard the back door close he looked through the window, and there she was hurrying down the path, out of the gate and over the road. He waited until Lottie took the tray away, exclaiming loudly on the uneaten fish; then tentatively he put his legs over the side of the bed. There was only one thing for it, he'd have to go and see her, face that fellow and get things straight. He couldn't let her do this. If he was let down for the third time it'd drive him insane. He didn't deserve this; hadn't he suffered enough for what he had done to her?

With the aid of the bedrail he stood on his feet, and felt so weak that he immediately sank down again. God, he never thought he would feel like this. Is this how he looked to her . . . a weakling? But once he got into his clothes he'd be all right.

The wardrobe door swung open at a touch, almost knocking him off his feet, and he grabbed at it, and for the moment was in peril of bringing the whole thing down on top of him. The effect of getting into his trousers tired him so much that he became afraid.

Even after four days at rescue work he had never felt like this. He was forced to lie back on the bed again, and as he lay he had the desire to drop off to sleep.

With a great effort he roused himself. He had done enough sleeping . . . enough lying; the bed had become like a drug; he didn't want to give it up. Dimly he realised he had dreaded getting better, really better, for then he would have to talk . . . and act, really talk and really act. As it was now, she said to him 'Lie still' and he lay still, 'Đon't worry' and he didn't worry, 'Go to sleep' and he went to sleep, and that had suited him, for deep within him he had a kind of dread of the day when he'd be forced to say, 'Jessie, will you marry me?' He knew he'd never be able to go really back and say 'Jessie, I love you,' yet in this moment he was fully aware that if Jessie took that fellow he would make an end of it, for he couldn't go on alone, he wasn't any longer sufficient unto himself. He did not think of her now as a housekeeper, someone to take the worry off his shoulders, but as a vital stay to his own life. He needed her.

The distance to the chest of drawers was a very long way. The room instead of having grown smaller with acquaintance had stretched, and the effort to pull open a drawer seemed beyond him. But he managed it, and was taking out a shirt when the door opened.

'Larry!'

He clutched for support at the top of the drawers, and the shirt fell to the floor.

'Larry. What on earth are you up to? What's the matter? . . . Come on this minute and get back into bed.'

'Jessie.' He still clung on to the drawers.

'Yes. Leave go.' She took hold of his hands. 'Come on . . . Why have you got up? You'll put yourself back for weeks.'

'Jessie.'

'Come on. There . . .' She supported him back to the bed.

But having sat down, he said, 'Wait . . . wait . . . Sit down.' He laid a hand on each knee in an effort to steady their trembling, and his head had the urge to droop on to his chest with weariness. He watched her pull up a chair and sit down, and when she sat facing him waiting, he dropped his eyes to his hands and said, 'I saw the fellow come.'

There was no answer from her, and he could not bring his eyes up to her face, but in line with his vision he could see her hands lying one on top of the other in her lap. They were not agitated and twisting, but they seemed to symbolise, even emphasise, her attitude towards him during these past weeks; they seemed to be calmly waiting.

'Jessie.'

There was no response to the plea in his voice, and he drew in a deep breath before murmuring, 'He wants to marry you, doesn't he, that's why he's come back again?'

'Yes.'

His heart bounded painfully, and he dare not ask,

'Are you going to?' But he raised his eyes to her face. It looked calm and somewhat sad and gave him no lead one way or the other. And he stammered, 'I . . . I wouldn't blame you if you took him; you're worth the . . . the best. But, Jessie . . . I want you . . . I want you as I never did before. I was a nowt in those days, I've always been a nowt' – he used the full-mouthed word of the northerner which portrayed the self-centred, egotistical big-head better than any other word. 'You were always too good for me. But more so now. But, Jessie, I' – his heart knocked at his ribs, his throat swelled – 'I love you again. You won't believe it, but I do.'

Drunkenly he swayed from the bed and on to his knees, and flinging his arms about her his voice went on incoherently: 'I do; I do. I couldn't believe it myself, but I do. Believe me, Jessie. It isn't only him, I've known for some time, but the pig-headedness of me . . . I couldn't bring myself. But now; now, Jessie.'

When he felt her hands strong and firm on his head he became quiet, and raised his face to hers. And there he saw his answer. The waiting had gone from her eyes, and under his gaze she became transfigured, beautiful as she had never been. Her face moved down to his, and his whole being cried out to her, 'Jessie. Oh, Jessie!'

THE END

THE UPSTART
by Catherine Cookson

Suddenly risen to power and influence, Samuel Fairbrother, manufacturer and retailer of boots, shoes and clogs, decided that his new station in life deserved a more imposing residence, so when a thirty-four roomed mansion, situated on the outskirts of Fellburn, became available, he found himself the owner of a property he saw as a suitable reward for his newly gained position in the business community. And that was not all, for with the house came the butler, Maitland, who at once made plain his belief that Samuel, far from being the gentleman his predecessor had been, was no more than an upstart.

So began a clash of wills between master and man, at which Samuel Fairbrother discovered he was at a distinct disadvantage, for Maitland was well skilled in the art of maintaining his indispensability. Fairbrother, for his part, was only too aware that he dare not dispense with Maitland's services. And so an uneasy truce was declared between them.

As the years went by and the century turned, Samuel Fairbrother saw his children, one by one, leave the big house to make lives of their own – all except his eldest daughter Janet who, by means of a legacy, was enabled to shape the destiny of her father's scatterd family and effect the reconciliation that he thought was impossible.

0 552 14037 9

THE SOLACE OF SIN
by Catherine Cookson

As soon as she saw the house on the wild moorlands near Hexham, Constance Stapleton was attracted to it. With her marriage to Jim on the brink of collapse, she had already decided to sell the large flat they shared. And a further visit convinced her that she could live quite happily at Shekinah Hall, despite its isolation and lack of basic amenities. Connie also sensed that the move would initiate the separation from Jim she knew was inevitable, especially now that her son Peter was old enough to go off to university.

Connie was told she must negotiate with Vincent O'Connor if she wanted to buy the house, although his abrupt manner and insistence that the papers must be signed the following day took her by surprise. She was to discover that mystery was a way of life for Vincent and began to rely on him increasingly as she settled into her new routine. However, when shocking revelations about the man with whom she spent so many years came to light, she realised that her life at Shekinah could be under threat
. . .

'Dame Catherine has done it again . . . a rattling good story with a satisfying ending, plenty of gritty dialogue, a tricky affair of the heart, and a strong, honourable heroine'
Val Hennessy, *Daily Mail*

0 552 14583 1

THE BONNY DAWN
by Catherine Cookson

For seventeen-year-old Brid Stevens, the day began at four o'clock on a summer morning, when her alarm clock roused her from a dream-filled sleep, for she had an appointment to keep with Joe Lloyd, whom she had met at the weekly dance. On the cliff-top at Stockwell Hill, overlooking the sea, they were to watch the sun come up. What was to occur after that was to bring a day of such promise to a tragic end.

The events of this powerful novel set on the Northumbrian coast in the 1960s, take place over one day, a period during which everyone involved discovers that the consequences of an innocent meeting between two young people are far more significant than the event itself. *The Bonny Dawn* is a remarkable *tour-de-force* by Britain's most popular novelist.

0 552 14531 9

THE DESERT CROP
by Catherine Cookson

Money is tight in the farming communities around Fellburn in the 1880s, so when Hector Stewart announces to his children that he is to marry wealthy Moira Conelly, who lives in a 'castle' in Ireland, it is his son Daniel who guesses the real reason for the union.

However, Moira has not been entirely honest about her background or finances. She certainly expects to become wealthy, although that depends on the generosity of an aunt whose money she has been promised. She had also assumed she would be marrying into money, but to her surprise finds the Stewart farm anything but gentrified.

Then, some years later when her aunt dies, to Moira's dismay she is not the one to benefit. The effects of this bombshell spread far and wide throughout the Stewart family, now without the means by which the farm could have prospered. Daniel, deprived of an opportunity to better himself, can see no escape, until a family tragedy opens up the way for him to expand his horizons and find the love and happiness he thought unattainable . . .

0 552 14156 9

THE LADY ON MY LEFT
by Catherine Cookson

Alison Read, orphaned at the age of two, had for some years lived and worked with Paul Aylmer, her appointed guardian. Paul, an experienced antique dealer whose business thrived in the south-coast town of Sealock, had come to rely on Alison, who had quickly learned the trade.

But when he asked her to value the contents of Beacon Ride, a chain of events was set off that led to the exposure of a secret he had for years managed to conceal. As a result, Alison's relationship with Paul came under threat and she knew that only by confronting the situation head-on would her ambitions be realised.

0 552 14569 6

A SELECTION OF OTHER CATHERINE COOKSON TITLES AVAILABLE FROM CORGI BOOKS

THE PRICES SHOWN BELOW WERE CORRECT AT THE TIME OF GOING TO PRESS. HOWEVER TRANSWORLD PUBLISHERS RESERVE THE RIGHT TO SHOW NEW RETAIL PRICES ON COVERS WHICH MAY DIFFER FROM THOSE PREVIOUSLY ADVERTISED IN THE TEXT OR ELSEWHERE.